## Books by Serena B. Miller

*The Measure of Katie Calloway*

*A Promise to Love*

# A PROMISE *to* LOVE

⸙ A NOVEL ⸙

## SERENA B. MILLER

**Revell**
*a division of Baker Publishing Group*
Grand Rapids, Michigan

Published by Revell
a division of Baker Publishing Group
P.O. Box 6287, Grand Rapids, MI 49516-6287
www.revellbooks.com

Printed in the United States of America

Library of Congress Cataloging-in-Publication Data
Miller, Serena, 1950–
    A promise to love : a novel / Serena B. Miller.
        p.    cm.
    ISBN 978-0-8007-2117-6 (pbk.)
    I. Title.
PS3613.I55295P76 2012
813′.6—dc23                                                        2012020283

This book is a work of fiction. Names, characters, places, and incidents are the product of the author's imagination or are used fictitiously. Any resemblance to actual events, locales, or persons, living or dead, is coincidental.

The internet addresses, email addresses, and phone numbers in this book are accurate at the time of publication. They are provided as a resource. Baker Publishing Group does not endorse them or vouch for their content or permanence.

12  13  14  15  16  17  18      7  6  5  4  3  2  1

To my grandmother, Elizabeth Allen Bonzo,
who married for love—who endured in that love—
and by enduring healed a broken family.

# ACKNOWLEDGMENTS

Many thanks to: Frank and Marilyn Markey, for hours of historical research; Joe Stockham, our local Civil War expert, for insight into the famed Michigan Cavalry Brigade; Ron Bloomfield, Bay City Historical Museum curator; Julie Miller, research assistant and proofreader; Heather Gragg, for equine information; Vicki Crumpton, editor, for knowing exactly how to improve my manuscripts; Paul Dillingham, for introducing me to the fascinating study of our country's past; Dr. Aaron Ellis, family physician, for brainstorming with me on possible causes of a young mother's death; the entire Revell editorial staff, for giving me an excuse to revisit the 1800s; and special thanks to so many precious readers who have taken the time to encourage and pray for this grateful writer.

Love bears all things, believes
all things, hopes all things,
endures all things.

— 1 Corinthians 13:7 NKJV —

# PROLOGUE

Joshua Hunter had survived four years of war, led men in battle, been honored for his courage under fire, and had turned sixty acres of lumbered-over Michigan land into crop-producing fields . . . but he was helpless in the face of his wife's agony.

"Maybe a cup of coffee would help," his father-in-law suggested. "Coffee sometimes cures my headaches."

His wife's father, Richard Young, was every bit as worried as he. Neither of them had ever seen a woman in such pain. She had not suffered this badly even in the birthing of their five children.

"Diantha," Joshua asked, "do you think you could sit up and drink some coffee?"

She nodded feebly and allowed him to put two pillows behind her back to prop her upright. Her mother went to fetch the coffee.

"It's lukewarm, honey." Virgie hurried back into the bedroom where her daughter lay. "It'll be easier for you to drink that way. I'm sure this will help. You know what a bad headache your daddy gets when he don't get his coffee regular."

Joshua brushed the damp hair off his wife's forehead as she reached for the cup. Diantha took after her mother's side of the family—a handsome people. Her skin was lovely, with an almost olive tint to it, but now it was the color of paste. Her pallor was greater than he had ever seen—even during her worst moments of labor. Beads of sweat clung to her forehead as she tried to hold the cup to her lips and her hands trembled.

"I can't do this," she said.

He grabbed the cup before it could spill onto the coverlet.

"Please try to sip some, sweetheart." He held the cup to her lips.

She took two swallows before she fell back against the pillows. "My head hurts so." She pressed both hands against her temples. "I can't stand it."

"Give the coffee a chance to work, honey," her father said.

"I'm so cold." Her teeth began to chatter, in spite of the fire Richard had built in the fireplace. "Josh, get me another blanket."

Virgie whipped a heavy quilt from the foot of the bed. "Here." She handed it to him, her face pinched with worry.

He tucked the quilt around his wife, wondering how she could keep from suffocating with so many layers over her.

Suddenly, she writhed beneath the quilts, grabbed her stomach, and threw up into an empty bucket her mother had placed beside the bed when she had first complained of feeling ill.

She fell back against the pillows once again, her eyes closed tight against the pain, her face twisted into a grimace. Joshua had seen a great deal of suffering in his lifetime, especially on the battlefield, but he had never seen anything like what his wife was experiencing.

"It doesn't make any sense," he said, as much to himself as to Virgie and Richard. "She was fine this morning at breakfast."

"What did she eat?" her mother asked.

"Cornmeal mush and milk." He shook his head, unable to think of anything that could have caused this. "She ate from the same bowls as the children and me, then she drank a cup of tea while we planned our day."

Virgie poured water into a washbasin on a nearby stand, dipped a washrag in it, wrung it out, and placed it on her daughter's forehead. "There, honey. Maybe that will help your head feel better."

"She went for a short walk in the woods behind the cabin," Joshua continued. "With that good rain we got yesterday, and with the dogwood tree blossoms the size of a squirrel's ears—she wanted to hunt for some morel mushrooms she could fry for supper tonight."

"Could she have gotten ahold of some kind of poison mushroom?" Virgie asked.

"The girl has enough sense to know the difference between a good morel and them poison mushrooms some people mistake for 'em—like the ones that killed that poor woman down by Forestville last spring," Richard said. "I taught Diantha myself. She knows how to be careful. I guarantee it ain't mushroom poisoning."

"I didn't eat any mushrooms," Diantha said, pulling the damp cloth from her forehead and dropping it on the floor. "Can I have some water?"

Richard left and came back with a tin cup. He held it to his daughter's lips. "Here, honey. I just now drew it up from the well so it would be nice and cool."

Diantha took one sip and began retching.

Joshua grabbed the bucket and held it while his wife emptied what little remained in her stomach. "My head hurts so bad!" Diantha pressed her hands against her temples again and rolled her head back and forth on the pillow. "Make it stop, Mama, make it stop. Please make it stop!"

"We need Dr. Allard," Joshua said. "We need him right now."

"I'll go," Richard said.

"No." Joshua looked up from where he was sitting on the side of her bed. "My horse is faster, and I'm a better rider. I'll go." He realized how arrogant that sounded. "I'm sorry, Richard, I meant no offense."

"It's true, though," Richard said. "After four years in the cavalry, you're a much better rider than me. You should be the one to go."

Diantha grappled at his shirt. "Don't leave me, Josh!"

Joshua had never been so torn in his life. He wanted to get Doc Allard as fast as possible, but how could he leave his wife when she was begging him to stay?

At that moment, her body began writhing in pain and then she started convulsing and tearing at her hair. A moan escaped her lips, her body arched, went limp, and she was suddenly and completely . . . still.

Joshua and his in-laws looked at each other, all three of them wild-eyed. Virgie began to shake her roughly. "Diantha! Wake up!"

Joshua reached for her wrist and felt for a pulse, but there was none.

"Don't you do this to me, Diantha Mae," Virgie cried. "Don't you lay there playing possum, a-trying to scare me like you did when you was a girl!" Virgie slapped her daughter in the face, over and over. "You wake up now. You wake up right this minute!"

"Stop it!" Richard grabbed Virgie and pulled her away from the bed.

Virgie shook him off, ran for the smelling salts, and waved them frantically beneath Diantha's nose. When there was no response, Virgie's shoulders slumped in defeat. She sat down on the floor beside the bed and began to wail, holding on to her daughter's hand, rocking back and forth in her great grief.

Virgie's cries sounded as raw and primal as those of a wounded animal. In some far-off place of Joshua's mind, he wondered if his mother-in-law could live through this after already having buried six other children.

"Not her too, Lord," she sobbed. "Not the only baby I got left."

"I'll go for the doctor now." Richard's voice was tired and resigned. He had endured this agony six times before, and the weariness of grief was already etched deeply into every line of his body.

Joshua was paralyzed with shock. They had four little girls and a three-month-old baby boy. The girls were upstairs in the loft playing. The oldest, twelve-year-old Agnes, was keeping an eye on her three younger sisters and baby brother.

He should go to them, but he couldn't seem to stop sitting there, staring at his wife, trying to pull his mind together, trying to absorb the fact that she was . . . gone. How could Diantha just up and . . . die?

The rhythmic hoofbeats of Richard riding off to fetch the now-useless doctor filled the room. Virgie lay sobbing on the floor. Joshua steeled himself against giving in to an outpouring of grief. He could not allow himself the luxury of falling apart. Not yet. He needed to go to his children.

Drawing upon every bit of willpower he had, he closed his wife's lovely green eyes, took one last look at her perfect face, ran his hand over her dark brown hair, placed a kiss on her forehead, and then pulled the sheet up over her body and face. She had never been a large woman, barely coming to his shoulder. Now, in death, beneath the sheet, she looked so very small.

# 1

## MAY 19, 1871

"You stupid cow!" Mrs. Millicent Bowers leaped to her feet and swished her rose-colored silk skirt away from the broken tea set lying on the floor. "Why my husband ever hired you, I'll never know! The cost of that steamboat ticket to bring you here from Detroit was a complete waste!"

Millicent was furious; her glossy brown ringlets—which took Ingrid forever to curl each morning—trembled.

Ingrid ducked her head, avoiding her mistress's blazing eyes, and fell to her knees, gathering the broken pieces back on to the heavily laden tea tray she had dropped.

"That set was imported from England and it cost the earth! What's *wrong* with you!" At that point, Millicent burst into tears, fell facedown upon the sofa, and began to beat the cushions like a child throwing a temper tantrum. In Ingrid's opinion, this was ridiculous behavior for a grown woman, but it wasn't the first time she had witnessed it. Millicent—an aging belle from Virginia who had not yet reconciled herself to living in the "wilds" of Michigan—was, in Ingrid's eyes, a spoiled brat.

She seldom understood why her mistress acted the way she

did, but it wasn't her place to understand. She only had to work for the woman, a job that was getting more tedious every day.

Still, she was aghast at the breakage. The tea set had been lovely, with hand-painted cabbage roses on a creamy white background, and it was not easy to come by nice things in this "godforsaken, backwoods hole in the ground." At least that's what Millicent told everyone within earshot on a daily basis.

Perhaps the state of Virginia *had* been next door to heaven before Mr. Lincoln's war. Ingrid didn't know and she didn't care. In her opinion, a woman with a roof over her head, money to spend, and a husband who doted on her did not have any reason to complain. However, if there was ever a woman determined to make a career out of being unhappy, it was Millicent Bowers.

"I am sorry." Ingrid struggled to speak the words correctly. Millicent hated it when she spoke in broken English. "It was a—accident."

As she mopped up the mess with a dishcloth, saddened by the waste of the good pastry over which she had labored, she felt a stinging sensation across her shoulders. She jerked around and, to her astonishment, saw Millicent leaning over her, a look of flushed triumph on her face and a riding crop in her hand. Before Ingrid could recover from her surprise, the crop came down upon her again and again, slashing across her face and ripping a tear in her dress before she could put a hand out to stop it.

"I'll teach *you* to destroy my things," Millicent crowed.

Ingrid fell onto her bottom and scooted backward, shocked speechless.

Her mistress was a fretful, thoughtless woman with no responsibilities and countless imagined illnesses. She frequently gave in to small, verbal cruelties to relieve her boredom, but she had never before physically attacked her.

As the blows rained down upon Ingrid's head and shoulders, she saw that Millicent's face had changed from complete despair to unabashed glee.

Fortunately, her mistress was not in the best of shape. Her indolent half-invalid state had robbed her of stamina. Her corset made it impossible for her to draw a full breath.

Millicent stopped, pressed her hand against her stomach, and tried to recover by breathing in short, shallow, dog-like pants. This gave Ingrid enough time to scramble to her feet.

For the first time since her decision to come to America, Ingrid felt real anger. Dropping a tea set was unfortunate, but being beaten for it was *not* acceptable. After working for Millicent this past month, she felt bottomless sympathy for the woman's former slaves.

She stepped over the broken china and snatched the riding crop away. Millicent raised her hand to slap her—just as a male voice sliced through the air.

"What's going on here?"

Millicent's hand dropped. In an instant, she arranged her face into a picture of simpering, sweet womanhood. Ingrid watched, amazed, as Millicent deliberately exchanged one facial expression for another, as quickly and efficiently as changing a hat. Ingrid had never learned the art of pretending to be anyone except exactly who she was, a twenty-four-year-old Swedish woman who could outwork anybody she knew.

"Oh—it's you." Surprisingly, once Millicent turned and saw the man, her voice did not drip honey.

"Is your husband here, ma'am?" the man asked.

"No."

She turned her back on him.

The rudeness of her attitude came as another shock. Ingrid had yet to see the man whom Millicent did not try to captivate.

"I came to the mercantile to pay my bill," the man said. "Your husband wasn't there."

"Leave the money on the table." Millicent nodded toward one of many useless decorative pieces of furniture crowding the sitting room. "Then, I'll thank you to leave, Mr. Hunter."

Hunter? Ingrid searched her memory. Why was Millicent, who loved the attention of a male—*any* male—being so dismissive? It was especially surprising because Mr. Hunter was an exceptionally handsome man. He was over six feet tall, broad of shoulder, and perfect in form.

He pulled some worn-looking bills from his pocket and laid them on the table. Something about the way he unfolded and smoothed them out made Ingrid think that the money had not come easily.

"Are you all right, ma'am?"

To Ingrid's surprise, he appeared to be speaking to her.

He was dressed in a farmer's work clothes, had the bluest eyes she had ever seen, and yes, they were most definitely looking straight at her. She noticed that his chestnut-brown hair, which curled over his shirt collar, was in bad need of a trim.

"You're bleeding," he pointed out.

Ingrid's hand flew to her face, where there was a trickle of blood. She wondered how much he had seen through the open door before he interrupted. Heat suffused her neck and face at the realization that he had seen her being treated like a disobedient dog.

"Don't worry about her," Millicent said. "This clumsy girl cut herself when she broke my tea set." She waved her hand dismissively. "Get back to work, Ingrid."

To Ingrid's astonishment, Mr. Hunter did not allow himself to be dismissed. "Shouldn't she have those cuts tended to first?" His voice held real concern.

Ingrid blinked. Her wounds meant nothing to her at the

18

moment. She was too busy studying this man who was taking up for her.

Mr. Hunter was worried about her—an overworked, badly treated housemaid.

It was the first real kindness she had received since arriving in White Rock, Michigan. At that moment, in the blink of an eye, Ingrid fell head over heels in love with a perfect stranger.

Millicent had a different opinion of Mr. Hunter. She slowly turned back around to face the man. "When I want the advice of a wife killer, I'll ask for it."

The man looked as though he had been punched in the stomach, but he quickly recovered.

"I'd take it kindly if you wouldn't go spreading that rumor around, Mrs. Bowers. I have little children to raise." He politely tipped his hat to them and left.

Ingrid's eyes followed him. There was something about Mr. Hunter, his concern for her, as well as the calm way he had dealt with Millicent's accusation, that made her wish she could follow him right on out the door.

"That tea set will be taken out of your pay, you know," Millicent hissed when he was out of earshot.

Ingrid wasn't at all surprised.

Shaken by Millicent's accusations, Joshua Hunter walked to his wagon outside the Bowerses' home. His daughter Agnes sat on the wooden seat, holding the reins of their patient driving horse, Buttons.

He had come to town to pay his bills and to pick up supplies. Although he knew that there had been some crazy talk from his mother-in-law about him being responsible for Diantha's death, he hadn't expected anyone to take her seriously. A coldness had developed between him and Richard, with whom he had always had a cordial relationship. He figured his grieving in-laws were resentful that their daughter was gone . . . and he was the one left alive.

But wife killer? Is this what people in town were saying about him?

No wonder there was going to be an inquest tomorrow into the cause of Diantha's death! The official who had given him the subpoena had not told him that he was a suspect.

Overwhelmed with the care of his children, dealing with his own grief, trying to get his fields planted—he had not realized that others might be echoing what Virgie had been saying.

He knew, of course, that a small town starved for news would manufacture its own, but Diantha's death had evidently set the gossips' tongues wagging in ways he had not anticipated.

When he returned to the wagon, a fight was brewing in the back between two of his little girls, Ellie and Trudy. It seemed like there was always some sort of altercation going on between those two. His wife had not been much of a disciplinarian, but things had gotten worse since she died.

Unfortunately, he had little idea of how to deal with the girls' disobedience and perpetual fussing with each other. Give him a regiment of men, and he knew how to lead them and keep proper discipline in the ranks. Give him a battle, and he would fight and, if given half a chance, would probably win.

He knew how to fight a war, but military battles had not prepared him for a house filled with little girls. Domestic issues left him at a complete loss, which reminded him of that young Swedish woman whom George Bowers had hired. She was definitely having a hard time of it. A whip, for goodness sake! Millicent had been using a whip on her! He didn't even use whips on his animals. The scene he had walked into had been a shock. He was glad he had been able to interrupt it.

The hired girl had worn a shapeless brown garment that was faded and worn. She was also as thin as a rail—shockingly thin. There was no excuse for this. George's store was well stocked and prosperous. The Bowerses could certainly afford to give her a new dress and enough to eat.

George was a decent enough man, except for being a complete pushover when it came to his wife. Joshua had never particularly cared one way or another about Millicent, but now he felt a real revulsion toward her.

"Pa! Pa! Ellie's a-hurting me!"

"Am not!"

"*Now* what's going on?" Joshua was exasperated. "What are you two fussing about now?"

Twelve-year-old Agnes seemed unperturbed by the battle taking place between her sisters in the back of the wagon. She rolled her eyes and shrugged at his questioning glance.

"Ellie keeps taking my marble." Trudy, his six-year-old towhead, wiped her nose on her sleeve and then pointed her finger at her sister.

"Why are you trying to take your sister's marble, Ellie?"

"I gots to have me somethin' to play with." Ellie, a solid little five-year-old with curly brown hair and freckles, stuck out her lower lip. "Aggie took my slingshot away."

Joshua climbed into the wagon. "Why did you take your sister's slingshot?" He took the reins from Agnes's fingers. One of the many challenges of raising his family alone was having to drag the girls along with him everywhere he went. Sometimes it felt like he was traveling with a circus. It was tempting to leave them all at home, but he was afraid he'd come back and find one of them strung up by her shoestrings.

"Ellie hit the rear end of Buttons with a big ol' rock," Agnes explained. "He nearly run off, but I held him back."

Joshua turned around and gave Ellie a hard stare. "Did you do that?"

"I didn't mean to," Ellie said. "My hand slipped."

"But you were aiming at Buttons when it slipped?"

"Yep," Ellie admitted. It might have been his imagination, but he could have sworn he heard a note of pride in the little girl's voice.

"I'll take that slingshot away from you for good if you ever let it 'accidentally' slip and hit that horse again." Considering how things had been going around his house, he added just to be on the safe side, "Or if it 'accidentally' hits one of your sisters."

"It won't happen again, Pa."

He made a clicking sound with his tongue, and Buttons obediently headed down the old logging road to their home. For a moment, he thought he had managed to establish peace among his girls. Then a wheel hit a rock and his youngest daughter, three-year-old Polly, let out a yowl. She had been in the process of standing up, and the bump had caused her to fall.

Ellie and Trudy scrambled over to comfort her. All three huddled in the corner of the back of the wagon, glaring at him like little animals—as though Polly's discomfort was all his fault.

Other men had daughters who were demure and well behaved . . . but not him.

Diantha had not been like other mothers. Some women endured childbirth, then forgot the pain and fell in love with their children, doting on them from the moment they were born. With Diantha it was the opposite. She always felt at her strongest while carrying a child, gave birth as easily as a cat, and then seemed to lose interest in each child soon after their birth. The older their daughters grew, the more disinterested she became. She went through the motions, but he could tell her heart was not in motherhood.

He had never figured it out. Coming home to his little girls every evening was his reward after a hard day's work—even if they *did* sometimes act like they had been raised by wolves.

Marriage to Diantha had meant being perpetually off balance because he had never known what to expect. During their courtship, he found her mercurial mood swings fascinating. After thirteen years of marriage, he wished her up-and-down emotions would even out.

Some days he would come home to domestic bliss. Diantha would be humming while doing some household task, and the girls would be gathered around the kitchen table, happily involved in some small project that she had created for them. She would be neatly dressed and she would have taken the time to smooth her hair back into a bun. She would greet him with enthusiasm, and the evening would be memorable.

Other times, especially after the birth of little Bertie, he would come home to find the children unkempt and hungry, the baby soiled and screaming in his cradle, and Diantha sitting on the front porch, her hair in tangles, staring into the woods, barely able to acknowledge his arrival.

He had been at a loss to know how to help her or how to read her. All he knew was that she sometimes struggled with emotions that he could not understand.

Well, at least she would no longer have to endure the hardscrabble life they had been living as they waited for his cherry tree orchard to mature. If he could hang on for one more year, and if the weather cooperated, he would have a good first crop next year.

His goal was to have enough to ship down to the markets in Detroit. If he packed the cherries well, they would survive the one-day steamboat trip just fine, and people were always hungry for fresh fruit after a Michigan winter.

Much of the land that had been opened by the timber cutters was not rich land. It had a thinner layer of topsoil than anyone had expected. The good first crop the farmers had gotten from the virgin soil had given everyone hope, but it was misleading. He was barely eking out a living with his oats, wheat, and corn. It was only a matter of time before the land played out. It had occurred to him that if there was one thing that Michigan soil appeared to be good at, it was growing trees. He figured if Michigan could grow giant pine trees and heavy forests of hardwood, it would also grow excellent fruit trees. A mixed orchard was his goal, to be built over a period of years.

There were already fine cherry tree orchards springing up all over the northwestern part of Michigan—progeny of the trees a Presbyterian missionary had planted back in '52 on Old Mission Peninsula. He saw no reason why he couldn't establish an equally lucrative cherry orchard. All it took was time and patience.

Sometimes he wondered if Diantha's strange behavior had been because her life was simply too hard—that it caused her to "go away" in her mind from time to time.

"I wish you were still here, sweetheart," he whispered to a wife who was no longer beside him. "Just one more year and your life would have been so much easier."

"Mama can't hear you," Agnes pointed out.

"I know. It just helps ease the pain to talk to her sometimes."

"But it don't make good sense—talking to someone who ain't here," she insisted.

Agnes had been born with more common sense than some people achieved in a lifetime. He seldom bothered to argue with her, because it never did any good. Agnes knew what she knew.

"You're right."

"Polly just filled her britches," Ellie called. "Pee-eew!" From the nasal sound of Ellie's voice, he knew she was holding her nose.

Joshua glanced back. Polly was sitting in the corner of the wagon upon a little mound of straw, hugging her rag dolly with a guilty look on her face.

"I reckon I got to go tend to her now," Agnes said. "I wish she'd learn to go to the toilet like a normal person. I'm sick of washing diapers."

Agnes climbed over the seat into the back of their small farm wagon, turned her little sister onto her back, and removed the gray flannel diaper.

"We're in luck," Agnes announced. "It ain't juicy."

After Agnes had changed the little girl's diaper, she propped Polly up, handed her the doll, and then leaned back against the side of the wagon with her arm around her baby sister.

"Did you get Mr. Bowers paid off?" Agnes called from the back of the wagon.

"I did."

"Took about everything we got, didn't it?"

"Mr. Bowers deserves to be paid."

"Still, it's gonna be a lean summer unless you get another carpenter job."

He couldn't argue with that. "Probably."

"You ain't planning on farming us out to other people like you did little Bertie, are you?"

Farming them out? Was that what his children thought he was doing? He couldn't care for an infant while doing his spring planting. Virgie might be angry at him, but she was wonderful with her little grandson.

"No. Of course not."

Not unless he was on trial tomorrow and did not know it. Millicent's comment worried him.

Another small altercation broke out between Ellie and Trudy. Joshua glanced back to see what the problem was this time. Evidently Ellie had managed to get her hand into Trudy's pocket, and now they were fighting over the marble again. Ellie refused to let go. Trudy held on, and the result was a pocket ripped and hanging by one corner.

"You girls stop fighting or I'll come back there and tan your hides!"

It was an empty threat, and everyone in the wagon knew it.

Agnes calmly reached over, captured the much-sought-after marble, and stuffed it into her stocking. Then she settled back again with her arm around Polly.

Ellie started to make a dive for the marble, but Agnes stopped her with one hand. "You just try it," she warned. "You'll be eating mush without any milk tomorrow morning."

Ellie settled back. If there was one thing the little girl loved, it was milk.

An uneasy peace settled over his family.

"We're going past Grandma's house," Agnes said. "You suppose she'd let us see little Bertie today?"

"Doubt it," Joshua said. "She wouldn't let me see him last week when I came by. She's having a real hard time getting over losing your mama."

"Maybe she'd let me," Agnes said. "Maybe she'll even let me hold him."

"I'll stop, but don't get your hopes up. Your grandma is going through a bad time. She'll be easier to get along with by and by after she has time to sort things out in her head."

Joshua pulled back on the reins and allowed Agnes to clamber out. He watched the girl knock repeatedly on the door of the cabin, but his mother-in-law chose not to answer. He wasn't surprised, but he did not understand. Even if she was embittered against him, there was no call to take it out on the girls.

Downcast, Agnes came back to the wagon. "She's in there, Pa. I heard her moving around, but she won't come to the door. Not even for me."

It hurt him to see Agnes's disappointment. Big gray eyes, dark hair in two long braids, and a heart-shaped face like her mother's. He hoped she had not inherited Diantha's penchant for melancholy, but there had been no sign of it yet. Agnes was the most stable person in their whole family.

"It's just that she's hurting so bad over your mama."

"Aren't we all?" Agnes muttered as she climbed back onto the seat beside him.

## 2

"Millicent doesn't mean to act that way," George Bowers said as he placed canned goods neatly on the shelf of his small mercantile. "She's truly a sweethearted woman. It's just been too hard on her following me here to the wilds of Michigan. She misses the elegant home we had before the war."

He was a medium-sized man in his late forties, balding, and he wore wire glasses that he polished obsessively when he was nervous—as he was doing now.

Ingrid was tired of hearing this area referred to by the Bowerses as the wilds of Michigan. In her opinion, the thumb area of the mitten shape of Michigan was beautiful beyond belief. Perhaps it was her Scandinavian background, perhaps some ancient Viking blood within her, but she loved living so close to the lake that she could hear the call of seagulls every time she walked out her front door.

Except that it wasn't *her* front door, it was Millicent's, and on Millicent's best day Ingrid felt like an unwanted, useless guest. The job that had drawn her here had turned sour the first day.

"Sweethearted? No!" Ingrid shook her head vehemently. "Not sweet."

"I know she was a little upset over the tea set . . ." George said.

"Upset?" Ingrid touched her cheek, where two red welts throbbed. "Look! Your wife is very mean person."

"Shush!" George looked about him nervously. "Someone might hear."

"Things need change," Ingrid said. "Or I not stay."

"Everything will be fine." George grabbed a feather duster and began to flick nonexistent dust off the shelves. "Just try not to break anything else."

Ingrid found it odd that George did a job that most wives would have been happy to do. It wasn't as though Millicent had anything else to occupy her time—at least not with Ingrid waiting on her hand and foot.

Suddenly, she had an idea that would fix everything. "I work here—you stay home." She smiled, pleased with herself. "You and wife spend more time together!"

He looked shocked. "That is not possible."

"Why?"

He seemed at a loss for words. "Because . . . I said so." He tucked the feather duster beneath his arm and nervously shoved his glasses higher up on his nose.

It was obvious to her that George was not anxious to spend all day every day with his wife, either. She gave up reasoning with him and brought up her most immediate problem.

"I am hungry."

"What do you mean, you're hungry?"

"Millicent punish me for breaking tea set. She not allow me to eat all day. She watch me all time."

"Oh, good grief," he muttered. "I finally get her a servant, and now she tries to starve her to death."

"Why you hire me?" Ingrid asked. "Millicent not old. She not sick."

"Because she was always used to sla . . . er, servants. She really doesn't know how to do much on her own, and besides that, her health is delicate."

"Delicate like horse," Ingrid muttered.

George overheard her. "Do not speak of my wife in such an insulting manner."

Obviously, there was not going to be any help from George. "I not work for wife anymore." Ingrid made up her mind. "I go. I want pay."

"I—I'm a little short on cash."

"Mr. Hunter leave money. When he see Millicent hitting me."

"Hunter saw that?"

"*Ja.*"

George rubbed his hand over his face and shoved his glasses up on his nose yet again. "I need that money to buy new stock." His eyes would not meet hers.

"You not pay me?" Ingrid was incredulous.

"Millicent said she would rather I not. Perhaps if you could stay on for a while longer," George wheedled. "Maybe then . . ."

"No." Ingrid walked over to a barrel, lifted the lid, and fished out a fistful of crackers. She was so hungry she didn't care what George thought.

George cocked an eyebrow. "I explained when you first came that you could not help yourself from our goods."

"I not eat all day. No food all time she mad. Millicent is mean woman!"

"Stop *saying* that!"

Ignoring his frown, she gobbled down the crackers and looked longingly at a small wheel of cheese sitting on the counter.

"Don't even consider it," he warned.

She paid him no heed. Those few crackers had whetted her appetite, and now she was consumed by an obsession to fill her hollow belly. She had worked sixteen straight hours with no food. She grabbed a knife and stabbed it into the cheese.

"Stop that!" he cried. "That is for paying customers only."

He started toward her, but some animalistic sense of survival came over her and she stood her ground—the knife held in front of her, keeping him at bay with one hand, while the other stuffed cheese into her mouth as fast as she could swallow.

Obviously seeing how hungry she was, he softened. "If you're that hungry—go ahead."

She focused her whole attention on consuming as much of the buttery cheese as she could manage. It had been a long, long time since she had been completely full. Millicent had been parsimonious when it came to her food. Now, it felt as though her ravenous body had taken over her mind and her willpower. She could not have stopped eating if she had tried.

Finally she drew a breath. A large wedge of the wheel of cheese was gone—and if Millicent found out, she would probably try to take the cost of it out of her nonexistent pay. A pickle barrel was close by, and she lifted the lid and looked at him questioningly.

"Why ask permission now?" He leaned an elbow on the counter. "Go ahead and eat one, but I'd appreciate it if you would put that knife down first. You're making me nervous."

She laid the knife on the counter and dredged a pickle, dripping brine, out of the barrel. She had been craving one of those ever since she had first seen a customer helping himself to one.

"Thank you," she said between crunches.

"I'm sorry." He patted her on the shoulder. "Obviously, Millicent has been treating you worse than I realized. I'll see what I can do."

He was not a bad man, nor an unkind one, but he was, in Ingrid's opinion, an extremely weak man when it came to dealing with his wife.

Ingrid felt tears form in her eyes at his small show of kindness.

At that moment, Millicent came through the door.

If Ingrid had thought that her mistress had been upset over the tea set, she had been mistaken. That tantrum had been mild compared to the towering rage Millicent exhibited upon finding her husband's hand on Ingrid's shoulder.

Although the moment between George and Ingrid had been nothing more than one decent person comforting another, Millicent gave it the worst possible connotation.

"So *this* is what you've been up to behind my back!" Millicent said. "Get out of my store! Get out of my house." Her voice took on a deadly pitch. "And you stay out, you little tramp!"

Ingrid skirted around the fuming woman as George began the placating speech she had heard before under different circumstances. "Now, calm down, sugar. Don't you go working yourself into a state. You don't want to bring on another sick headache."

Three whole weeks of her life and the only thing she had to show for it was a torn dress, some whip marks, and a belly full of cheese. There wasn't much she could do with that, but she had no choice but to try.

While Millicent fumed, and George talked, she marched across the street, into the house, and up the stairs to the attic where she had been living. There wasn't much to pack, but what there was, she wanted. She stuffed everything she owned into the same battered valise that had seen her across the ocean.

Millicent had put the money Mr. Hunter had left in a small

drawer in the table. As far as she knew, it was still there, and it tempted her mightily. They owed it to her, but she could not in all good conscience take it. She was not a thief—even if they were.

Lugging the battered valise, she walked north, out of town.

The children would be hungry when they got home. They seemed to always be hungry, no matter how much he fed them. He had never fully realized before how much time it took Diantha to feed their brood. Now that he looked back, he realized that she had been at it pretty much day and night except for the days when it all became too much and she developed that terrible, blank stare.

Now it was his most difficult challenge, coming up with ways to feed four children, three times a day. Agnes helped, but she was too young to take on the full load of a grown woman. She already had too much responsibility as it was. She had shouldered too much of it when her mother was alive as well.

There were other chores that had now become his on top of all his other work. It seemed like Polly was constantly in need of another clean diaper, and he didn't have the slightest idea how to train the little girl. All the children's clothes were perpetually in need of laundering. There were dishes to wash, noses to be wiped, scraped knees to be tended, and repairs waiting to be made to clothing that seemed to wear out on an almost hourly basis.

His list of responsibilities was overwhelming. It was impossible to even contemplate bringing little Bertie home because Joshua was seriously afraid the infant wouldn't survive in this household right now. His chest ached with missing his young son, and he felt like giving up—but real men didn't give up. Men soldiered on. Always.

The children were half-asleep now, jostled by the rolling motion of the wagon. Ellie and Trudy had given up their fight and leaned against each other, their eyes closed. Agnes's head lolled against her chest. Polly was curled up asleep in a nest of hay he had thrown in to cushion their trip.

He brought his mind back to what he would feed all of them when they got home. Cornmeal mush and warmed-over soup beans were the best he could come up with. They had been having a lot of that lately.

It almost made the rations he had eaten in the war look tasty.

"I don't need no hired gal." The old woman's face lit up when Ingrid knocked on her door with her battered valise in hand. "But you're as welcome as rain to stay here with me awhile if you've a mind to."

Ingrid had met Hazel Smith when the older lady had come calling on Millicent. Hazel was nearing seventy and lived alone on the outskirts of the village with a dog that looked like it had more wolf in it than dog. At the moment, the wolf-dog was quietly positioning itself between her and Hazel. Its behavior was not yet threatening, but Ingrid could tell it was giving the situation careful thought.

Millicent had told her that Hazel had moved here with her trapper husband long before White Rock had become a village. The old woman had unkempt gray hair and wore men's britches, a belted calico shirt, and an old battered hat. She grew her own garden, shot her own meat, and ate fish that she caught and cleaned.

Millicent, needless to say, did not approve of Hazel, her life, or her choice of apparel. The feeling appeared to be mutual.

Hazel had dropped by the Bowerses' home only once while

34

Ingrid was there. She had ended up quarreling, quite heatedly, with Millicent over the war. Ingrid discovered later that the only reason Hazel had stopped by at all was to see the young immigrant girl who had answered the advertisement George had placed in a Detroit newspaper. There wasn't a lot happening in White Rock, and for a few days the news of her arrival had apparently been the town's primary source of gossip.

For a short time, Millicent had enjoyed the attention Ingrid brought. It made her the first woman in White Rock to employ a "servant," which is what she insisted on calling her. Ingrid preferred the term "hired girl," which was what the other townsfolk called her—to Millicent's annoyance.

"If that woman ever gets on your nerves," Hazel whispered as Ingrid walked her to the door after her one memorable visit, "you just come on over and stay with me till you figure out what you want to do."

It seemed an odd thing for the old woman to say, but Ingrid had tucked it away in her mind just in case.

"I have no place to sleep," Ingrid said. "Millicent tell me . . . get out."

"I figured that might happen," Hazel said. "What did you do to upset her?"

"I broke tea set."

"That fancy china teapot all the way from England?" Hazel whooped with laughter. "I bet that was one furious Southern belle you had on your hands."

"It was accident."

"Well, of course it was an accident. A girl like you don't go around smashing good china on purpose. How did you get those welts on your face?"

"She whip me."

Hazel's laughter stilled and her eyes narrowed. "She what?"

"She hit me with whip."

35

"Well, I'll be." Hazel's mouth formed a rigid line. "That woman's crazier'n I thought. She's probably walking around with her corset laced too tight again. Forty-two years old and still trying to have the waistline of a girl. I've heard she even sleeps in it—is that true?"

Ingrid nodded. "She have sleep corset, day corset, and party corset—very tight, that one."

Hazel shook her head. "Imagine sleeping in something made of bone and steel, laced so tight you can't breathe."

"She say girl-childs need wear too."

"Are you making a joke?"

"No. I hear her tell Mrs. Burnett to lace her *dotter* up tight at night."

"Little Lucy? For goodness sake. That sweet child is only seven years old!"

"Millicent say it best when the bones still soft."

"I hope the mother refused."

"Mrs. Burnett say she do when girl is eleven."

"Goodness! Well, you're just as well out of there. Come on in and we'll find you a place to sleep."

Hazel's indignation about the way she had been treated made Ingrid feel enormously better. She hadn't been certain if getting beaten by an employer was considered normal in America. Now she knew that not only was it not normal, it was considered crazy.

Even though Hazel's house was small, Ingrid immediately felt at home. Instead of every corner being stuffed with furniture, there was a barrenness that appealed to her Swedish love of cleanliness and order.

Except it wasn't really all that clean. Hazel, after all, was not young. She no longer had the clearest eyes or the sharpest nose. Perhaps in return for a bed, Hazel would allow Ingrid to give the place a good scrubbing.

"You can sleep in the loft," Hazel said. "There's a bed and a bit of furniture up there. Go on up and get yourself settled."

Ingrid mounted the narrow stairs and was pleased with what she saw. The roof was steep, and the loft felt roomier because of it. A small, glassed-in window was at one end, allowing a ray of late afternoon sunshine to dance upon the wooden floor. There had been no window in the Bowerses' attic.

Pegs were set into the logs for hanging clothes. There was a single rope bed with a plain dressing table and oil lamp beside it. A footstool was pulled up to a small rocking chair.

It was more than enough, especially since she was grateful to have a roof over her head at all. She scooted her one piece of luggage beneath the bed and went back downstairs.

"Thank you," she said. "I pay with work. I clean now? Sweep floor?"

"You'll be paying me back by giving me some company in the evenings," Hazel said. She patted the dog's head, which came up to her waist. The wolf-dog could easily have made a meal of Hazel with a few bites, but it not only tolerated Hazel's loving hand on its head, it also closed its eyes with pleasure when the old woman stroked it.

"She-Wolf here isn't much of a conversationalist at night, but she can scare the daylights out of anyone that might try to take advantage of me."

The dog gave Ingrid a straight, meaningful look, as though making certain Ingrid knew she was there on a probationary status only.

"She bite?" Ingrid was uneasy about the glare she was getting from the wolf-dog. "She *look* like she bite!"

"Not unless I tell her to."

Ingrid tried to ignore the giant wolf-dog. She rubbed her hands together and looked around. "Give me job."

"Let's get you settled first. That bed up there ain't been

slept in for a while," Hazel said. "Might be a good idea to shake the mice out of it and tear some fresh corn shucks to put in. I got some I been saving since last fall. Hadn't seen the need till now."

"I help!" She was pleased to have something productive to do.

"Good then." Hazel dragged a large bag of dried corn husks from beneath her own bed, which was placed in the only other room on the first floor. "It's gonna be good having company around here again. Old She-Wolf here is tired of listening to me telling my stories over and over, aren't you, She-Wolf?"

The wolf-dog had settled down on the floor next to Hazel's rocker with her muzzle on her paws. Now she looked up at Ingrid and whined softly as though in agreement that she would be happy to be relieved of the burden of listening to Hazel's stories.

Had the dog not been so large and intimidating, Ingrid would have been tempted to laugh at her self-pitying expression. She chose not to risk it. She-Wolf might not have a sense of humor.

"Go up and throw down that mattress," Hazel said. "Then take it outside and empty it. We'll see if there's any damage."

Ingrid did exactly as Hazel asked. Unfortunately, the mattress *had* been used as a cozy place to raise a family of mice. She took the mattress outside and shook the contents into the field beside the cabin.

Then she went back inside and repaired the small hole the mice had made, and Hazel built a fire against the cool spring night. It was companionable sitting in the solid little cabin, a small fire burning in the grate as they tore husks and stuffed them into the mattress.

"Why'd she stop whipping you?" Hazel asked.

"I take whip away."

"You did?" Hazel's eyes were admiring. "Did she put up a fight?"

"She try. Mr. Hunter stop her."

"Joshua?"

"Millicent call him 'wife killer.'"

Hazel's hands stilled. "To his face?"

"Ja."

"She *would* do that!" Hazel grabbed a large handful of corn shucks and started ripping them with renewed vigor. "I been trying to squash that rumor for weeks now. Joshua has enough on his hands without dealing with that kind of foolishness. I wish the Bowerses would move back to where they belong."

"Millicent much like that."

"I know. I've heard her singing the praises of Richmond ever since the two of them got here. She doesn't seem to realize how it sounds to those of us here in the North, especially them that's got menfolk in the ground because of that war. The biggest mistake of my life was selling my husband's store to George. I miss visiting with the customers."

"Why you do?"

"I was going through a sickish spell. Thought it was the end. Couldn't take care of the place like I wanted. I got better, but by then it was too late."

"Why they want store?" Ingrid reached into the sack for another handful of corn shucks. They were so dry they felt like thin paper.

"There was no money down South after the war. Michigan is where the money is, now that it's the lumber capital of the world. George is not dumb. He knew a store in a place growing as fast as White Rock is, and especially a town near the lumber camps, would be a gold mine. It was a good business decision for him, and I didn't have anyone else standing in line to buy it from me. Now that wife of his is spreading gossip about Josh, one of the finest men I know. I could just wring Millicent's neck."

"Did he?"

"Who, Joshua? Kill his wife? Of course not. Never saw a man so besotted with a woman, and with that passel of little girls of his. He can't even keep his daughters under control, let alone hurt that pretty wife."

"She pretty? This wife?"

"I don't think I ever saw a woman more perfect in form or face. Had an air of mystery about her too, that seemed to fascinate all the boys that hung around before she married Josh. She never told anyone what she was thinking, not even other women. Josh worshiped her from the moment he laid eyes on her, and from what I could see, he never got over it."

"But Millicent say . . ."

"Millicent is enjoying herself at Josh's expense. That big mouth of hers is one of the reasons they've called for an inquest. Between you and me, sometimes I suspect the real reason George moved north was because there was no one left in Virginia who could tolerate Millicent."

"When is this . . . this . . . inquest? I get word right?"

"Yep. That's right. Where did you learn English, anyway? You sure don't sound like you just got off the boat."

Ingrid felt very pleased at the compliment. She had worked hard learning the language of what was going to be her adopted country.

"We have English neighbor. She marry Swedish man. We children, me and brother, go next door and visit her every day. She very lonely. She play games, bake cookies, teach us English just for fun. Very kind." Ingrid sighed, missing their friend. "When we decide to go to America, she work very hard so we be ready."

"Well, that answers another question I had," Hazel said.

"What is that?"

"How a Swedish girl wound up having a British accent."

"That is bad?"

"No. Not at all. Just a little confusing," Hazel said. "Are you talking about the brother I heard was supposed to meet you in Detroit?"

"Ja." Ingrid marveled at the way news traveled in a small town. "Hans is my twin brother. He go to America, get work on farm in Ohio and send money for Ingrid's trip. He say he make more money in lumber camp in Saginaw, Michigan. He say come in spring to Mrs. Baker's boardinghouse in Detroit. He say wait for him. I do. He never come and never come. No letter. No Hans. I run out of money and take job in White Rock. Think if I come close to where Hans work, I find him."

"You poor child." Hazel shot her a pitying look. "Did he write you regular-like before then?"

Ingrid nodded.

"And then the letters stopped?"

"Ja."

"We'll pray that you find your brother." Hazel laid a comforting hand on her arm. "But don't get your hopes up. Lumber camps can swallow a man whole."

"You think Hans is not alive?"

"He could be the governor of Michigan for all I know." Hazel shrugged. "I'm just sayin' it might be wise to have a plan that don't involve pinning all your hopes on finding your brother."

Ingrid winced at Hazel's words. They too closely echoed her own fears. She knew that if Hans had any way of getting word to her, he would. A lumber camp very well might have "swallowed him whole" as Hazel had put it.

She didn't want to cry in front of her new friend, so she fought down the panic that threatened to overtake her at the thought of losing Hans and tried to force herself think about something else—something that would not make her sad.

"You say Mr. Hunter is good man?"

"Why?" Hazel shot her a glance. "Are you interested in Josh?"

Ingrid looked away. "He was . . . kind to me."

"Well, I'll be," Hazel said, smiling. "You're sweet on him."

Ingrid felt her face turning red.

"Can't say that I blame you. Josh is definitely a looker. A war hero too. There'll be more than a few women in this county setting their caps for him—once the inquest puts the rumor about his wife to rest."

The thought of other women pursuing Mr. Hunter bothered Ingrid.

"You do realize," Hazel continued, "that anyone who snags Josh will be taking on a poor dirt farmer with five children to feed."

"I like children." Ingrid shrugged. "I like farm."

"Well, the inquest will be tomorrow at the Rogerses' house. Maybe we'll find something out then. No one really knows what happened to Diantha, including Josh. It's the biggest mystery we've had around here since we quit trying to figure out why a nice man like George would marry a woman like Millicent."

Joshua managed to get all the children fed, heard their prayers, and tucked each girl into bed. Now he had to get their clothing ready for the inquest tomorrow. Earlier in the day, Agnes had taken the clean clothes off the line, sprinkled water on them, rolled each piece up tight, and then put everything into a laundry basket to await ironing.

He folded a small dish towel into a palm-sized pad, used it to grab the hot flatiron from on top of the woodstove, and spit on it. It sizzled, so he knew the iron was hot enough. He laid Ellie's church dress on the ironing table and pressed the hot iron onto it. His girls needed to look nice for the inquest tomorrow.

As he ironed, his mind fell back into the well-worn path of trying to figure out, yet again, why Diantha had died. It was the strangest thing he had ever experienced. She had been healthy, strong, and in a better mood than usual when she fixed breakfast for them that morning. A few hours later—he was building a coffin.

No wonder people were talking.

He carefully laid Ellie's little dress over the back of a chair, sat the cooled flatiron back on the stove, grabbed the second iron which had been heating, and began pressing out the wrinkles in Trudy's dress. His ironing would not come up to a woman's standards, but it was as good as he knew how to do. The trick was getting the wrinkles out without scorching the material.

"Pa?"

He glanced up. A small face looked down at him from the top steps. Ellie was the one who looked the most like Diantha. Dark hair, dark eyes, pretty little face. Trudy, on the other hand, looked more like his father's mother, who had been blonde. Polly was a combination, a mixture of both his and Diantha's families. And Agnes was at that age where she was all knees, elbows, and freckles. She was either going to be odd-looking when she grew up or a real beauty. Regardless, whoever married her would be getting a prize—as long as he didn't mind complete honesty.

"Yes, Ellie."

"Is Mama looking down at us from heaven?"

"I suppose. Why?"

"Because she told us that if anything ever happened to her she would be looking down at us from heaven."

Joshua paused in his ironing. "When did she tell you this?"

"Right before she went away."

This struck him as exceedingly strange. Diantha was not given to conversations like this with her children. "Why do you suppose she told you this?"

"I dunno." Ellie shrugged.

"Go to sleep now," he said. "It's going to be an early morning tomorrow."

As he listened to Ellie's footsteps pitter-pattering back to bed, he wished he could ask Diantha why she had said such a thing to a small child. Had she received a premonition about her own death? If so, why hadn't she told him? Or was there a deeper meaning behind her words?

"What did you do, Diantha?" he whispered. "Did you leave us on purpose?"

A noise on his front porch startled him. It was much too late for a visit. He grabbed his gun from above the door frame, blew out the wick of the oil lamp, unlatched the door, and eased it open. No one was there now, but someone *had* been there. On his porch, illuminated by starlight, lay a neat bundle of twigs bound together with string.

He kicked it as far off his porch as possible. Never had he expected to see such a message left upon his own property!

Men in this area didn't put up with someone who abused or neglected his family. They gave the man one warning, and one warning only—a bundle of twigs left on his porch late at night. It meant, treat your wife and children right, or we—the men of the community—will give you the beating of your life.

The message was so ominous that he had seen the presence

of that bundle of twigs alone sober old Fred Jones right up last year. A coward at heart, Fred had turned into a model citizen overnight.

There was no call to leave such a message on Joshua's porch. He was not a drinking man. He had always treated his family with as much love and respect as he knew how. There was no call for this . . .

Unless . . .

Someone else, someone besides Millicent Bowers, thought he was responsible for Diantha's death. Maybe even a great many people. Either that, or Virgie had decided to play a cruel trick on him. It didn't take a man's hands to make a bundle of twigs.

A smell of scorched fabric wafted to him as he stood on the porch with his gun in his hand. He rushed back inside and jerked the heavy iron off of the fabric. His heart sank. Sure enough, there was the vivid imprint of a flatiron on the back of Trudy's best dress.

It was going to be a very long night.

# 3

"The inquest starts in an hour."

Ingrid sat up and saw Hazel's head sticking up through the opening in the floor of the loft. "You don't want to miss it. This is the most excitement we've had around here in ages." Her expression grew thoughtful. "Frankly, it's the most excitement I've seen here since the last Indian uprising, and that's a very long time." Then her head disappeared again.

Ingrid blinked at the sunshine streaming through the little window. She hadn't slept this long in ages. Her first thought the moment she had opened her eyes this morning was fear that Millicent would be angry that she had not brought her morning tea on time. Then she realized, with an enormous sense of relief, that she was no longer living beneath Millicent's roof.

"I got some coffee boiling on the fire and flapjacks on the table. You were dead to the world, so I let you sleep, but now you got to hurry if we're gonna get a good seat."

Ingrid tumbled out of bed and trotted downstairs. With only Hazel and She-Wolf there, it wouldn't matter that she was still in her nightgown.

Upon the table were two plates of the flat, round cakes

that were called flapjacks here. Hazel seated herself across from her, said a brief prayer of thanksgiving, and then, after pouring warm sorghum over their flapjacks, they both dug in.

"Thank you much." Ingrid had eaten better, but she had never appreciated a meal more.

"No thanks needed. It's nice seeing another face across the table from me for a change." Hazel tossed a buttered flapjack to the great dog sitting on guard beside her. "Begging the pardon of She-Wolf here, of course."

She-Wolf's teeth snapped as she caught the flapjack in the air and consumed it in one gulp. Ingrid caught a flash of gleaming teeth that made her shiver.

"Gonna do some fishing this evening." The old woman slathered more butter and sorghum on her flapjacks. "You ever seen my boat?"

"No." Ingrid shook her head. "I have not."

"Her name is *Wind Dancer*. She's a sweetly balanced little twenty-foot dory who rides the waves like a cork. She's no young thing, but *Wind Dancer* is still seaworthy and remembers where all the good fishing spots are. Kinda like me. My husband bought her from an old trapper, and we had a high old time exploring the shoreline together. Many a night we roasted fresh perch on a beach somewhere and ate like royalty."

Ingrid was impressed. "Such a good life you and husband have."

"A life worth living is built on good friends and good choices. I've made a whole lot of both. As long as it wasn't against the Holy Scriptures, I've done what I thought best, instead of doing what people told me I oughta do."

Ingrid pondered this. There had been many people back in her village who had told Hans and her that they were foolish to spend every penny they had on a boat ticket. She had to admit, it had felt like stepping off the edge of a cliff with nothing to catch them except faith in God, faith in each other, and a dream of a better life.

Then the Lord gave her the gift of this kind woman who had offered her food and shelter. Coming here had been a good choice, and she had a feeling that being friends with Hazel was another one. Now, if only she had her beloved twin at her side! Hans would love Hazel.

"You about done with breakfast?" Hazel said. "There won't be much room over at the Rogerses' house if we don't get there early."

It didn't take long for Ingrid to throw on her dress and braid her hair. Her hair needed washing, but it had been awhile since Millicent had allowed her the luxury of preparing a bath for herself. The woman had, instead, told her that she could use the leftover water from *her* bath. Ingrid balked at that. She would rather go dirty than allow her body to touch water in which Millicent had bathed.

"Is that all you got to wear, girl?" Hazel said when Ingrid came back downstairs.

"Ja."

"I'm sure not a woman who needs fancy clothes," Hazel said, "but that dress looks like you've been wearing it ever since you left Sweden."

"Ja."

"What? You only own one dress?"

"Two." She held up two fingers. "I make many pretty dresses for new life in America." Ingrid shook her head sadly. "All gone."

"What happened?"

"Ship crew leave trunk behind. It was accident." Ingrid shrugged. "I have one dress in handbag, one dress on Ingrid, one nightgown, and one pair shoes. Soles wear out. Millicent give me George old shoes."

"Oh, you poor child," Hazel said. "We'll have to do something about that, but you'll do for now. Come on. I don't want to be late."

White Rock was too small to warrant a courthouse. Instead, their local justice of the peace, A.J. Rogers, had made his own front room available for the proceedings. By the time Hazel, She-Wolf, and Ingrid arrived, several horses were already tied to the various trees and fence posts surrounding the Rogerses' home. A few hard-looking men lounged on the porch. The women present had dressed as though for church. A handful of children played hide-and-seek.

Hazel led Ingrid over to where one of the tough-looking men was lounging and struck up a conversation.

"Is the judge here yet, Paul?" Hazel asked.

"Rode in about an hour ago," he said. "They should be starting soon."

"Is Diantha's mama and daddy or Joshua here?" Hazel asked.

Paul jerked his head toward the door. "Virgie is sitting in there right now, front and center, ready to hang Josh from what I hear."

Hazel frowned. "Last I heard, he hadn't been formally accused of anything."

"He will be after that mother-in-law of his has her say. She's mad as a hornet."

"It ain't fair." Hazel shook her head with regret. "I'd stake my life that Josh had nothing to do with Diantha's death."

"I would too," Paul said.

Hazel nodded toward the other men sitting, leaning, and standing on the porch. "I never seen these fellows before," Hazel said. "You know them?"

"Know them?" Paul gave a mirthless laugh. "I know them, ate with them, fought with them, and pulled them out from under their horses when they fell. These men are some of what's left of those of us who served with Captain Hunter. Word got out about what was being said about him, and we know it's a pack of lies. If ever there was a man who loved his wife, it was Joshua Hunter. These men rode a far piece today to give him their support. Some of us wouldn't be alive today if weren't for Captain Hunter."

"Virgie is after his scalp," Hazel said. "That poor woman has been through too much, and she's bent on blaming it on Josh. There's no telling what she might say."

Paul's gaze traveled to Ingrid. "Who's this 'un you got with you?"

"Ingrid Larsen. Until yesterday, she was the Bowerses' hired girl."

Paul looked her up and down with a friendly sort of interest. His eyes lingered on her feet.

"It looks like the job didn't turn out so well for you, did it, girlie?"

Ingrid glanced down, embarrassed. Not only was her dress practically worn out, she was wearing cast-off boots that had belonged to Mr. Bowers. He was not a large man, and she had had to cut slits into the boots so her feet would fit. She had hoped no one would notice her at all, let alone look her over so closely.

"No. Not good," Ingrid said.

"I can see that." Paul's voice was kind. "Seems to me like a shopkeeper could manage to keep his hired girl in shoes. Business must be real poorly, or else he's a stingier son of a gun than I thought."

"George is all right," Hazel said, "except when he's trying to keep Millicent happy."

The sound of a wagon rattling over rutted ground interrupted them. She-Wolf pressed protectively against Hazel.

Paul and the others lost interest in everything except the appearance of Joshua Hunter and his four little girls.

Ingrid caught her breath at the sight of him and his family. The children were as handsome as their father and as polished as it was possible for young children to be. The girls' braids were neat and their hair still bore the traces of a comb in the wet furrows of their part. Their hair ribbons matched their dresses, and their clothes were neatly pressed.

Joshua Hunter wore a freshly pressed white shirt with navy blue pants that looked as though they had once been part of a military uniform. He was clean shaven and sat erect on the seat of the farm wagon. His eyes, as they surveyed the group of people in the yard, were steely.

Mr. Hunter had been a sweaty, unshaven farmer yesterday when she first laid eyes on him, but the man who rode into A.J. Rogers's yard was no farmer. This was a soldier going into battle. Ingrid felt her pulse quicken at the sight of him.

He climbed down out of the wagon, and then his oldest daughter handed down his littlest girl, dressed in a light blue dress. Holding her in his arms, he walked toward the men clustered around the porch. The other three girls clambered out of the wagon and followed close behind him.

To her surprise, Paul left off leaning against the porch railing, took his hat off, and stood up straight. "It's good to see you, sir."

The other men who had been lounging on the porch did the same. "We're here if you need us, Hunter," one of them said.

"I'll take care of your horse and wagon, sir," another man said.

"Thank you." There was deep gratitude in Mr. Hunter's voice. "You men didn't have to come today, but I appreciate the fact that you did."

"We wanted to," Paul said.

Mr. Hunter caught sight of Ingrid standing beside Hazel and Paul.

"Are you all right now, miss?" His blue eyes drilled into her as though he actually cared about her well-being.

Joshua Hunter, in his semi-uniform, clean shaven, standing so tall, with that darling little girl in his arms, was a picture that made Ingrid's heart do a flip-flop in her chest—and then she completely forgot how to speak English.

Hazel came to her rescue. "She's doing just fine. The girl had the good sense to come to me after what Millicent done. I'll see to it that she don't never have to go back."

"Good." He nodded his approval. "I'm glad you got away from that woman, miss."

As he walked on into the makeshift courtroom, Ingrid saw several men give each other meaningful looks, and then they closed ranks behind him.

Something deep and permanent happened in Ingrid's heart as Joshua Hunter strode into the courtroom. Something that she knew would never, ever go away. This man had stopped, on this day of all days, when he had so much else to worry about—and he had noticed her.

"So there goes Captain Joshua Hunter." Hazel's voice was as proud as if he were her own son. "One of the bravest men ever to ride with the Michigan First Cavalry. He stood with General Custer at Gettysburg against Jeb Stuart. That thin line of our Michigan boys held their own against the superior numbers of Jeb Stuart's Southern cavalry and kept them from coming to the rescue of the Confederates. If Joshua and his men had given way, we would have lost the battle."

Ingrid had little understanding of the war these Americans had fought with themselves a few years back—but she liked hearing how brave Joshua had been.

"Those men would walk through fire for him, but walking

through fire won't shut up a few yappy-mouthed women. His mother-in-law seems bent on getting that man hung if she can. She's got her sister, Almeida, all up in arms over this too, and now Millicent is flapping her lips. I hope the judge has enough sense to see through all that fiddle-faddle."

"I never see a man I want to marry . . . until I see him," Ingrid whispered.

"Don't get your hopes up," Hazel said. "He was awful in love with that pretty little wife of his. I'm afraid it might be a long time before he has the heart to go courting again—which is a shame because those children surely do need a mama."

# 4

Joshua tried to take the measure of Judge Cornelius Carver, who now sat at a table, reviewing some papers that A. J. Rogers had given him.

Carver looked like a man who had ridden hard for too many miles and was not particularly happy to be here. His black suit was dusty and his eyes were red-rimmed. He did not strike Joshua as a man who intended to put up with much. There was only so much territory one judge could cover, and although this was life-and-death to him, Joshua knew that it was just another crowded makeshift courtroom to this court official.

Joshua settled himself stiffly on a chair, with Polly on his lap and the other three girls grouped around him. His in-laws were seated only a few feet away, but except for one guilty glance from his father-in-law, neither of them looked at him.

Little Bertie was nowhere to be seen, which was a disappointment. Aunt Almeida was probably keeping the child at home. A courtroom was no place for an infant—but it would have been nice to catch a glimpse of his son.

"Pa." Ellie tugged on his shirtsleeve. "I gotta go bad."

Joshua nodded toward the open door. "Go ahead but come back quickly."

"I will."

Ellie escaped the confines of the cabin. Through a window, Joshua watched the little girl head straight for the outhouse. Unless he missed his guess, that would be the last they saw of Ellie for a while. After finishing up in the outhouse, she would find a toad, or an ant colony, or some other child to play with. Sitting still was not Ellie's strong point.

"Tell the people to come in now, if they're going to," the judge said to A.J. "I do not intend to tolerate interruptions." Carver continued to peruse the sheaf of papers he had been studying earlier.

Joshua saw Hazel and the hired girl find a place on the benches that had been placed around the wall. It irked him that Millicent wore silk while allowing her to be reduced to wearing rags and what appeared to be George's cast-off shoes.

She was in good hands with Hazel, and he knew Hazel could use the company. If he could afford help, he would give the poor girl a job himself. It would be wonderful to have someone who would come and cook for the children every day.

Polly squirmed on his lap.

"Please be good, Polly," he whispered.

The little girl stuck her thumb in her mouth and settled back against his chest.

"Can I go outside, Pa?" Trudy asked. "Ellie's still out there and it's getting hot in here." She ran a finger around the collar of her dress for emphasis.

Even though it was nice outside, the makeshift courthouse was filling up, and it was already getting stuffy.

"Go ahead," he said. "But please try to keep your dress clean."

"I will, Pa."

After ruining that one little dress, he had been up half the night trying to get their clothes ready without scorching anything else. His own shirt and pants were easy compared to the girls' little things.

"Is Joshua Hunter present?" Judge Carver said.

"I am, sir."

"I'll take your testimony now."

He handed Polly off to Agnes. He hoped she wouldn't be too much for her big sister to handle. This was not a good time for his children to misbehave. As he made his way forward, there was a slight murmuring among the people who had wedged themselves into the small space. He saw that the windows had been opened so that the people outside could watch and hear.

The judge nodded to A.J. "Swear him in."

Hand on the leather-bound Bible, Joshua promised to tell the truth.

"Were you the husband of the deceased, Diantha Hunter?" the judge asked.

"I was."

"Please have a seat, Mr. Hunter," Carver said. "And tell the court what happened the day your wife died."

Joshua took the seat they offered. "Where do you want me to start?"

"This is an inquest, not a trial, Mr. Hunter," the judge said. "Just start with that morning and tell us anything you consider important."

He cleared his throat. "My wife fixed breakfast about six o'clock that morning. Then she took a walk in the woods while the children and I ate. Afterwards, she sat and drank a cup of tea with me while we made our plans for the day. She then took the children down to her mother's to help her with some spring cleaning. About two hours later, she started complaining of a bad headache. She died about twelve-thirty, about two hours after the headache started."

"Had she complained about any symptoms or pains prior to that morning?"

"No, sir."

"Was she given to walks in the woods in the morning?"

"Sometimes. She said it calmed her nerves."

"Did your wife have trouble with her nerves?"

"Occasionally."

As the judge wrote something on his papers, Agnes spoke up from where she sat with Polly on her lap.

"Mama said me and my little sisters got on her nerves a lot, sir."

Soft laughter rippled through the courtroom.

"I can imagine that she did," Carver said kindly. "But I'm asking your father questions right now."

"Sorry." Agnes's face had turned red from the laughter.

"Please continue, Mr. Hunter."

"Later that morning, Agnes came running to the barn where I was working and said that her mother had fallen. I ran down to the Youngs' farm, thinking Diantha had hurt herself, but when I got there, she came walking out to the gate. I asked her if she was sick. She laughed a little and said she had just gotten a little dizzy-headed, and then she went back into the house."

"And what happened then?" the judge asked.

"I helped my father-in-law load some lumber, then went to check on Diantha to see if she'd had any more dizzy spells. I found her out in the backyard drawing water from the well to start dinner. She said she felt fine. While Diantha and Virgie cooked, I went inside and visited with Richard for a while. About that time, my wife came into the sitting room from the kitchen and said her head was hurting."

"That was the first she mentioned a headache?" Carver asked.

"It was. She sat down a spell, and I asked if she was sick in any other way. She said she wasn't. Then she got back up and went on out to the kitchen again. It must have been after eleven o'clock by that time. I was there about five minutes when Agnes came to get me. She said something was wrong with her mother again. I went into the kitchen, and my wife was sitting in a chair, saying her head ached. I helped her go into her parents' bedroom and lie down."

Joshua looked out over the crowd. The rapt expressions on some of their faces made him feel slightly nauseous. It seemed as though some were practically feeding on the story of the events preceding his wife's death. Others, his closest friends, were staring down at the floor as though trying to give him some privacy as he recounted the most painful hours of his life.

"What measures did you take to help her?" the judge asked.

"We put a wet cloth on her head and gave her some coffee to drink. She started getting chilled, and we built up the fire and tried to make her warm."

At this, his voice choked up. He closed his eyes for a moment, trying to pull himself together.

"Please go on, Mr. Hunter," the judge said impatiently.

"It was so hot in there that I was sweating, but Diantha was shivering. Her mother put an extra quilt over her, and Richard built the fire up even hotter. Soon after that, she started complaining that her head was worse. I started to go for the doctor, but she grabbed hold of me and begged me to stay with her.

"At that point she started writhing around underneath all those covers. She started convulsing and . . ."

"And?"

Joshua took a deep breath. "She died about a minute later. Her father went for Dr. Allard, who got there about one o'clock. He said he thought the cause of her death was some sort of burst blood vessel in her brain."

"Did he mention any other possible cause of death?"

"He did." This was the moment that he had been dreading—the comment the doctor had made that had set Virgie off. "He said that the convulsions we described could also be symptoms of strychnine poisoning."

There was a gasp in the courtroom.

The judge nodded as though acknowledging that this is what he had expected him to say. "At any time previous to her death, did you hear your wife say that she was tired of living or that she would commit suicide?"

Joshua was blindsided by this question. This was private information—something he thought was just between him and Diantha. He had never mentioned it to anyone.

Judge Carver noted his hesitation and glanced up from his papers. "Please answer the question, Mr. Hunter."

"She was in one of her bad moods one day." Joshua picked a piece of lint off his army pants. "She said she was tired of living and wanted to drown herself. There were some days when she would talk like that to me when the children weren't around. She didn't mean it. It was just something she would say to let off steam. The next day she would laugh about it."

He wished he had been warned that he was going to have to repeat these words. If so, he would have sent Agnes out of the courtroom.

There was a buzz in the air as everyone absorbed this shocking information. He had planned to go to his grave never telling anyone about those conversations with Diantha.

He glanced at Agnes, who was sitting stone still. Her eyes were wide with shock. She leaped up, hiked Polly onto her hip, and ran out of the courtroom. He wished he could run after her, but Judge Carver was already following up with another question.

"Had you secreted about your house previous to her death any strychnine or other poison?"

"No." He shook his head emphatically. "I have small children in my home. I would not have risked keeping that sort of thing anywhere around them. Richard told me he hadn't bought any, either."

He didn't tell the court that he had been so afraid that Diantha might do something to herself on one of her bad days that he had made certain there was nothing about the house which she could use to hasten her death. He had even hidden his guns away in the barn and had removed all but the dullest knives from the house.

Judge Carver seemed to have lost interest in his testimony. The next question was so trivial he wondered why the judge even bothered to ask.

"What was your wife's age?"

"She turned thirty November first of last year."

"Describe your wife for the court."

"Her hair was brown, her height was five foot and two inches, and her eyes were green . . ." He hesitated. Those words seemed so inadequate to describe someone like Diantha—a woman he had loved with all his heart. "And she was the most beautiful woman I have ever known."

The judge scribbled something on a piece of paper. "You may go back to your seat. We'll take a short break."

During the break, Ingrid saw Mr. Hunter standing outside beneath a large tree, talking earnestly to Agnes, who had obviously been wounded by the things he had been forced to reveal about her mother. Her heart broke for him and his daughter.

"Why do they do this to him?" she asked Hazel.

"Diantha's mother and her aunt Almeida, who came over right after her death, were in the room when Dr. Allard mentioned the possibility of poison. Neither of them have let up since. Evidently, Diantha had told them how unhappy she was, and at least one of them brought Millicent in on it. Diantha and Millicent were friends."

"I did not know," Ingrid said.

"It does seem odd. They weren't exactly thick. Diantha had too many young children for them to spend a lot of time together, but she was closer to Millicent than anyone else."

At that moment, Millicent arose and started out the door. She seemed surprised to see Ingrid.

"So that's where you got to," she said. "I need you back at my house at once."

Ingrid was taken aback. "You make me leave."

"I changed my mind. It will take time to find someone to replace you. In the meantime, I have no one to do your chores."

"She's fine just where she is," Hazel said.

Millicent sniffed. "You don't need a servant. You could never afford to pay one in a million years, no matter how wretched the servant might be."

"You might be surprised what I can afford," Hazel said.

"Come along, Ingrid," Millicent commanded. "I'll take you home now. There are dishes to wash."

Ingrid pressed her back against the log wall. "No."

"Excuse me?"

"I stay with Hazel."

"Hmm." Millicent pursed her lips and cocked her head. "I wonder how Hazel will feel about that when George stops ordering the medicine he keeps in stock for her heart condition."

"He would not do that," Ingrid said.

Millicent's mouth curved in a knowing little smile. "George will do anything I tell him to."

"You have heart problem?" Ingrid asked Hazel.

"Nothing to worry about," Hazel said. "Besides, I can order it my ownself—ain't like I never kept a store before. I was only having George order it to give him some business." She glared at Millicent. "The man needs all the business he can get if he's gonna buy this one here all the fancy doodads she wants."

"I hope you're prepared to order everything else you need for the rest of your life once I tell George you stole my servant." Millicent glanced back and forth between the two women as though trying to figure out her next move.

Ingrid put her arm around Hazel. "All she do is give me a bed when you throw me out."

"You have a perfectly good bed at our house. I'll expect to see you in it by this evening, or I'll make certain that Hazel's money won't do her a bit of good in our store."

And with that, Millicent swished away. She-Wolf growled softly, watching her go.

"My sentiments exactly," Hazel said, patting the dog's head.

Ingrid did not want to risk bringing misfortune on her friend, but she could not bear the thought of going back to work for Millicent. The only relatives she had left in the world were an ocean away, and she had no money to get back to them. There was no other job to be had for a woman in this small, out-of-the-way place.

Mr. Hunter came back in and sat down. He moved like a man who was heart sick and bone weary. She felt so sorry for him that she shoved her own worries aside.

"I'm gonna go see if that boy needs anything." Hazel patted

Ingrid's hand. "You stay right here. Don't let Millicent get to you. We'll be just fine. Millicent must have forgot that they still owe me quite a few more payments on that store. George will get me whatever I need. Millicent doesn't have *that* much power over him. The man does have a backbone. We just don't get to see it very often."

Ingrid watched Hazel approach Mr. Hunter, wishing that she, too, had the right to go over and talk to him. Although what she would talk about, she had no idea.

Soon, Judge Cornelius Carver took his seat, and people poured back into the room. Hazel resumed her spot beside Ingrid. Agnes returned with Polly on her hip and the other two girls in tow.

"You should stay outside," Ingrid heard Mr. Hunter say to his daughters.

"We ain't leaving," Agnes said.

The two little girls who had been outside were red-faced as though they had been running and playing hard. Obviously, they were too young to understand the gravity of the situation. Their ribbons had come undone, the lace on the youngest's pantalets was torn and dragging, and both of their faces could use a wash. Agnes sat Polly down and began to rebraid Trudy and Ellie's unruly hair.

"How is he?" Ingrid whispered when Hazel had settled back down beside her.

"He's taken a pretty big hit, but Joshua is tough," Hazel said. "He's faced worse enemies than Diantha's mother and this court, but never with his children beside him. I'm so mad at Virgie I could just spit. She's probably the one who told the judge about her daughter spouting off about wanting to die just to make Josh look bad. Every woman says things she don't mean sometimes."

Ingrid could not imagine ever saying anything like that. Not with those beautiful children to care for.

"Now people will always wonder what Joshua did to make her feel that way," Hazel said. "Oh. It's starting again. I want to hear what Virgie has to say for herself."

# 5

There was a time when Joshua had liked Diantha's mother. Up until now, she had always been civil to him. In fact, when he had bought 160 acres of adjoining land from Diantha's parents after the war, he thought that since his wife was not a woman to be easily separated from her mother, the acreage he purchased next to them was as good a place as any to live.

Now, a hundred miles would not be enough distance to put between him and the Youngs as far as he was concerned. After Virgie had accused him publicly to whoever would listen of killing her daughter, he didn't have a whole lot of use for the woman, even if she was grieving.

After facing the enemy in battle, he had never dreamed the enemy would take the form of a woman in whose face he saw the shadow of his beloved wife's.

"Would Virgie Young please come forward and be sworn in?" the judge said.

Virgie was a small, slender woman like Diantha. She had seen so much trouble in her life that her hair had turned completely white even though she was only in her early fifties.

"Please tell us what happened on the day your daughter died, Mrs. Young," the judge said after she had sworn to tell the truth.

Virgie dabbed at her eyes with a wadded-up handkerchief,

and for a few moments, while the entire courtroom held its breath, she seemed unable to speak.

"Did your daughter appear to be in good health on that morning when she came to your house?" the judge prompted.

"She did."

"Do you remember anything different from what your son-in-law testified?"

"That man is not my son-in-law." Virgie pointed at Joshua. "Not anymore. Not after what he done."

"No more of that, please, Mrs. Young." The judge's voice was firm. "I repeat. Is there anything you want to add or subtract from Joshua Hunter's testimony?"

"Well, she didn't make no complaints until about ten o'clock. I started out back to get me some greens for our dinner, and Agnes comes to the back door and she says, 'Grandma, come in here quick!'

"When I come in, Diantha was lying on the floor. I asked her what was wrong. She got up, brushed herself off, laughed, and said that nothing was the matter. I asked if she had fainted, and she said she didn't think so. She started peeling some apples I was going to bake and then I heard her make a real curious noise. I looked over, and she had her head laid down against the table and her eyes shut. I shook her and asked her what was the matter. But she didn't say nothing. That's when I told Agnes to run get her pa.

"When Josh come in, he talked her into laying down on my bed." Virgie's eyes narrowed. "I know it sounds like he was all helpful, but he was just trying to make us think he hadn't done nothin' to her."

"I'll come to my own conclusions," the judge said. "Was there anyone else on the place?"

"Besides me and Richard?" Virgie thought. "Right after Diantha died, Almeida walked in."

"Who is Almeida?"

"My sister. She says to me maybe Diantha had some kind of spasm. 'Let's rub her,' she says. Sometimes people come out of it if you rub them. So we rubbed her and put camphor under her nose, but it didn't do no good."

"Where was Mr. Hunter all this time?"

"In the other bedroom just a-talking to the children. He weren't helping us try to bring Diantha back to life at all."

"Did the doctor mention a need for an autopsy?"

"Dr. Allard said he didn't think there was any reason for one. He seemed worried about a baby he had to deliver, and he was in a big hurry to go," Virgie said bitterly. "He didn't stay no time. Just up and left. Next thing I know, Richard and Joshua are a-putting my daughter in the coffin."

"Did you ever hear her say that she wanted to kill herself?"

"Yes, but I think that's just 'cause she was afraid of Josh."

Virgie hesitated, and Joshua was afraid he knew what was going to come out of her mouth next.

"Go on," the judge instructed. "Explain what you mean by that comment."

"That last Sunday, when she come for dinner, she said that she thought Josh was a-trying to kill her."

There was a rumble in the courtroom at this information.

"Ma'am." The judge shot a sideways glance at Joshua. "Do you have any idea why your daughter would say such a thing?"

"No sir." Virgie stared innocently at her entwined fingers. "But them's her exact words. She said, 'That Josh, he's gonna kill me one of these days if I don't get away from him.'"

Joshua wished he could say that his mother-in-law was lying, but he couldn't. She wasn't lying. He was quite certain that his wife had said those words to her mother. She had said them to him.

Diantha was tired of bearing and caring for their children.

She hadn't even wanted little Bertie, and she had informed Josh there would be no more children between them ever again.

He had agreed to her terms. It was not what he wanted for their relationship, but he was willing to do without physical intimacy if it would make Diantha's black moods go away.

Then one night, a few weeks after Bertie's birth, during one of Diantha's brief, sparkling, joyful periods that she sometimes had for no apparent reason, she had turned to him in the night whispering love words, and he had responded.

Was he going to have to explain all of this in front of his friends and neighbors? In front of his daughters? In front of the men with whom he had served? Did a man have to strip himself naked in a court of law?

The one thing he had chosen not to share with the court or anyone else was that on the day Diantha died, she was certain she was with child once again, and she was furious about it.

Ingrid had stopped paying attention to the court proceedings. It was late afternoon, and after Richard's testimony, the words were becoming repetitive. The headaches. The chilling. The dizziness. The death. Even the doctor had little to add except to hold to his original diagnosis that Diantha had died of something bursting inside her brain. He even said that his comment about strychnine had been the mere musings of an overworked physician. A.J. Rogers reported that a search had been made of both the Hunter and Young farms and no strychnine or any other poison had been found.

Ingrid wasn't really listening. She was far too absorbed in watching the four little girls squirming in their seats beside their daddy. Her hands ached to take a needle and thread to the one child's torn pantalets, and she wished she could neatly braid the other girl's hair that was coming undone once again from the braid the big sister had tried to do. She could tell that the oldest girl was doing her best, but no twelve-year-old could care for children like a real mother.

If only she could work for Mr. Hunter, she would be so good to those little girls!

The judge finished questioning the doctor and checked his pocket watch. Ingrid suspected that a man as important as Judge Carver could not linger long in any one spot.

"Does anyone else have something they want to say to the court?" the judge asked. "If not . . ."

"Your honor?" A lone man stood at attention in the back of the courtroom. His left arm had a hand hook on the end of it. There were scars about his left lower jaw and neck.

"Yes?"

"Private Lyman Wilson, your honor. I just want to say that I fought with and followed Captain Hunter for more'n three years when I served in the First Cavalry. I never saw a braver soldier or a more honest man. He saved my life, sir. Saved it at the risk of his own. When we weren't fighting, he'd tell us about his pretty wife back home, and the one little girl they had then, and how bad he wanted to get back to them. There's not a one of us who served with the captain who thinks there's a word of truth in whoever's been telling folks that he kilt that poor woman."

The former soldier lifted his chin and looked around the courtroom. "Anyone who says Josh Hunter hurt his wife is a yellow-bellied liar, and I challenge ever' last one of you to a fair fight!"

A raucous cheer went up from the back of the room where the knot of former soldiers stood, all of them evidently itching for a chance to lick somebody on Joshua's behalf.

"I fought with the Third Infantry myself, Mr. Wilson."

The judge gazed thoughtfully at the remnant of the First Cavalry that had come to support Joshua. "In my opinion, no one knows a man's nature better than those who have fought alongside of him. Your words carry a good bit of weight with me."

"They do?" Private Lyman Wilson looked startled.

Judge Carver picked up the gavel he had brought with him and twirled it in his hands.

"Based on the fact that there has been no evidence whatever of foul play, based on the fact that there has been no evidence provided of strychnine or any other poisonous substances found upon the premises of the Young or Hunter farms, based on the fact that the doctor who examined the body saw no basis for doing an autopsy or for believing Diantha Hunter was poisoned, based on the character witnesses I see today in the presence of the men who served with Mr. Hunter, *and* based on the fact that I am due in Port Hope in four hours—I am hereby ruling Diantha Hunter's death one of unknown causes." He hit the table with his gavel. "Court is dismissed."

Ingrid saw Mr. Hunter whisper a few words into his oldest daughter's ear, and then he walked to the back of the room to talk to the former soldiers who had come to support him. Several people pumped his hand and patted his back as he made his way through the crowd. People in the courtroom, tired from sitting and surfeited with about as much drama as they could absorb, began gathering their things for their journey home.

Suddenly, there was a stir up front. She saw Diantha's parents in deep conversation with the judge, and then she heard the judge's gavel come down hard.

"Will everyone please take their seats?" the judge said.

People sat down but looked at one another, puzzled.

"Another serious matter has been brought to my attention

regarding this case," the judge said. "Richard and Virgie Young are accusing Joshua Hunter of negligence in his parental duties and have petitioned the court for protective custody of all five of the Hunter children."

"You can't take away my children!" Mr. Hunter exclaimed. "They're all I have left!"

"I sympathize with you, Mr. Hunter," the judge said, "but it is not the court's responsibility to protect the parent's feelings. It is the duty of the court to protect the best interests of the children. From what little I've seen today, the Youngs' accusation that you are overwhelmed and unable to give your children the care they need is justified."

Ingrid saw Agnes try to tuck the torn lace of Ellie's pantalets out of sight.

"Pa's doing the best that he can," Agnes said, unwittingly hammering the nail deeper into her father's coffin. "He can't help it if he can't cook nothin' much but corn mush and Polly don't have no diapers on most of the time when she's playin' outside. He can't help it if he can't iron Trudy's dress without burning a hole in it. That's no call to make us go live with Grandma and Grandpa."

"It will only be temporary," the judge said kindly. "In a year I'll come back through here and reevaluate the situation. Perhaps your father will have found a new mother for you by then."

"But Grandma won't even let Pa see baby Bertie!" Agnes protested. "If you do this, she won't let Pa back inside the door. She won't let us see him at all, and Judge . . . our pa really needs us."

"You girls need a competent woman taking care of you." The judge's face grew stern. "I've made my decision." He raised the gavel.

Ingrid saw Mr. Hunter's eyes dart around the courtroom,

as though desperately searching for an answer. She didn't blame him. She would not want her children being cared for by someone who hated her, either. His soldier friends mumbled among themselves, but this was not a fight they knew how to wage.

Her eyes fastened upon the gavel as it began to descend, almost in slow motion. Joshua bowed his head—whether in prayer or defeat, she did not know. Instinctively, she knew that if the children were wrested from him, it would destroy him. She also knew that if Virgie was as hateful to the children as she was to him, the girls would be permanently damaged by living with her. Ingrid was only a witness to this terrible thing, but it was tearing her apart.

"Stop!" She surprised everyone—including herself—by leaping to her feet amidst this room full of people she had originally hoped would not even notice her. "I take care of children!"

There had been no conscious thought before she jumped up. It had felt almost as though an unseen hand had propelled her there.

Her face burned as everyone swiveled to stare at her, but in spite of knowing she was probably making a fool of herself in front of dozens of witnesses, she lifted her head and squared her shoulders. Ingrid knew her own worth—even if no one else in the room did. She knew she could absolutely make a good home for those little girls—and their father—if given the chance.

"I take care of children," she repeated. "I marry him."

In spite of the fact that dozens of people were openly gaping at her, she had eyes only for Joshua.

"I . . . marry you," she said, praying that the Lord would open Mr. Hunter's eyes and allow him to see into her heart. Praying that Mr. Hunter would see the woman she was.

They were practically strangers, but she had never felt so sure of anything in her life than that she could build a good life with this man. She had seen the kindness in his eyes when he had stopped to inquire about her well-being this morning—when he had bigger things to worry about. She had seen the esteem in which his men held him. Most of all, she had watched him fight for his children when too many men would have gladly handed the responsibility over to their in-laws.

Well, she would help him fight. Even if it meant making a fool of herself in front of all these people. She looked hard into his eyes, willing him to see past her ragged clothes and the whip marks on her face. Her heart hammered inside her chest, and she held her breath, waiting for his response.

When she had awakened this morning, it had never occurred to her that before nightfall, she would propose marriage to a widowed stranger with five children.

Someone sniggered on the front row. The judge cast a warning glance at them and they stopped, but Ingrid knew that if Joshua did not speak soon, the whole courtroom would burst into laughter.

She had taken a desperate gamble.

"This is ridiculous!" Millicent stood and pointed at Ingrid. "That girl is my servant. She doesn't even know the man!"

"Is this true?" the judge asked.

"Now, everybody just hold your horses." Hazel shot to her feet and put a protective hand on Ingrid's shoulder. "And I'm talking to you too, Judge. How about you just put that little wooden hammer down and give us a minute to sort this out."

The sight of an old woman might not have been enough to stop the proceedings, but the sight of an old woman with a wolf-dog the size of a small moose standing beside her, with its hackles raised and teeth bared, definitely captured the judge's attention. He laid the gavel to one side.

"How are you involved in any of this, ma'am?"

"My name is Mrs. Samuel Smith, your honor." Hazel drew herself up to her full height. "Me and my husband founded this town, and before I say anything else, I got a question to ask you."

"Please make it brief."

"Were you serious when you said if these children get a new mama, they can stay with their daddy instead of having to live with a woman bent on punishing a good man because she's hurting so bad?"

"If it appears that the stepmother will make a good home for the children, then yes, I would allow them to live with their father."

"Welllll," Hazel drew the word out as she cocked one eyebrow and gave Mr. Hunter a stern look. "It appears that there's been some courtin' being done around here that nobody but me's known much about. Josh here has been sparkin' my good friend Ingrid these past few days. From what I understand—and I might be wrong about this—but from what I understand, he was thinkin' of popping the question his ownself in a few months." Hazel once again cocked an eyebrow and gave Joshua a meaningful look. "Ain't that so, Josh."

A dead silence fell over the courtroom as everyone gawked back at Joshua.

"That's a lie!" Millicent fumed. "Joshua Hunter has not been courting that girl!"

"I don't see as you can know that for sure," the judge said. "You wouldn't be the first woman to not know that her hired help was seeing someone behind her back." He glanced at his pocket watch again. "What's it going to be, Mr. Hunter? It appears that you have a serious marriage proposal from a woman you evidently care about. I can perform a quick ceremony right now or the children can go home with their grandparents until I come back—which won't be soon. Your choice—but you'd better make it fast."

Hazel motioned for Ingrid to bend down, and the old woman whispered in her ear. "Sorry about that little bitty exaggeration of mine!"

Ingrid knew that what Hazel had told the judge was a whole lot closer to a lie than an exaggeration, but she also knew that now would not be a wise time to correct her.

Joshua saw the look of longing in the hired girl's face and knew that she was only waiting for a word from him. It had taken incredible courage for her to do what she did—or incredible desperation. He had nothing but pity for the girl, but he had been placed in a terrible position. He could refuse and humiliate her *and* Hazel—and in so doing have all of his children end up in Virgie and Richard's care, where they would be well fed and well clothed. But with the venom that existed against him in that household, he did not want to gamble with how his children would feel about him a year from now. He knew that Virgie was capable of trying to turn all five of them against him.

His only other option was to go along with Hazel in this charade of having been courting this poor immigrant girl.

During the war, he had learned to use whatever means possible to win a battle with the fewest casualties. In this case, if he did not win the battle, the casualties would be the hearts of his children.

Hazel knew the girl. She would only have spoken up if she believed the girl would treat his children well. He had little to offer except food and shelter, but apparently she had nothing at all. If he was very lucky, it might turn out that she could cook—which would be quite a blessing.

It wasn't the best solution, but it was better than having to fight Richard and Virgie every time he wanted to see his children. Another pair of hands to help around the farm would be a welcome thing, and it wasn't as though he expected to ever love another woman after Diantha. One woman was as good as another to him—as long as she was good to his children. He had heard of men sending off for mail-order brides and of it working out. At least in this situation, she wasn't a complete unknown. Hazel vouching for her meant something. That woman had an eagle eye when it came to assessing a person's character.

But if he was going to marry this girl in front of all these people, it was going to be on his own terms. He would not allow this courtroom to think that he had been railroaded.

He rose, walked to where she stood, and leaned over to whisper into her ear. "What *is* your name?"

She whispered back. "Ingrid Larsen."

He got down on one knee and took her calloused hand in his. He took in the battered men's boots, the faded dress, and the emaciated body. Then the soldier within him said in a voice loud enough for the entire room to hear: "Miss Ingrid Larsen, would you do me the honor of becoming my wife?"

## 6

"This is a joke," Virgie Young shouted. "He doesn't even know the woman! Do you see what kind of man he is, Judge? He's marrying a complete stranger just to keep our grandchildren away from us . . . and . . . and he's a murderer!"

"Madam," Judge Carver said, "what I see before me is an honorable man who has lost a wife and does not want to lose his children. I see a grandmother who is so distraught with grief that she has wasted the court's time with unfounded accusations."

"But what about my daughter saying he was going to kill her?"

"Your daughter had just been delivered of a baby a few months earlier. I am certain other women have said such things about their husbands in similar circumstances."

"But—"

"Stop it!" Richard put both hands on Virgie's shoulders and gave her a shake. "None of this is going to bring Diantha back."

"This court is adjourned," Judge Carver said. "Whoever wishes to witness the marriage between these two people can reconvene in exactly five minutes."

Millicent stomped over to where Hazel and Ingrid stood, but Joshua stepped in and blocked Ingrid from her view.

"What do you want, Millicent?" he said.

"This is ridiculous," Millicent said. "You never met the girl until yesterday."

"As the judge pointed out"—Joshua's voice took on a dangerous-sounding edge—"you aren't the first woman ignorant of what your hired girl has been doing."

"Well, I know she hasn't been seeing you!"

Several grouped around, watching and listening to this conversation.

"Would you like for me to describe the scene I saw yesterday in your living room, Mrs. Bowers?" Joshua drawled. "I am absolutely certain your friends here would love to know the method with which you discipline your help."

"You wouldn't." Millicent's voice was low and vicious.

"I would." Joshua leaned in and lowered his voice. "If you *ever* try to hurt this woman again, in any way, you will answer to me. I promise you that you will not like my response."

Millicent took a step backward. It was obvious that she had finally met her match.

Any doubts Ingrid might have had about this makeshift marriage dissolved as she watched her former mistress back into the crowd. Having a man who would stand up for her against an opponent as formidable as Millicent was worth every risk she was taking.

"There was a bundle of switches left on Josh's porch last night," Virgie yelled desperately from the front. "Everyone knows that's a sign he's not fit to be a father."

"I didn't tell a soul about that," Joshua said, "including the children. Exactly how do *you* know about that, Virgie?"

"I . . . I . . ." Her eyes darted around the courtroom. "Somebody told me."

"If anyone here had a hand in laying that bundle on my doorstep," Joshua asked, "I'd take it kindly if you'd speak up."

Not one person said a word.

"I told her not to do it, Josh," Richard said. "But her and Almeida were set on making you think you were going to get a beating."

"I kind of figured that," Joshua said.

Ingrid had no earthly idea what she was supposed to do next. Was she supposed to just walk over to the judge and start saying her vows?

"Hello." A sweet-faced young woman neatly dressed in a dove-gray dress came up to Ingrid. "My name is Susan Cain. My father preaches here in White Rock when he isn't out circuit riding to other churches."

"Hello." Ingrid had no idea what circuit riding meant, but it must have been a good thing, because Susan sounded like she was proud of her father.

Without another word, Susan stood up on a chair and raised her voice until it carried over the crowd. "It is customary for a bride to have something borrowed upon her person on her wedding day."

Ingrid wondered if George's boots qualified.

Susan hopped down and pressed a lace hankie into Ingrid's hand. "Please accept this handkerchief as something borrowed. You can return it next week when you and your new husband come to call. My mother and I will be expecting you."

Ingrid marveled at how Susan took charge of the situation. The preacher's daughter gave a meaningful look to all the other women clustered about. "I believe it is also customary for a bride to have something blue, something old, and something new?"

There was a hesitation as the other women looked at each other. Then another woman, middle-aged and stout, pushed her way through and took a lovely fringed shawl from her own shoulders. "This is something new." She draped the shawl around Ingrid's back and arms. "My oldest girl just sent it to me all the way from New York City, and I have a perfectly good one at home. You go ahead and keep it."

"Thank you." Ingrid was so grateful. The shawl was a deep maroon color and beautiful. As she settled it around her shoulders, she was grateful to have at least one pretty thing to wear for her wedding.

Another woman who appeared to be an older copy of Susan fumbled with the collar of her dress and unpinned a small brooch with tiny blue beads. "I just remembered. I have something blue! Here, dear." She fastened it onto Ingrid's dress and gave it a pat. "That will do nicely. I'm Emma Cain, Susan's mother. My husband planned to be here today, but our old cow that's about to calve wandered off and he's out trying to find her."

Ingrid did not remember any of these women ever coming to call on Millicent, so she thought it was a safe guess that they were not friends of her former mistress.

"Well, lookee here what I just found." Ingrid saw Private Lyman Wilson nudge Joshua's shoulder with his own. "This ole wedding ring just flopping around in my pants pocket. You suppose it would rate as something old?"

"I can't take that," Joshua said.

"Sure you can." Lyman held it out. "A woman needs a ring on her wedding day. Besides, it's not doing me any good without a left hand to wear it on."

"You could wear it on your right," Joshua pointed out.

"My Leah has been gone these past two years," Lyman said. "I'm fixing to start courting again myself soon. Sorry if it's a little big, but you can get it fixed later on if she wants. It would be an honor for me to know your wife is wearing it."

"Thank you, Lyman." Joshua accepted the ring and put it safely in his breast shirt pocket.

"So you're gonna be our new ma, huh?" Agnes, still toting the littlest girl on her hip, butted her way through the crowd. People backed off to watch the confrontation between the new stepmother and Joshua's oldest girl.

It was the first time Ingrid had seen Agnes up close. Now she saw that the girl's eyes were way too old for a child her age. The other people faded into the background as Ingrid focused all her attention on Agnes. "I be good mother to you and little ones."

"Well, I guess I could use some help with these younguns." Agnes motioned for Ingrid to bend over. "Can I tell you a secret?"

Ingrid leaned down until her ear was even with Agnes's mouth.

"If you're ever mean or hurtful to my pa or my sisters, I'll cut your heart out with a dull spoon while you're a-sleeping and I'll feed it to the coyotes. Do you understand, lady?"

"Ja!" Ingrid straightened up and looked at the child with concern. "I understand."

"Good." Agnes turned an angelic smile toward everyone standing around. "Ellie and Trudy—come say hey to our new ma."

Ingrid was still absorbing Agnes's threat when the judge called for everyone's attention.

"Will the wedding party come forward?" Judge Carver's voice boomed across the room. "I really do have to get going."

"Come and stand up with me," she heard Joshua say to Lyman.

Lyman looked dumbstruck. "Well, I'd be honored!"

Ingrid turned to Hazel. "Will you . . . ?"

"Why, sure, me and She-Wolf would love to stand up with you."

Susan, who had disappeared outside for a few moments, ran back in with a bouquet of dandelions. She shoved them into Ingrid's hand. "Here. This is the best I could do. Every bride should have a bouquet."

With a borrowed lace hankie, some woman's new fringed shawl, the preacher's wife's brooch, a bouquet of dandelions, and She-Wolf and Hazel as bridesmaids, Ingrid covenanted herself to a stranger while an ant that had been clinging to the dandelions crawled up her elbow.

And with that, Ingrid Larsen's new life began.

As he drove his family home, Joshua held the reins loosely in his hands and pondered the strange turns a man's life could take. Never in his wildest dreams would he have imagined that morning when he left his cabin that he would be bringing a new wife back with him.

He had no earthly idea what to say to the woman.

Ingrid rode in silence, her battered piece of luggage at her feet.

Even the girls seemed awed into silence by the fact that there was a strange woman going home with them.

"It will be late when we get home." Joshua cleared his throat. "I'm afraid there's not much to eat, and I didn't have time to tidy things up before we left."

"I can cook," Ingrid said. "I can clean."

Silence.

"I have a good start on a nice cherry orchard." Joshua made another attempt. "I'm hoping to have a good crop next spring. The trees should be mature enough by then."

"Cherries are good."

"Yes, they are."

Silence.

"You got any idea how to make biscuits?" Agnes spoke from the back of the wagon. "Pa's are as hard as rock. I almost broke my tooth on one last week."

"I make good biscuits."

This was of great interest to Agnes. "Do you know how to make gravy?"

"Ja." Ingrid nodded.

"Biscuits and gravy sure would be tasty tonight before we go to bed," Agnes hinted.

Ingrid looked at Joshua. "You want I make biscuits and gravy?"

"Yes!" He spoke so emphatically that the woman jumped and looked at him with concern. He hadn't realized until Agnes began talking about food how hungry he was.

"That is fine, then," Ingrid said.

"Can you sew?" Agnes pressed.

"Ja, I sew fine."

He waited, but the woman never said another word. She seemed content to sit in silence, so Joshua stopped trying to make conversation and concentrated on other things—like where, exactly, he would sleep tonight. His stomach rumbled. It really would be helpful if the woman could cook.

Ingrid had a hundred questions on the tip of her tongue, but she did not have the nerve to ask even one. If only she had had time to prepare herself for all of this! The judge, however, would have thought something was strange if Joshua had not taken his new bride home with him tonight.

A new bride.

She had never been a bride before. She wasn't certain how she should act or what she should do.

"This is it." He stopped the wagon and horse in front of a small, sturdy-looking log cabin.

Ingrid drew a deep breath and looked around. There was much she could do with this place. There was a fine, big barn to the right of the cabin with a large corncrib. Neat split-rail fences created a roomy pasture where a healthy-looking dairy cow and two well-muscled plow horses stood contentedly cropping grass. To the left of the cabin was a large vegetable garden. Next to it was a smokehouse. Then came a low chicken house and a pigpen with two lean young hogs rooting in the earth. Behind the cabin, on a small rise, she saw the cherry orchard, which had a few white blossoms. Seeing all this gave her great pleasure. Joshua was no slovenly farmer. He took pride in his home.

"You and the girls go on in," he said as he leaped down from the wagon seat, "while I put the wagon away and take care of the horse."

Ingrid had seen George help Millicent down from their buggy many times. She had watched other men helping their wives down from various buggies and wagons. Perhaps this was what married women in America were supposed to expect. She did not want to make a mistake so soon after her marriage. She lifted her valise onto her lap and waited. While she waited, she fingered the unfamiliar wedding ring Joshua had placed upon her hand.

"Something wrong with your legs?" Agnes said as she jumped off the wagon.

"No." Ingrid hurriedly climbed down.

"Oh," Joshua said, rushing over. "I forgot to help you down. I'm sorry."

"Is fine."

"So many things on my mind."

"Is fine." She stood in the middle of the yard, unsure of what to do next. Although she was now supposedly the mistress of the house, it felt odd to walk into a strange home without first being invited. Joshua was no help. He had already gone back to unhitching the wagon.

"Don't be scared." Trudy took hold of Ingrid's hand.

That small act of kindness gave Ingrid courage. Together, they entered the cabin.

The chaos inside was appalling.

Dirty dishes were piled on the table. Dirty clothes lay abandoned in a corner. A cold fireplace was filled with dead ashes, many of which were spilling across the hearth and out onto the floor. The remains of what appeared to be the family's breakfast sat in two skillets on top of the wood cookstove. Flies buzzed around the cold stove and blanketed the leftover food.

A little girl's yellow dress lay across a chair rung, the perfect imprint of a too-hot iron upon the bottom.

"It's even worse than I remembered," Joshua said as he came through the door. He scratched his head. "It usually isn't this bad. I didn't want to be late to the inquest, and I was trying to get the girls ready this morning, and . . ."

"Is fine." Ingrid sat her one piece of luggage on the floor and rolled up her sleeves. This, at last, was something she knew how to handle. "Is all fine."

"I'll, uh, just put this in the bedroom." Joshua opened a door and shoved it inside. She caught a glimpse of an unmade bed.

"I need water. And soap. And kindling." Ingrid put her hands on her hips and took stock. The cabin had only two rooms: the big sitting room with the kitchen area at the end, and the small bedroom. Narrow stairs led to a loft.

"Of course." He hurried out the door with a bucket.

"Are you gonna make us something to eat or what?" Agnes was still holding Polly. "Those biscuits and gravy sure did sound good back there."

"We wash dishes. Then cook."

"I don't mind washing dishes," Agnes said, "if that's what we gotta do to get some food around here."

The stove had a water reservoir that had retained some warmth from the morning. With the girls showing her where everything was kept and Joshua bringing her water, kindling, and firewood, Ingrid built a good fire in the stove, then helped Agnes deal with the stacked and dirty dishes, pots, and pans while they waited for the oven to heat. When the fire warmed to a temperature hot enough to bake biscuits, she could finally create the meal she had promised, and more.

It was difficult cooking with four hungry children underfoot, but by the time Joshua came in from caring for his livestock and doing his evening chores, she was setting supper out on the table. Fried potatoes. A pyramid of biscuits. Sliced ham from the smokehouse. Plenty of ham gravy made with flour and drippings. Plus a bowl of honey still in the comb. It was the best she could do with such little notice.

Joshua stopped and stared. "Oh, my." A slow grin spread over his face. "Real, honest-to-goodness food. Thank you, Ingrid."

She did not feel comfortable sitting down with her new family. Instead, she stood beside the stove, ready to serve them.

"Sit down." Joshua grasped her hand and tugged. "Eat with us. You must be so tired after everything that's happened today."

She obeyed, as she believed a good wife should. Inside, she was greatly pleased. Many men would have gobbled the food with no thought for their wife's comfort, but her Joshua was not such a man.

Her mind was spinning with possibilities for the future. She had married a fine man who was respected by other men. He owned his own farm and a promising orchard, and took care of his animals before taking thought to his own needs. The fact that he had wrestled with an unfamiliar flatiron trying to make his daughters presentable melted her heart.

She could hardly believe that she was sitting here with her new husband who had eyes the color of the ocean she had crossed, and best of all—oh, how blessed a woman she was—he had just led their family in a fine prayer of thanksgiving before he put so much as a bite of food into his mouth.

One of the reasons she had longed to come to America—apart from the fact that there were jobs and inexpensive land here—was because she and Hans were Pietists, a group that strove to lead lives of piety and personal holiness. Those in charge of the well-established Lutheran church back home were not pleased that there were those who did not accept church doctrine without question. They were especially displeased that there were those who felt it necessary to study the Scriptures for themselves instead of putting blind trust in the Lutheran clergy. Things had gotten to the point that there had been some persecution, and many Swedish Pietists were immigrating to this new land for that fact alone. Hans had written her the good news that many American churches were now emphasizing the need for Bible study and personal accountability over the trappings of tradition and form.

Although the Bowerses occasionally drove a great distance to some church that Millicent approved of in a larger town, there was no church building in the small village of White Rock. However, there must be some sort of church since Susan had mentioned that she was a preacher's daughter. Perhaps, like the Pietists back home, there were people here who worshiped in one another's homes.

As Joshua and the girls dug into their heaping plates, she prayed her own silent prayer of gratitude and asked that the years would be good to them. That she would learn to be a good mother to these children. That someday her husband would give her children of her own. And that somehow, some way, God would give her a miracle and Joshua Hunter would learn to love her.

Two hours later, Ingrid rolled her sleeves back down. Joshua was busy tucking all four girls into their beds in the loft in the cleanest clothes she could find. The dishes were all put away. The bits and pieces of leftover food had been thrown to the hogs. She had rinsed a kettle of beans, which was now soaking for tomorrow's dinner, and she had swept the fireplace clean. Much had been accomplished.

Joshua came downstairs and sat down at the kitchen table, looking tired to death. There were dark circles beneath his eyes. She could only guess at the emotional toll this day had taken on him.

"You're still working," he said. "What can I do to help you?"

"Nothing," she said. "Go. Rest. I will come to bed soon."

Joshua didn't argue. He disappeared into the bedroom. With pounding heart, she went out to the well to draw one last bucket of water. She drew the dripping bucket up and sat it on a small bench near the house.

She felt shy about getting ready for her wedding night inside the house, so she slipped her dress off outside in the dark and dipped a clean rag into the bucket of cold well water. With a sliver of lye soap, she washed herself as well as she could and then slipped on the only nightgown she owned.

She threw her bath water away and then quietly entered

her new home. Pulse racing, she opened the door to the small bedroom she and Joshua would share.

He was sound asleep, fully clothed, facedown, sprawled out as though trying to claim every square inch of the bed for himself. Trying not to take up any more space than absolutely necessary, she carefully moved his arm and curled up beside her new husband.

A wolf howled in the distance, a mournful, lonely sound. She decided that she would not allow herself to be afraid of that wolf—or anything else. She would defend her new home with her life, whether the man of the house ever learned to care for her or not.

# 7

Joshua awoke in the early morning darkness from a vivid dream in which Diantha and he were still young and very much in love. It was in this half dream, while clothed in a foggy happiness, that he put an arm around the warm body next to him and pulled her close.

That was when he fully awoke. This person he had reached for was not Diantha. His wife had been a small, soft handful. Just the right size for a man to wrap his arms around. The person he was embracing was all bones and angles and nearly as large as himself. She also smelled of lye soap instead of the French-milled rose-scented soap that Diantha had hoarded for herself.

"Good morning," the woman said.

Had her body been made of hot coals, he could not have let loose of her more quickly.

"G-good morning." He scrambled out of bed so fast, his feet got caught in the blankets and he stumbled and fell. As he lay on the floor, tangled in blankets, she rose from the bed and knelt beside him.

"You are hurt?" she asked.

The shock of falling had jarred a little sense back into his dream-muddled brain, but for the life of him, he could not remember the name of the woman he had married yesterday.

"No, no, I'm not hurt." He untangled himself from the bedcovers, grateful that he was still fully clothed.

"I fix breakfast?" the woman asked.

What *was* her name?

"Yes, that would be good, thank you."

To his surprise, she immediately set to making the bed. But instead of simply drawing the covers up, which had been Diantha's habit, she unbuttoned one side of the straw tick and reached in and smoothed the mounds of straw out more evenly. Then she straightened and tucked the bedcovers.

"I'll go milk the cow," he said for lack of anything better to say.

"Ja. That is fine." She gave the neatly made bed a satisfied pat.

What was this woman's *name*?

By the time he had finished milking, strained the milk, set it to cool in the small cellar out back, and brought yesterday's already-cooled milk into the kitchen, she was completely dressed, her hair was neatly braided, and she was standing in front of the stove.

"I'll go get the eggs now," he said.

"I already do." She nodded toward the cast-iron skillet, in which eggs spluttered in bacon grease. Thick pieces of fried bacon from the smokehouse lay on a platter nearby.

"Oh."

"Coffee is ready. Please sit." She gestured with the spatula. "I take care of everything."

And so Joshua sat at his own kitchen table feeling like an awkward guest while she placed a cup before him and filled it with coffee.

"Good?" She avidly watched as he took a sip.

It was the blackest, strongest coffee he had ever tasted.

"Yes," he lied, "very good."

She studied his face with a worried expression. "Not good."

"It's a little strong, and I like cream."

"I fix." She poured hot water into his cup and added cream that she skimmed from the top of yesterday's milking.

He sipped again. It was rich and delicious. "Very good."

Her face lit up like he had given her a gift. Smiling, she turned back to the stove.

An aroma of something sweet came from the oven. She folded a dish towel and brought out what smelled like a bit of heaven. Somehow she had managed to find some raisins and nuts, which now studded the golden pastry.

"How in the world did you manage *that*!"

She shrugged modestly.

He pinched off a piece of the hot pastry, placed it on his tongue, and felt it melt in his mouth.

She waited for his appraisal.

"That is delicious, um . . . ma'am."

Her face fell. "I am Ingrid."

"I know." It was a lie, and they both knew it.

She turned back to the stove while he chastised himself for having unintentionally hurt her. Living with a woman he barely knew was not going to be easy—even if she was a good cook.

Silence descended upon the kitchen. He watched while she carefully spooned hot bacon grease over the frying eggs. The girl was certainly no beauty. Everything about her looked used, from her borrowed men's shoes to her frayed brown dress.

She brought the eggs, still spluttering in the skillet, and sat them in the middle of the heavy oak table. Then she refilled his cup, took her place at the table, and sat with her hands folded in her lap and her head down. Waiting.

Her submissive posture unnerved him. She was trying so very hard to please that it made him uncomfortable. Something needed to change if they were going to get through this.

"Do you like coffee, Ingrid?" He deliberately used her name.

She nodded.

"How do you like it?"

"With sugar." She started to rise.

"No." He put a hand out. "Don't." He took one more sip of the coffee she had brought him. "Let me."

Hoping to break the ice between them, he rose from the table, filled a cup, put in a heaping teaspoon of sugar, and brought it to her. She accepted it with wide-eyed wonder.

"Thank you," she said softly.

"Is the coffee to your taste?"

She took a sip and nodded. Her eyes were a light blue, and her eyelashes were the same light blonde of her hair. Her features were even, and her complexion was creamy white. Her body—well, the shapeless work dress she was wearing didn't give away much. Her hands were roughened and red from work. When she was standing, she was only a couple inches shorter than him, and he was not a short man. Had he tried, he could not possibly have brought home anyone more different from Diantha.

"Breakfast looks tasty," he said lamely.

"Do you want I wake the children now?"

"Yes, please." He desperately wanted to have the girls sitting here at the table with him, absorbing some of the awkwardness between him and his new . . . wife.

Few things had ever pleased Ingrid more than the sight of those four little girls lapping up her breakfast like hungry puppies. Of course, it was a challenge to find things to cook when she had not been the one to choose the contents of the family's food supply, but she had long ago mastered the art of putting together things that tasted good even when ingredients were sparse.

"Should we make a trip to town?" Joshua asked. "For supplies?"

"Today?" She shook her head. "No."

He seemed relieved. She didn't blame him. The last thing she wanted to do was go back into town the day after their very public wedding.

By nine o'clock in the morning, she had gathered eggs, set a nice, even fire in the cookstove, fed her new family, washed the dishes, swept the floor, put the overnight-soaked beans to simmering on the back of the stove, and, while the children helped their father weed the vegetable garden, scrubbed the wooden floor on her hands and knees with lye soap. She threw the dirty water outside and stood surveying the damp, clean floor with satisfaction.

"You gonna do the wash today?" Agnes asked. "It sure has piled up lately."

"Ja. I do laundry," Ingrid agreed. "Today is fine day for drying."

"And there's some mending that needs doing."

Ingrid nodded. "Tonight I mend."

Agnes contemplated her through narrowed eyes, as though evaluating how far she could push.

"I sure could use me a new dress," Agnes said. "And so could Trudy. I've about grown out of this one, and Pa ruined Trudy's best dress with the iron."

Ingrid put both hands on Agnes's shoulders and turned her around. The dress was shorter than it should be for a girl her age, and it was getting too tight beneath the arms.

"You have . . . material?"

"Not that I know of, but Mama had some real pretty dresses. Do you think it might be possible to cut one of them down to fit me?" Agnes's voice, usually so very grown up, grew hopeful. It was the first time Ingrid had heard a hint of the child's voice hidden beneath Agnes's prickly grown-up one.

"I sew you fine dress."

"Can you do smocking?"

"Ja. I smock too."

"Huh." Agnes stared at her in amazement. "How about that."

Ingrid was amused at the child's surprise. "After we wash, we sew."

"Sounds good to me, lady."

Lady? That did not seem like something a child should call a mother—not even a new stepmother.

What she secretly longed to hear coming out of these children's mouths was "mama," just like she had called her own mother, but it was too soon to hope for such a thing.

"Please call me Ingrid," she said. "Not 'lady.'"

"You sew me a nice dress," Agnes said, "and I'll call you anything you want."

Joshua had carefully explained to her exactly where he would be if she needed him. He had even taken her outside and pointed to the far pasture where he would be plowing ground for corn. This made her feel protected and cared for.

Before he left, he had also taken the time to show her his new pride and joy, a John Deere plow, which he said was going to revolutionize farming. It was a fine thing, indeed, and Ingrid, who had helped Hans plow their small acreage back home, genuinely admired the exquisitely made tool. It had been a nice, friendly moment between them.

With a light heart, Ingrid drew water from the well and filled the two washtubs. Then she lit a fire beneath a large kettle outdoors. It was a beautiful spring day, and laundry was one of her favorite chores when the weather was fine. Agnes brought the washboard, and without a word, the child began to scrub a dress while Ellie and Trudy played with Polly beneath a large maple tree nearby.

Ingrid stood back, watching Agnes with her skinny arms trying to do a grown woman's job, and it made her ache to think of how hard this child had struggled to care for her family since her mother's death. Agnes was a force to be reckoned with, but she was still, deep down, just a little girl.

"You want to play with sisters, ja?"

Agnes looked over her shoulder at the three little girls. "We got work to do," she said and went back to the scrub board.

"No." Ingrid gently pulled the wet dress out of Agnes's hands and turned her away from the washboard. "You go be little girl."

"Are you serious, lady . . . I mean, Ingrid?" Agnes cocked her head to one side, taking her measure. "You want me to go play? There's an awful lot of clothes here."

"This job, for *me*, is play." Ingrid nodded toward the laundry tubs. "You go be *liten flicka*, a little girl."

Agnes's big gray eyes slowly filled with tears, and her skinny arms suddenly encircled Ingrid's waist. For one brief, fleeting moment Ingrid felt the thrill of an unexpected hug from her new daughter. Then Agnes ran to her sisters.

The rest of the morning went by like a song.

Their dinner was not elaborate, but Joshua, once again, seemed inordinately grateful for her cooking, and the children had good appetites. She had noticed, when she came back inside after hanging out the laundry, that the cabin smelled much better from all the cleaning she had done.

"You scrubbed the floor," Joshua said. "You didn't have to do that."

He had noticed. She smiled modestly down at her plate. She was enormously pleased with how this day was going. She intended to astonish Joshua with his well-ordered home.

As odd as it felt coming home to see a stranger presiding over his wife's kitchen, Joshua certainly couldn't fault the woman's work ethic. An enormous burden had been lifted from his shoulders today at noon. He had come home for dinner and found the cabin filled with productive domestic activity, and his children were not cross with each other for a change. Agnes had even smiled a couple of times while they ate, and he had not seen his oldest daughter smile since she had lost her mother.

By the grace of God, he was once again free to work his land. The children were being well cared for. Life was far from perfect, but it was survivable . . . until he walked into the cabin in the late afternoon and smelled the familiar scent of his wife's perfume wafting from within their bedroom.

The sweet smell of roses brought such a flood of memories that it nearly brought him to his knees. It was as though his wife were physically present . . . tangible . . . waiting for him in their bedroom, just beyond the half-closed door.

He managed to walk through that door and found Ingrid going through his wife's things.

The top drawer of Diantha's bureau was open and empty, and various articles of her clothing were stacked in small piles on the bed. The precious bottle of his wife's perfume sat on the dresser.

And Ingrid reeked of it.

He was usually a patient man, slow to anger, but the sight

of this immigrant girl pawing through his wife's things threw him into such an instantaneous rage, he wanted to slam her against the wall. The woman smelled as though she had bathed in Diantha's perfume. Was she too stupid to know any better? Or did she think he'd fall in love with her if she wore enough of his wife's scent?

"What do you think you're doing, you stupid cow?" Without realizing it, he repeated the very same hurtful words he had heard Millicent fling at her. "You have no right!"

Ingrid seemed surprised by his anger. She dropped the article of Diantha's clothing she had been holding and cowered against the wall.

"Speak up!" he roared. "Tell me why you think you have the right to touch my wife's things!"

"She was doing it for me, Pa." A child's frightened voice sliced through his anger and brought him to his senses.

Joshua had not realized that Agnes was directly behind him.

"Ingrid was going to cut down one of Ma's dresses for me if it was all right with you. We were going to ask your permission before we did anything."

He turned around and his heart sank. Not only was Agnes directly behind him, but so was little Ellie. He saw Ellie's hand stealing into Agnes's while both of them stared at him with frightened eyes.

"I asked Ingrid to do it," Agnes said. "My dresses are too little for me, and I didn't think you would care."

Joshua's anger evaporated, leaving him empty and ashamed—but the scent of roses still swirled around him, tickling his senses, making him feel unsettled and disoriented.

"That doesn't excuse her for using your mother's perfume."

"She didn't, Pa." Agnes shook her head. "Trudy was playing with the bottle and she accidentally spilled some. The only thing Ingrid did was clean it up."

Joshua could not meet Ingrid's eyes. He stumbled over his apology. "I—I'm sorry . . . I didn't realize."

Ingrid hurriedly lifted the piles of folded clothing and stuffed them back inside the dresser drawer with trembling hands. She shoved the drawer closed and tried to pass by him in the doorway. He touched her arm to stop her. "Ingrid, I'm so sorry—"

"Please excuse." She had her head down and did not look at him.

He stepped aside, as did the girls, and Ingrid walked right out of the cabin.

"Now see what you done?" Agnes complained. "We finally get some good help around here and you scare her off."

Had he scared her off? She wouldn't leave, would she?

In all honesty, he wouldn't blame her if she did. Who would want to live with a man who went into a rage over a few items of clothing and some spilled perfume—especially a man who had been accused by some of killing his wife.

With shame, he remembered the cruel thing he had said to her. What he had called her was unforgivable.

It was the first time he had wished that Ingrid didn't have such a good grasp of the English language. He went to the front door and watched, helpless, as Ingrid walked toward the large woodlot that adjoined their farm, but unlike Diantha, who would sometimes spend hours walking alone in the deep woods, Ingrid stopped at the edge, hesitated, looked back at the cabin, and took a seat on a stump.

"You oughta at least go talk to Ingrid." Agnes jabbed an elbow into his side as they stood there. "Go tell her you're sorry again. Sweet-talk her or something. Go on, Pa. We need her here bad."

"Give me a minute or two, will you?" Impatience with his daughter rushed over him. His relationship with Ingrid was awkward enough without Agnes thinking it was her place to give him pointers.

"That woman makes the best biscuits I ever ate," Agnes said. "We're sure gonna be in a sorry fix if she walks out on us, and then I'll *never* get me that new dress."

"Would you quit talking like that?" Joshua said. "She's not your hired hand. I actually *married* the woman, for Pete's sake!"

"Then go on out there, Pa." Agnes turned accusing eyes on him. "Go apologize. We need her."

## 8

"Hello, the house!"

Ingrid heard a familiar voice, and her spirits lifted. It was Hazel. Never had she been so grateful for the appearance of another human being.

She-Wolf loped along, a self-appointed advance scout in front of the wagon that Hazel was driving. The dog came right up to where Ingrid sat on the stump and sat back on her haunches with her tongue lolling, and Ingrid could have sworn that the animal was grinning at her. Perhaps it was nothing more than Ingrid's desire to feel welcome, at least by something, but she was ridiculously grateful the animal seemed happy to see her.

Hazel drove the wagon over close to her. "Whoa!" She pulled back on the reins and from the high seat of her wagon looked down at Ingrid sitting at the edge of the forest.

"What are you doing way out here a-sitting on that stump in the middle of the day?" She sniffed the air. "And why do you smell like you've been smearing roses all over yourself?"

Ingrid shook her head in despair. There was so much she needed to say, and so much English required to say it. She grew tired of forever translating in her mind for these people.

"I cook. I clean. I try to find mother's dress to make dress for Agnes. Joshua get angry because I touch wife's precious clothes." Her voice broke. "He yell at me."

"Angry, huh." Hazel's eyes narrowed. "He yelled at you? Well, I'll just have to go over there and show him what angry looks like! *Hi-yup*!"

With that, the old lady tore into the front yard of the cabin. The wagon had barely come to a stop before she leaped off. Ingrid saw Joshua walk outside and give her a quick glance. Right before she turned her back on him, she saw Hazel wagging her finger beneath Joshua's nose while she gave him what appeared to be a good talking to.

Ingrid, in spite of her hurt feelings, was delighted. If Hazel chose to chastise him, that was fine with her. Even though she was several yards away, she could hear the angry tone of Hazel's voice and Joshua's conciliatory tone in return.

A few minutes later, out of the corner of her eye, she saw him jam his hat on his head and stride toward her while the children and Hazel gathered together in the doorway. She pretended not to notice and feigned a great interest in pulling petals off of a daisy she had plucked from a clump growing next to the stump.

"It appears I have not yet apologized enough," Joshua said when he was a couple feet away.

She kept her back to him and did not acknowledge his presence. She had scrubbed the man's dirty floor, washed his dirty dishes *and* his dirty underwear only that morning. He was not going to be forgiven so easily.

He walked around the stump so he could face her. "Will you please look at me?" he asked. "I'm trying to tell you that I'm very sorry."

So, he wanted her to look at him, did he? Well, she would look at him! He was not the only one who was angry. She gave him the full force of her anger.

"I cook, cook, cook. Clean, clean, clean. I try to find dress for Agnes. She is young girl. She need pretty things!" She lowered her voice. "And you say mean things to me."

"It was the perfume. For a second I thought Diantha was back."

She sniffed. "I not want wife *parfym*! It stink."

"I'm sorry. I overreacted." He put a hand in his pocket and pulled out a small perfume vial.

"What? You bring to me? No!" Ingrid folded her arms across her chest and shook her head emphatically. "I not want."

"I know." He took the vial and flung it as hard and as high as he could.

She saw it glistening in the sun as it arched into the sky and then disappeared into the deep foliage of the forest.

She cocked her head. "Daughters not want?"

"My daughters might want it, but I need to get that scent out of the house. Obviously, it does bad things to me." He tried to smile, but it was halfhearted. "It makes me say mean things to someone who has done nothing but 'cook, cook, cook, and clean, clean, clean.' I did not mean the terrible things I said to you." He held out his hand. "Hazel can stay with the children. Come take a walk with me."

Ingrid took his hand and rose from the stump. He led her to an opening in the woods where there was the hint of a path.

"Diantha used to love to come here," he said. "There was something about a forest that always calmed her. Her father's people were hunters, and she must have inherited some of that desire. Sometimes she would actually take my gun and kill game for our family."

Ingrid was not in the mood to hear about what a wonderful outdoorswoman his wife had been. There was entirely too much to do. For one thing, the children needed to be fed supper and she was longing for a chance to visit with Hazel. A walk in the woods with a man who wanted to talk about his deceased wife was not part of her plan for the day.

"I have dough rising." She pulled away. "Time to put in stove."

To Joshua's surprise, Ingrid stalked away from him without so much as a backward glance. He took his hat off, scratched his head, and put it back on again. He put his hands in his pockets and took them back out. He had no idea what he was supposed to do now as Ingrid marched back to the house.

He had been a fool to start talking about Diantha. Even though he'd just been trying to make conversation and had said the first thing that popped into his mind, he didn't blame Ingrid for walking off like that. Who would have guessed that the immigrant girl who had been so eager to please would have that much spunk when she felt mistreated?

He walked back into the yard, intending to go into the cabin and wait for supper, until he saw that Ingrid, Hazel, and the four girls were huddled in a tight circle and Ingrid was talking and gesturing. It did not take a genius to figure out what she was talking about when she stopped and six pairs of disapproving female eyes trained themselves on him. Even She-Wolf appeared to be unhappy with him.

Who would have guessed that his daughters would take Ingrid's side so quickly? Weren't stepmothers supposed to be suspect? Wasn't there supposed to be a sort of probationary period before children accepted them into the home? He had expected to have to ease Ingrid into their lives. He had especially expected there to be problems between her and Agnes. Instead, in less than twenty-four hours, he felt like the outsider!

Girls were fickle creatures. All it had taken was some good cooking, a clean house, freshly laundered clothes, and the promise of new dresses for them to firmly take Ingrid's side.

It made him long to bring his little son home, if for no other reason than to have another male around. In fact, now that he thought about it, there was no reason he couldn't go get little Bertie now. Ingrid already had the house and children under control. It was reasonable for him to want to bring all his children back under one roof, and his girls had been begging for him to go get their little brother.

It would not be a pleasant task to confront his former in-laws, but the judge had said that if he had a wife, he could have his children. His in-laws didn't have a legal leg to stand on.

Besides that, going to get little Bertie seemed infinitely preferable to entering a cabin filled with irate females. He decided to take a detour to the Youngs' farm down the road before going in to supper. It would give everyone, including him, a chance to cool off.

"I brought you some supplies," Hazel said. "With all these children, I figured you could use 'em."

"George not mind?" Ingrid asked. The wagon was filled with interesting-looking bundles and boxes, and she couldn't wait to find out what Hazel had brought. It really had been stretching her abilities to come up with meals for the family with what Joshua had on hand.

"No." Hazel grinned. "George didn't mind. Millicent may think she's got that man of hers wrapped around her little finger, but he does have a backbone. When I gave him the list I'd made out for you, his eyes practically bugged out of his head. He could hardly wait to fill it."

"He know this is for us?" Ingrid asked.

"He did," Hazel said. "He even stuck some candy in there for the children. It wasn't on my list, but George always has a soft spot in his heart for children. It's too bad he married a woman who couldn't carry a child full term. She lost two that I know of after they moved here."

"Ingrid, look!" Agnes exclaimed. "A whole bolt of pink calico! And ribbons! You won't have to use my mama's clothes to make me a dress after all!"

"I do not think my husband has monies to pay," Ingrid said.

"I'm quite sure that he doesn't." Hazel laughed. "Actually, I'd be surprised if Josh has two cents to rub together until his cherry orchard comes in—if it ever does come in. He's pretty much invested every dime he has into those cherry trees. Lots of people wondering if it will pay off."

"A cherry orchard is fine thing," Ingrid said defensively.

"Absolutely," Hazel said. "Actually, I owed Joshua for helping me build a fence around my pasture, but he wouldn't accept anything for it. I'm not a poor woman, in spite of the way I dress. My husband and I got here before the town ever got started. He had the good sense to put our name on the land where White Rock stands, and then he sold building lots to the people who wanted to move there. I owe Josh, and I can afford to pay him for his help, but I know he won't take money from me—and I was pretty certain you and the girls could use a little help."

Ingrid bit her lip, considering. "For you I come work to pay back."

"Nope. No need for that. Me and She-Wolf don't need any help." She turned to her wolf-dog. "Do we, girl? But we do need some company from time to time. I'm fine, but She-Wolf tends to get lonesome. In fact, I was wondering if it would be an inconvenience if we spent the night here. It took me longer than I expected to get all this stuff loaded. By the time we get it unloaded and put away, it'll probably be dark. Especially since it appears like Joshua has decided to visit your neighbors instead of helping us unload."

Ingrid looked. Joshua was, indeed, walking toward Diantha's parents' place.

"Oh, I almost forgot. I have something for you." Hazel dug a pair of women's everyday shoes out of the wagon. "I hope they fit."

"Ah!" Ingrid immediately sat down on the porch, pulled off George's boots, and pulled on the new shoes. "So much better! Thank you, thank you. Where you find?"

"George had ordered them a few days ago, without telling Millicent. They just came in yesterday."

"I never take off!"

"Well," Hazel said, "I wouldn't sleep in 'em if I was you."

"I put the bread in oven, then we unload. Have fresh bread and *soppa* after."

Hazel seemed taken aback. "You're making soap for supper?"

"No, no, no." Ingrid made a motion as though dipping and slurping out of a spoon.

"Oh! You mean soup!"

"Ja. I make soup."

"Soup and bread sounds good to me. I never did have the knack for making bread. Drop biscuits was about as good as I could manage." Hazel lifted Polly from Trudy's arms. "And how are *you* doing, you little sweet 'tater?"

Polly grinned, unplugged her thumb from her mouth, and offered it to Hazel.

"Oh, you got some sugar for old Hazel? I been needing me some sugar. Yum!"

She pretended to put Polly's thumb into her own mouth and made loud smacking noises. This tickled Polly so thoroughly that she started belly laughing. Ingrid saw Joshua glance back at them as he walked down the road to Diantha's parents'. Ingrid turned her head so he wouldn't think that she was bothering to watch him.

She desperately longed for a heart-to-heart talk with Hazel, so she asked the girls to go upstairs while she finished making supper. She put a few more sticks of good ash wood into the firebox, then held her hand inside the oven to test the heat. She counted the seconds and made it to twenty-five before she had to snatch her hand away. Perfect! Twenty-five seconds was just about the right temperature to bake bread. Forty-five seconds was her standard for anything that required a moderate oven. Sixty seconds for more delicate foods.

"I am so sorry," Hazel said once the girls were out of ear-shot. "I don't know what came over me yesterday. I saw this smirk on Millicent's face when the judge said he was going to give those girls to Virgie, and it went all through me. I spoke up before I thought. Now you two are in a mess, and it's partly my fault. I came out here hoping for a chance to tell you, privately, that I'm pretty sure you can get this marriage annulled. It'll take awhile and it will cost money, but since I got you into this, I'll pay for it."

"Annulled?"

"It means the marriage would be over."

"Where I go?"

"I got friends in Port Huron. Nice people. The wife is an invalid. They've been looking for just the right person to come help out. Pay is decent. It's just the two of them. I had planned to get you set up with them before I lost my mind yesterday and told the judge all that hogwash about you and Josh being a couple."

Ingrid sat down at the table and gave Hazel's words thoughtful consideration. Finally she said, "No. I stay."

"I don't understand," Hazel said. "I come here and find you sitting out on a stump, Josh upset, and the girls all in a state. It's obvious to me that things aren't working out. Why would you want to stay?"

"I already love girls . . . and Joshua. He is good man. Someday, he make a fine husband. I pray he loves me someday."

"Josh Hunter"—Hazel crossed her arms and leaned back in her chair—"would be a greater fool than most men if he didn't."

"You ain't taking the boy," Richard Young said. "And that's that."

If Joshua thought getting his son back just because the judge had given him permission would be easy, he had been mistaken. He kept a careful eye on the Kentucky long rifle that his father-in-law cradled in the crook of his arm. It had never occurred to him that he would have to arm himself to enter a home that had once been as much a part of his life as his own.

"The judge said I could have my children."

"Well, the judge ain't here now, is he?" Virgie chimed in. "You got all the girls. Now, leave us the boy and get out of here."

"But he's my son."

"And Diantha was our daughter and you went and kilt her."

"Virgie, you know that's a lie. I never harmed a hair on Diantha's head."

Her jaw was set—a bad sign. The woman could be as stubborn as a mule. "We're keepin' the boy."

"Richard . . ." He wished he could get Richard alone so they could work this out man to man. His father-in-law had always been reasonable.

That estimation of his father-in-law's reasonableness evaporated when Richard very deliberately cocked the gun and pointed it straight at him.

"Git on out of here, Josh," Richard said. "Whether or not you had anything to do with Diantha's death is no never-mind now. She's gone. The thing is, Virgie's gotten attached to the boy, and you ain't gonna take him away from her. She's suffered enough."

There really was no choice. Joshua knew it was best to retreat and regroup when going up against overwhelming odds, and so he walked away. That cocked rifle worried him. When it came to guns, Richard was a very careful man. Josh had never known him to point a gun at something he did not intend to kill.

Richard wasn't playing around when it came to Bertie.

The problem was, Josh didn't know how to regroup in a situation like this. To come back here armed and ready for battle was ridiculous. There was no way he would allow bullets to fly around his infant son, nor did he want to hurt Richard or Virgie. For the moment, he was stumped.

Admitting temporary defeat, he went back home.

Ingrid, Hazel, and the girls were having a spirited discussion over the use of a bolt of pink calico when he slipped through the door. He was hungry, and even from outside the house, he could smell the aroma of fresh-baked bread and bean soup. Ingrid made a point of ignoring him. The girls barely noticed him. It was obvious that they had eaten without him. It was Hazel who finally acknowledged his presence.

"Where've you been, Josh?" Hazel asked. "Me and the girls had to unload the supplies out of the wagon all by ourselves."

"What supplies?"

"The ones I brought. And not a moment too soon, from what I see."

"I was going to make a trip into town tomorrow."

"I made the trip for you," Hazel said. "I'll repeat, where've you been? Trying to make peace with your in-laws?"

"I went to get little Bertie."

All conversation stopped. Once again, six pairs of female eyes were focused on him.

"You *what*?" Agnes asked.

"I went to get your little brother."

"Well, I don't see him anyplace." Agnes mimed looking around the cabin. "What happened?"

"Your grandfather refused to give him up."

"You're bigger and stronger than Grandpa."

"Not when he's pointing a gun at me."

"Grandpa pointed a gun at you?" Agnes was astonished. "Our grandpa? The one who always tells us to never point a loaded gun at anything we don't want to kill?"

"And he cocked it."

"Oh!" Agnes frowned. "He must be awful serious about keeping Bertie."

Suddenly, no one was angry at him anymore.

"You are *hungrig*." Ingrid ran over and sliced him off a thick chunk of bread and buttered it. "Give father a bowl," she told Agnes.

Agnes didn't argue but placed a deep, savory bowl of bean soup in front of him. Ingrid brought him a cup of coffee. His spirits rose a bit when she delicately lightened it with cream. She had remembered how he liked it.

"Richard and Virgie are too caught up in grief to think straight," Hazel said. "They'll soften. You're too good of a father to be deprived of your child. Goodness, you all live so close they could see Bertie every day if Virgie would quit that craziness we had to listen to at the inquest."

"I hope you're right." He dipped a piece of bread into the soup.

"We get baby." Ingrid patted his arm and dipped another ladleful into his bowl. *"Snart."*

He had no idea what she had just said. *"Snart?* What does that mean?"

"Soon," Ingrid explained. "We get baby soon."

Later that night, he lay alone in his room and listened to what sounded like a party going on overhead. Ingrid had chosen to share the loft with Hazel and the girls tonight. He heard Agnes spluttering with laughter—probably at his expense.

Although he felt left out of the fun, he was intensely grateful. His house, which had felt so desolate, had come alive.

# 9

Ingrid sprinkled water from a bowl onto a pair of Joshua's line-dried pants, then picked up the flatiron, licked her finger, touched it to the iron, heard a satisfying sizzle, and knew it was hot enough. Ironing was not her favorite chore, but it was a necessity for a well-ordered home. She had spent most of the afternoon pressing the family's laundry.

Joshua came in just as she finished ironing a sheet for his bed.

"You iron sheets?" he asked.

"Ja." She folded it neatly and laid it on the table.

"Why do you bother?"

"Because it look good and feel good. This is a problem?"

"No." He shook his head. "But even my mother didn't iron the sheets unless company was coming."

"My company is you and children."

She meant it. She cherished having her own family to care for. Even if that family felt a little . . . borrowed.

"Don't try to argue with her, Pa," Agnes said from her seat at the kitchen table. "Ingrid has her own ways of doing things and you better not try to change it. The woman even has a certain way of putting clothes on the line."

"How is that?"

"Sheets go first." Agnes ticked items off on her fingers. "Then towels, then long pants, then dresses—then Polly's diapers. It has to go in order of length. I pegged a washrag beside the sheets and I thought she'd faint."

"Neighbors see laundry," Ingrid said. "They judge us."

"But we don't have any neighbors," Joshua pointed out.

"Someday." Ingrid smoothed out another sheet and began to iron it. "Somebody come on wash day. They say . . ." She frowned and shook her finger in the air. "That Ingrid, she is bad housekeeper. Her washing *krökte*—crooked."

Joshua laughed. "I doubt anyone will ever call you a bad housekeeper, sweetheart."

Her heart flip-flopped in her chest. He had called her a love name. Only two weeks into their marriage and he had not gotten angry at her again, and just now he had called her a love name.

Her eyes sought his, to see if his words had meant anything, but he didn't seem to notice what he had said, nor did the girls, who were busy cutting out chains of paper dolls from an old newspaper.

"Hey, Pa," Agnes said, picking up the section from which she was cutting, "listen to this. President Ulysses S. Grant signed something called the Ku Klux Klan Act." She looked up at him. "Aren't them the people who burn crosses and scare people?"

"Sometimes they do a whole lot more than scare people. It's a good law, Agnes. I'm glad Grant signed it. It's the kind of thing we fought for."

"What was it like?" Agnes's eyes were avid with curiosity. "Fighting with General Custer?"

"Dusty."

Ingrid waited for him to say more, but all he did was reach

around her for a cup from the cupboard and the coffeepot from the stove. The nearness of him made her lose her English again.

"*Noggran. Kaffet är hett!*"

He paused. "What did you just say?"

"I say, 'Careful, coffee is hot.'"

It was embarrassing that his nearness had flustered her so.

"With you in the house, there is always coffee, and it's always hot." Joshua saluted her with his cup.

He had started coming in each afternoon for a small bite of something to eat and drink. It was becoming a habit of his, and she had begun to make little surprises for him each day. Her mother had taught her that a man who was well fed was a good worker, and a good worker meant prosperity for a family.

"There is cookies," she said. "Fresh bake. In top of stove."

His face lit up as he opened the warming oven of the woodstove and drew out a plate of sugar cookies.

"Can I have some, Ma?" Ellie asked when she saw them.

The sound of "ma" coming out of the child's mouth made everyone stop what they were doing, except for Ellie, who continued cutting out paper dolls.

"Ingrid ain't—" Agnes started to correct her sister, but Joshua shook his head at her.

"Leave it be," he said quietly.

Agnes gave it some thought and then nodded. "You're right, Pa."

Ellie, absorbed in her play, did not notice the exchange.

The fact that he did not want the little girl corrected made Ingrid very happy. "There is cookies enough for all." Ingrid's heart sang from the child's slipup.

While Joshua admired the girls' handiwork, Ingrid took the bedsheets into the bedroom and proceeded to make up Joshua's bed.

And it *was* Joshua's bed. Even after Hazel left, she had continued sleeping upstairs with the girls. She had no intention of coming back to Joshua's bed until he invited her.

She did not know that he was even in the room until he spoke.

"You can sleep here with me tonight if you want."

She gasped and jumped.

"I'm sorry. I didn't mean to startle you." He was leaning against the doorway, a half-eaten cookie in his hand, watching her.

"You are sure?" she said.

"No," he answered. "I'm not at all sure. It's only been two months since I buried my wife. To be honest, I'm not sure about anything anymore."

She considered his words. "I sleep with girls, then."

"Please, Ingrid. You are so wonderful with the children. Let us at least attempt to be husband and wife."

As Joshua went back out to his fields, he was furious with himself for what he had just done. His invitation had been a momentary impulse stemming from sheer, overwhelming gratitude for the order she had made out of the upheaval of his life.

At first, he was relieved when she had taken to sleeping with the girls. Night after night he had lain awake smiling as he listened to his daughters giggling as she told them stories. And then, truth be told, a deep sense of loneliness began to wash over him every night, an emptiness that he wondered if she might be able to fill after all.

She was a pleasant enough woman. Could sheer gratitude be a strong enough emotion to take the place of romantic love?

He had no idea, and there wasn't one person on earth he

knew to ask. He had never known anyone who had been thrown into this sort of situation before. Now, he was angry at himself for opening his mouth, and he dreaded tonight and what might or might not happen.

"How come you're fixing a bath?" Agnes asked as she and the girls watched Ingrid fill the large round tub with water she had heated on the stove. "It ain't Saturday night."

Joshua would not come back to the house for a while. He always spent at least an hour after supper doing chores, but just to be safe, she had put three of the high ladder-backed kitchen chairs in front of the tub and draped them with a quilt to give her a little privacy in case he did walk in.

She should have realized that privacy was impossible with all these curious little eyes watching her.

"I work hard, little one. I want bath tonight."

"So, Swedish people bathe even in the middle of the week if they feel like it?" Agnes probed.

Ingrid smiled. That Agnes—so quick-witted with her never-ending questions.

"Ja. Some *Svenska* people bathe even in middle of week." She disrobed and sank into the warm water.

She had to sit cross-legged in the tub for it to come up to her waist, but she unbound her hair and used a dipper to sluice warm water over herself. Hazel had been thoughtful enough to include a bar of precious scented soap in the supplies she had brought. Ingrid did not know if it was an accident or if Hazel simply knew—but that bar of soap smelled of lilacs, not of Diantha's roses. In fact, she didn't think she would ever be able to tolerate the scent of roses again.

Her bath would be absolutely delightful if not for the questions coming from the other side of the quilt.

"So, you gonna do this every night from now on?"

"No. Not every night."

"Too much work to get it ready, right?"

"Ja." She worked up a nice lather and smoothed it into her long hair. "Too much work."

It *was* a lot of work, but oh, what a pleasure to wash the week's worth of toil and labor off her body. Best of all, she had a secret she had managed to keep from the girls' prying eyes. Hazel had seen her shabby nightgown the night she had slept at her cabin and had somehow secretly slipped a brand-new, store-bought nightgown into her old valise. Hazel hadn't even told her about it until the next morning.

"I left something behind for you in that old bag of yours," Hazel whispered as she was leaving.

Ingrid had investigated the minute the girls' backs were turned. It was a lovely, floor-length, white cotton nightgown with a square-cut neckline, lace on the bodice, and a few sprigs of pretty pink flowers printed here and there.

She had not dared to even try it on until today, after Joshua's surprising invitation, while the girls were outside playing. It had fit her well, and best of all, had made her feel pretty.

She now rinsed her hair and then scrubbed her body with a rough washrag until her skin glowed.

"You about done back there?" Agnes asked.

"Ja. Why?"

"Well, I was just thinking," Agnes said. "Polly's starting to smell a little ripe—can I stick her in there with you?"

One thing that Ingrid did *not* want tonight was to smell like a ripe Polly.

"Wait!" she said. "Almost done." She rose from the tub and wrapped around her the quilt with which she had covered the chairs.

"Now all girls can take bath!"

With glee, the two littlest girls shucked their clothes off and dove in—the unexpected pleasure of splashing in the tub on an unprecedented middle-of-the-week night was too delightful to pass up. Even Agnes was grinning as she stripped Polly and lifted her in.

While the children splashed in the water, Ingrid, still wrapped in her quilt, sat in front of the opened door of the still-hot oven, drying her hair and reading a ragged copy of her Swedish Bible. Seeing the familiar words made her homesick for her country and for her language. She had not heard a word of Swedish spoken for months.

At home, Bible study and prayer had been a major part of her life. Now that things were settling down here, she intended to get back into her routine of reading from the Scriptures every night before bed. Tonight, it felt especially appropriate to read 1 Corinthians 13, the chapter about love.

"What are you reading?" Agnes asked, looking over her shoulder.

"My *Bibel*."

"Your Bible? It don't look like any Bible I ever seen."

"It is *Svenska* Bible."

"Huh," Agnes said. "I guess that would explain it. How about reading some of it to me?"

Ingrid repressed a sigh. More translating when she had been looking forward to escaping into her mother tongue for a while. It would be too difficult and time consuming to translate the entire chapter, so she decided to focus on a few verses that she especially loved in this chapter.

"Love last long time . . . and love is kind," she read.

For Agnes's sake as well as her own, she tried to translate the Swedish words into the simplest English possible.

"Love does not envy, and love does not brag on self."

She glanced over and saw that Agnes, sitting on a small stool beside her, was listening intently.

"Love is not rude or selfish or angry."

She turned a page.

"Love does not have evil thoughts, it hate sin, and is always glad of truth." Agnes, the teller of blunt truths, nodded her head in agreement with that verse.

"Love bears always, trusts always, hopes always, endures always." She smiled as she repeated her favorite words in the entire Bible. "Love never fails."

She was surprised to see tears welling up in Agnes's eyes.

"Why you cry?" she asked.

"Do you believe what you just read?" Agnes asked. "Or is it just some fancy words—that part you read about love enduring?"

"Ja. I believe the *Bibel*."

"Does that mean you ain't gonna run out on us if my sisters act bad?" Agnes stared at her hands, twisting and untwisting her fingers. "Or if I get cranky and say something stupid, or if Pa gets mad and starts yelling again like he did when Trudy spilled Ma's perfume? Isn't that what 'endure' means? Sticking around even if sometimes you don't feel like it?"

"Why you ask this?" Ingrid was concerned. It wasn't like Agnes to avoid her eyes, and it was highly unusual for the child to cry.

"I know you and Pa aren't in love or anything mushy like that. You're just here because you don't have anyplace else to go, and he only married you because you were handy. What I want to know is, before I get too attached to you, are you gonna take off and leave us the first time you get a better offer?"

Ingrid closed her Bible and considered how to answer the

child. Agnes was too smart to accept a pat answer. She would expect and most definitely deserved the truth.

Ingrid leaned over and grasped Agnes's chin. "Look at me."

Agnes turned her eyes to her—eyes that were open and vulnerable. Eyes that were begging not to be hurt.

"I not marry your father because I have no place to go. I marry him because I love him already. First time I see you girls, I want to be your *moder*. Your father does not know this. He is not ready to know this, but I promise you I not run away. Ever."

"So, love endures, huh." Agnes's voice had a catch in it.

"Ja." Ingrid let go of the child's chin. "Love endures."

When Joshua came in from the barn, his kitchen smelled like lilacs and the floor was wet. He climbed the narrow stairs to kiss his girls good night, and they all had wet hair and also smelled of lilacs.

"Swedish people sometimes take baths even in the middle of the week, Pa," Agnes informed him. "Not just on Saturday."

He had a sinking feeling he knew why there had been a bath in the middle of the week. "Is that so?"

"Yeah, and Ingrid says that Polly kicks her in the side when she's sleeping here with us, so she's bunking with you tonight."

"Is she now?"

"If you ask her to," Trudy said, "she'll tell you a story before you go to sleep. She always tells us one."

"I'll remember that."

He heard the girls' prayers, marveling at their sweet innocence. How had he and Diantha, with all their faults, managed to create such beautiful little creatures? His heart caught when he saw Bertie's cradle standing empty in the corner. His son should be here.

He went back downstairs and wandered into the kitchen area. He checked, and there were still a couple of sugar cookies left in the warming oven. Tomorrow there would probably be another treat for him put there by Ingrid's competent hands, but the fact was, he had no appetite. He was simply putting off walking into his own bedroom.

His gratitude to Ingrid was boundless, but he dreaded going in there, and he didn't know what to do about it.

Ingrid heard him enter the house. He had stayed in the barn later than usual. She thought perhaps it was his way of being thoughtful to her, his way of giving her time to get the children tucked into bed and herself ready for him.

Joshua and Diantha had made beautiful children together, but she too would give him children. Some would have light hair like hers, and some would have wavy dark hair like their father.

All their children would be treated the same. There would be no favorites, no loving the children of her flesh more than she loved the others. That was not how one wove a strong family together. She knew she had enough love in her heart to cherish a whole houseful of children.

She heard him as he went up to the loft, a little disappointed that he had not come to speak to her first, but she could not fault him for listening to the girls' prayers. He was a good father. Once the girls were settled, he and she would have their time to be together.

One candle was still burning on the thick window ledge of their bedroom, because she wanted him to be able to see her in her pretty new nightgown that Hazel had purchased. She wanted him to see her with her blonde hair unbound and falling in shining waves around her shoulders.

She was sitting up in bed, her back pressed against the freshly laundered pillowcases that smelled of sunshine, waiting . . . waiting . . .

He went downstairs and . . . into the kitchen.

Why was he going into the kitchen when she was here waiting for him—waiting with so much love in her heart?

She heard the small squeak of the door on the warming oven. Why was Joshua searching for cookies on a night like tonight? Her own stomach was in such a state of nerves and anticipation that she could not have eaten had she tried.

Then his footsteps came right up to the outside of the bedroom door. She had left the door slightly ajar, just enough to let him feel her welcoming him but closed enough to leave her a little privacy.

There was a long hesitation outside the bedroom door. Too long of a hesitation. She did not understand.

And then the door opened.

She saw him taking it all in, the clean, neatly ironed sheets folded back, her new white nightgown, her unbound hair, the glowing candle.

The expression in his eyes was unfathomable. She did not know him well enough yet to discern what was going on in his mind. Was he thinking she was beautiful? Was he thinking he might be able to love her?

Her breath caught in her throat, waiting . . .

"I can't do this," he said. "I am so very sorry, Ingrid, but I just can't. I'll be sleeping in the barn if you or the girls need me."

And her world crumbled in.

# 10

Scalding tears soaked Ingrid's pillowcase as she rehashed the hopes and dreams she had held in her heart as she had prepared for this night. What kind of man turned away from a woman, his legal wife, who was waiting and willing to give him her heart—a woman who had worked miracles with his family and home in such a short time?

She knew the answer to this question. It was the kind of man who was still in love with his first wife, a man whose heart was still bound to Diantha.

Her romantic dreams of love with this handsome stranger evaporated. Like drops of water casually flung upon a hot stove, they turned into a fine mist and floated away upon the breath of his rejection.

Of course, it was hard for him to turn his affection toward her so soon after his wife had died. She did not blame him for being divided. That, in itself, was understandable, but tonight had not been her idea. She had not been the one who suggested they spend the night together.

How dare he do this to her? She, who had spent so many nights with the girls, entertaining them with her stories, loving them, and watching after them while he snored away, alone, in his own bed downstairs. She had not once complained; if anything, she had gone out of her way to make things easy for him. She had deliberately allowed this husband of hers, this widower, the time and space to grieve.

Well, he could spend the rest of his life grieving as far as she was concerned.

Ingrid did not sleep a wink. Instead, she lay awake, thinking, reflecting, redefining, and planning her life as it would be from now on.

It was clear that there would be no more children. Even if he changed his mind someday, she would never allow herself to be put in the position of being rejected by him ever again. Instead, she would love the children she had even more, and she would not visit her disappointment in the father upon the little girls who had so innocently accepted her into their lives.

Nor would she visit her disappointment upon the man who had been forced, because of his love for his children, to marry her. It would be foolish to attempt to punish him for not loving her. She had seen the fruits of such things in other women's lives, those who complained and nagged about inattention from their husbands—their tongues effectively pushing men away who had once presumably loved them.

No, when Joshua came in from the barn for breakfast in the morning, she would act as though nothing was the matter. She would act as though he had not broken her heart with his rejection. She would act like the happy mother of a brood of children.

He would not know the difference. After all, he was only a man. As long as his belly was full and his children were alive, he would be content. Then he could grieve his wife, the wonderful Diantha, all he wanted!

Long before the rooster crowed to greet the sunrise, Ingrid rose to begin her day. She plaited her hair, removed her new nightgown, put on her old work dress, and went outside to split the day's kindling with Joshua's sharp axe. This was a chore he was becoming lax about doing. She had to remind him nearly every morning this week that she needed kindling to start the fire.

He was always apologetic—him with the beautiful blue eyes—and he would hurry to bring an armful in, but she was tired of reminding him.

Awakening before the rooster crowed gave her enough time to do the chore herself and saved her from having to ask him to do something he should have done without being asked. She would wager that Diantha had never had to ask him for kindling. No doubt he had anticipated her every need.

The pain of Joshua's rejection made her longing, worry, and grief over her brother's disappearance even more acute. It would be comforting to know that there was one person on earth who truly loved her. But she would never allow Joshua to know the emptiness she felt inside.

Unless it was an emergency or something important for the children, she would never ask that man for another thing as long as she lived!

Joshua slept fitfully in the hayloft. The scurrying of mice over the horse blanket under which he was sleeping and the sound of the livestock stirring beneath him had kept him awake most of the night as he tried to forget the memory of the hurt he had seen in Ingrid's eyes as he had turned away from her. Finally, he fell into an exhausted slumber in which Ingrid's and Diantha's faces blended together in a bizarre collage.

The sound of an axe splitting wood roused him from that restless sleep. This was not a sound he was used to hearing unless he was on the other side of the axe. He threw back the horse blanket and climbed down the ladder to investigate.

It took a moment for his eyes to adjust to the sight of a tall, slender woman illuminated by a lantern glowing nearby, wielding an axe as expertly as a man. Her golden hair gleamed in the lamplight as she swung the axe in a perfect circle over her head and brought it dead-center on each piece of wood she was splitting.

Apparently, Ingrid had decided to take care of the kindling herself, and taking care of it she was! She could not be more energetic with that axe than if she had been going after a nest of rattlesnakes.

In the lantern's glare, he checked his pocket watch. It was three o'clock in the morning. Even on his best work days, he didn't awaken for another hour.

"Good morning?" he said. After what had happened last night, he wasn't entirely certain what sort of morning it was going to be.

She froze with her back toward him, and then she lowered the axe and slowly turned around to face him.

"Good morning!" she said with a wide smile.

She looked reasonable enough, he thought, as he slowly approached her. Maybe she had just wanted to get an early start.

"I'll get the rest of the kindling in." He cautiously reached for the axe. "But, Ingrid, do you have any idea what time it is?"

"It is early. Better to get work done before children awake." She blithely handed him the axe and sauntered on into the house.

He stood there looking at the axe, then at her, then at the woodpile. He had always hated splitting kindling, a tiresome job for which he'd been responsible since he was big enough to handle an axe. Because he hated it, he tended to split just enough to get them through each day, but today, he decided it might be wise if he went ahead and got a nice big pile of it together for her. Perhaps enough to see her through the entire week.

"Here you go." Joshua filled the wood box nearly full and headed back outdoors for another armload.

"Thank you." Ingrid was engrossed in beating up a batch of something in a large bowl.

When he came back in, she had the stove blazing, a thin pastry spread out over nearly the entire table, and she was industriously layering it with butter, sugar, nuts, and dried fruit.

"What is that?" he asked, dropping another armload of kindling into the box.

"Strudel."

"Is that what we're having for breakfast?"

"No," she said without looking up.

He waited for her to explain, but she was so engrossed in her task that she seemed to barely notice that he was standing there. He had absolutely no idea what to do next—so he went outside and split another armload of kindling.

"I keep the bed," Ingrid said as he mounded kindling in what had been an empty box.

"Excuse me?" he asked.

"I keep." This time she looked straight at him. "I keep the bed. Not right for *moder* to sleep in loft with girls all the time."

Now he understood. Perfectly. She was staking out her territory, claiming his bedroom for herself.

"Where am I going to sleep?"

"I no care." She made a dismissive gesture with her hand. "Barn. Kitchen floor. On roof. On moon. I no care."

She finished sprinkling the pastry with cinnamon and

began to expertly fold it. The folding of it was intricate and would have been fascinating to watch—except he was still trying to puzzle out where he was going to sleep.

"But really, Ingrid, where—"

"Barn good enough last night, good enough other nights."

"It was miserable out there."

She paused in the middle of folding the pastry, and he saw a slow smile spread over her face as she savored the idea of him having been miserable.

"Ingrid, I want to apologize—"

"*Kaffee?*" She whirled around with the coffeepot in her hand.

"Sure," he said. "About last night . . ."

"We need eggs." She brushed butter over the folded strudel. "You get?"

"I guess so."

He slunk off to the henhouse—thinking it was a whole lot easier to deal with a riled-up rooster and twelve sleepy hens than the woman who was slinging pastry together in his kitchen.

He wondered, given Ingrid's mood this morning, if it might be wise to hide the axe she had been wielding so expertly.

"Something sure smells good." Joshua came back inside after milking the cow and gathering the eggs. "Is it that strudel you were working on this morning?"

Ingrid bent to take a pan out of the woodstove and sat it on the table. The pastry had turned out beautifully.

"That looks delicious, Ingrid." He reached to pinch off a piece.

"Not for you." She smacked his hand. "For neighbors."

He looked at her like he could not believe his ears. "What neighbors?"

"Diantha's parents."

"They won't want to see you. These are not people we can be friends with, Ingrid. They hate me."

"But they not hate *me*. Ingrid nothing but *dum Svenska* girl. They think I not know better than come for visit."

"My father-in-law has a gun."

She grinned. "But Ingrid have strudel."

"You're a great cook, Ingrid, but they aren't going to soften toward us just because of some pastry."

"We see. You stay with children. Breakfast in skillet. Soup on stove for dinner. I come back—maybe late."

"Please," he said. "Don't go down there. Or at least let me go with you."

"No. You stay with children."

She had a plan, but it was not one she wanted to discuss. It involved an emotional tug-of-war that might or might not work. If it failed, she would rather no one know what she had attempted to do.

"You do not worry." She patted his cheek like a bustling housewife. "Diantha's persons like."

This particular strudel was a complicated dish and not even native to her country. She had learned it from a German girlfriend, who had told her that good strudel was irresistible to men. This was important, because she had gotten the impression at the inquest that Richard Young might not be quite as unreasonable as his wife.

She took two flat, clean bricks she had heated in the oven and placed them in the bottom of a basket. Then, she carefully wrapped the steaming strudel in a clean cloth and laid it on the hot bricks. That would make the pastry not only stay hot but be at its most aromatic when she arrived. She had used extra cinnamon for that reason alone.

"Richard might not shoot you, Ingrid, but I'll guarantee

he's not going to be happy to see you," Joshua warned. "Virgie's a good cook in her own right."

"It is time I visit neighbors." She wrapped her maroon shawl around her shoulders and lifted the basket.

Because she did not speak perfect English, she knew that Joshua had sadly underestimated her. She hoped Diantha's parents would also. Now that she knew there would be no children born between her and Joshua, now that she understood that their marriage would remain a marriage of convenience, she was absolutely determined to come back with Bertie in her arms. She wanted that baby more than anything in the world right now. For all she knew, little Bertie would be the only infant she would ever get to nurture as her own.

She was on Richard and Virgie's doorstep before either of them knew she was on the place, which was exactly as she had hoped. She had walked so quietly she had even escaped the notice of their old dog until she was knocking on the Youngs' front door. Then the dog began to bark.

Richard heard the dog and came hurrying from the barn just as Virgie opened the door to her.

"Good *morgon!*" Ingrid deliberately thickened her accent and made herself sound as Swedish as possible. "Ingrid bring neighbor gift."

"What are you talking about . . . 'neighbor gift'?" Virgie's eyes narrowed. "Ain't you that Swedish girl Josh married to keep us from getting the girls?"

"Ja. I marry to Joshua." She peeled back the corner of the cloth covering the strudel and put a vacuous smile on her face. "Nice gift. Friends now?"

"Look at this, Richard." Virgie barked out a laugh. "The girl thinks we're gonna be friends just because she baked us some kind of a pie."

"Strudel," Ingrid corrected.

"Whatever you want to call it, it don't make no difference. You turn yourself on around, missy, and—"

"Take it easy on her, Virgie."

Richard, as Ingrid had hoped, intervened. "She's just a young immigrant girl. In her country it's probably some kind of custom to take this, this . . ."

"Strudel." Ingrid supplied the word, still smiling.

"This strudel to their neighbors. She probably don't know no better." He came closer and sniffed. "What's that thing got inside of it, girl?"

"Nuts, eggs, flour, butter—much butter—raisins, cinnamon, sugar." She pulled the covering completely back and revealed the pastry in all of its glory.

The strudel, carefully brushed with beaten egg whites, glistened brown and delicious-looking. The cinnamon, sugar, and butter—still hot—oozed out of the slashes she had made with her knife into the many layers. Even Virgie seemed impressed and reached for the basket.

This was the pivotal moment. Instead of relinquishing the basket, she held on to it and affected a hurt sound to her voice.

"No invite Ingrid in for *kaffee*? Strudel much, much hard work."

The delicious aroma surrounded them, but there was another smell, one not quite so pleasant—and Ingrid was delighted.

"Good golly, Virgie," Richard said as he caught a whiff. "You done gone and burnt the potatoes!"

With a screech, Virgie rushed inside, leaving the door open. Ingrid immediately stepped inside as though invited. Richard, following the pastry, did not try to stop her.

Their home was pleasant enough. It was a little larger than Joshua's, but her eyes were drawn to only one thing—the corner where a small cradle lay. It rocked a little as the infant inside it kicked and gurgled.

"Bertie?" she asked.

"Yes," Richard said.

"May I see?"

"No." Richard plucked the baby from the cradle, carried him into the bedroom, and kicked the door closed.

She was devastated.

"Well," Virgie said, "them taters are hog food now, thanks to you a-knocking at our door. All I can say is that strudel better be good! We ain't had breakfast yet."

"Strudel very good." Ingrid sat the basket on the living room table. There was no reason to hold on to it anymore. The golden pastry had gotten her through the door, which had been her intent. Virgie and Richard could bathe in strudel now for all she cared.

She seated herself on a small horsehair sofa. It was the nicest piece of furniture in the room.

"Why are you sitting down?" Virgie asked. "You ain't staying."

"Ingrid so tired." She gave a great sigh. "All week long. Cook, cook, cook. Clean, clean, clean. You care I sit down? Rest a little minute? Joshua, he no help."

"Honey, I hear you." Virgie's face softened. "A woman can get a bellyful of work out here on these hardscrabble farms—but you can't stay here."

"Ingrid leave—with Bertie."

"You little sneak." Virgie's eyes smoldered. "The only reason you came here was to take our little boy away!"

"Bertie needs grow up with *systrar* and with father."

"Did Josh put you up to this?"

"No. He say, 'Don't go there. Diantha's parents mean.'"

Virgie seemed taken aback. "We're not mean."

"Then give Bertie . . . judge say."

"Richard!" Virgie yelled. "Get your gun!"

Joshua fed the girls breakfast, then dinner, and later on, he fed them leftovers for supper. It had been hours and hours since Ingrid had left for the Youngs' with her hopeful little basket of strudel, and she had not returned.

Had they shot her? Or had she handed them the basket of strudel and then just kept walking? He wouldn't blame her a bit if she did.

He tried to put the girls to bed early, but it was like trying to put a hutch of rabbits to bed. About the time he got one down, another one would pop up full of questions about when Ingrid would be coming home.

It was starting to get dark. What would he do if she never came home?

# 11

"Bertie needs be with family," Ingrid said for the umpteenth time.

This statement had become a recurring refrain that had woven itself through the whole weary day. Ingrid had lost track of how many times she had said it. She was discovering that being an unwanted guest in two angry people's home was more tiring than anything she had ever done.

Richard had tried threatening her with his gun.

"Big mess." Ingrid was unimpressed. "Have to clean Ingrid off of floors and walls." She did not move from the spot she had staked out on the horsehair couch.

Virgie had tried reasoning with her. "You already got four children to take care of and you're not even their real mother. What's a girl like you need with another baby to care for?"

"Bertie needs be with family," Ingrid had repeated.

"I think the woman might be a little slow-witted," Virgie said to Richard, tapping her finger against her own forehead.

Richard tried bribery. "I'll give you five whole silver dollars to leave our house."

"You keep money. I take Bertie."

The baby began to cry back in the bedroom where they

135

had put him away from Ingrid's sight. Virgie went in to tend to him. While she was gone, Richard attempted to physically remove Ingrid from the cabin.

It turned into a wrestling match that was not pretty and did not last long once Richard realized he could not win. He soon discovered that if he was going to remove Ingrid from the house, he would have to remove both her and the heavy horsehair couch to which she determinedly clung. There was one long, awkward scuffle in which Ingrid clung tenaciously to the couch and Richard pulled and strained, trying to pry her off of it.

"What in the world do you think you're doing?" Virgie asked when she reentered the room and found him dragging the sofa across the living room floor with Ingrid still firmly attached.

"I'm trying," he huffed, "to get her out of here!"

"Leave her be. You ain't gonna be able to toss her out. She'll just grab something else to hang on to. Besides, she'll get fed up with this soon enough. She can't sit there on that sofa forever."

They had sorely underestimated Ingrid's endurance. She sat and sat some more as she watched Richard and Virgie attempt to ignore her as they went about their daily chores. Ingrid did not intend to be ignored. Virgie washed and dried the breakfast dishes, and Ingrid watched.

"You need put those dishcloths out in sun," Ingrid advised. "Be much whiter."

Virgie cooked dinner, and Ingrid watched.

"Tablespoon of vinegar in beans make cook faster," Ingrid pointed out.

"No, no!" she exclaimed when she saw Virgie salting them. "Salt make cook time too long!"

Richard ate the noon meal Virgie prepared, and Ingrid

watched every bite he took from her vantage point on the sofa. Soon, his meal half-eaten, he escaped to the barn, leaving Virgie alone to deal with both Ingrid and the baby.

Virgie self-consciously swept the floor.

"You miss spot," Ingrid pointed out.

"I don't need you a-telling me how to keep house!" Virgie exclaimed tearfully.

It was at that moment, with Virgie on the point of tears, that Ingrid knew things were beginning to go her way.

From her place on the sofa, Ingrid graciously dispensed free advice on everything that Virgie did for the rest of the day. When Bertie began to cry again, Ingrid kindly offered to hold him so that Virgie could work more efficiently.

Virgie declined. "You'll just run out the front door with him," she said, "the minute my back is turned."

"Ja," Ingrid agreed cheerfully. "Probably I do that."

In the late afternoon, with Bertie asleep in a cradle near her feet, Virgie released a thin rope that was attached to the wall and lowered a quilt frame from where it hung near the ceiling. It held a quilt that had been pieced from various shades of blue and white.

"Ah!" Ingrid said. "That is some pretty quilt. You make?"

Virgie preened a bit. "It's a new pattern."

"I quilt good. I help?"

Virgie looked confused. "I don't know . . ."

"I sit here anyway." Ingrid shrugged. "Nothing to do."

Virgie looked down at the baby sleeping soundly beside her.

"I suppose it wouldn't hurt. Frankly, I'd like to get the thing done. It's the piecing I enjoy the most, not the quilting. It's so tedious."

For the first time that day, Ingrid left the couch and pulled a kitchen chair up to the quilt frame. It felt heavenly to move about. Now, if she could only empty her bladder without being locked out of the house! Hunger she could deal with. Dirty looks she could deal with, but the need to go to the toilet was beginning to be a problem. She estimated she was good for about another hour before things got critical.

Virgie handed her a needle and thread, and Ingrid inspected the quilting done so far.

"Good work," she said admiringly. "Tiny stitches."

"I try." Virgie smiled, then she realized that she was smiling and frowned.

"I try make tiny stitches too," Ingrid said. "I want not to spoil beautiful quilt."

Virgie waggled a needle at her. "Now, just 'cause I let you help quilt, this don't mean you get to take Bertie home."

"I know," Ingrid replied.

Quietly, almost companionably, the two women set to work.

"How are the girls getting along?" Virgie bit off a piece of thread. "I ain't seen 'em since the inquest."

"They fine," Ingrid said. "But they miss grandmother and grandfather."

Virgie looked up from her work. "Did they say that?"

Ingrid nodded. "Agnes, she say, 'Grandma Virgie make best corn bread. Wish we have corn bread like Grandma Virgie do.'"

Virgie smiled. "Well, I do make a good pone of corn bread, even if I do say so myself."

"I not know how make right," Ingrid said sadly.

"Well, that strudel thing you made was right tasty."

"You like?"

"Very nice. Wish there was some left. Richard ate most of it. I didn't have much of an appetite at the time."

"I make again sometime. You come visit?"

"I'll never set foot inside that house again. Not while Josh is there. But tell me more about the girls."

"They miss mother. They miss grandmother. They miss little brother. But all right. Not sick."

"And Josh?"

Ingrid sighed. "He miss Diantha so very, very much."

Virgie's voice took on a hard edge. "You made a mistake marrying that man, you know."

"I know." Ingrid shrugged. "Too late. I do best I can now."

It was the truth, and Virgie apparently heard the truth of it in her voice. She glanced up, eagle-eyed. "You aren't happy with him?"

"Joshua love Diantha. I love children. I cook. I clean. We do all right."

"You aren't afraid of him?"

"Joshua?" Ingrid scoffed. "No. He so easy on girls. He let Agnes talk back all the time. I not afraid."

"That Agnes does have a mouth on her." Virgie chuckled. "I'm not saying I'd ever let you take Bertie or anything, but if I did, would I ever get to see him again?"

"Of course!" Ingrid said. "You baby's grandmother."

"And you'd let the girls come visit me?"

"All the time."

"I've missed those girls something awful," Virgie confessed. "But I don't want to see Josh or be around him."

"No worry," Ingrid said. "You visit Bertie and girls when Josh in fields."

"Are you sure you could handle everything? You might be having a baby yourself before long."

"*Nej*," she said sadly. "No baby. Joshua sleep in barn."

Virgie's eyes widened. "Josh sleeps in the barn?"

"Ja," Ingrid said. "Bertie only baby I maybe ever get."

"Oh." Virgie digested this piece of information. "So you and Josh haven't . . ."

"I cook. I clean. I care for the children." She rethreaded her needle.

"I'll admit," Virgie said, "it's been a little hard taking care of an infant. I'm not as young as I used to be."

Ingrid quietly sewed and nodded as she listened to Virgie argue with herself. She hoped Virgie would come to a conclusion soon, because she didn't know how much longer she could hold on to the coffee she had been foolish enough to drink that morning.

"Richard has been complaining a bit," Virgie said, "about me not being able to help him with his outdoor work as much as I used to."

Ingrid held her peace as she diligently worked the thread in and out of the lovely quilt.

"You sure you'd let me see the baby any time I wanted?" Virgie asked.

"Ja. And girls too," Ingrid agreed.

There was a silence for many minutes as both women plied their needles.

"Do you know why my Diantha died?"

"No," Ingrid said sadly. "But I very sorry for you."

Virgie threw down her needle and thread. "Let's go take a walk."

When Ingrid didn't move from her place, Virgie picked the baby up from the cradle.

"I'll let you hold Bertie while we walk, but I gotta go out to the barn and talk to Richard."

Ingrid held her arms out for the baby, trying not to tremble in her eagerness. The girls would always have memories of their mother, even Polly might have some fuzzy ones that would stay with her, but Bertie would be *her* baby, and hers alone.

It was getting dark, and he could do nothing but pace the floor and worry about Ingrid. He had completely given up on getting the girls to stay in bed.

"I need to go look for her. Can you watch over your sisters?"

"Sure," Agnes said. "Do you think Grandpa might've shot her?"

"I hope not." He lit a lantern and reached for his gun. "I should never have let her leave," he said as he went out the door. His first stop would be Richard and Virgie's to ask if Ingrid had been there. He had only taken a few steps out onto their lane when he saw a tall figure cresting the small rise between their cabin and his in-laws'. It was Ingrid, and she was still carrying that basket with her.

He went back inside and hung his gun in its place above the door. "Ingrid's coming. You girls go to bed now. I want to go talk to her."

He didn't really expect to be obeyed, and he wasn't. Before he had left the yard, four little girls were huddled, barefoot and in their nightgowns, in the doorway behind him.

"Try not to scare her off again, Pa," Agnes advised. "We really need her."

"I know." He was surprised at how strongly he agreed. In two weeks, she had become like a comforting flame within their home around which they all huddled, hands outstretched, warming themselves. The house had felt empty all day without her.

She seemed completely unafraid of the dark as she walked toward him, even though the forest loomed on either side of them. In fact, her step seemed surprisingly buoyant for having been gone so long. The large basket swung from one hand, still heavy with those bricks she had heated and placed within.

"Are you all right?" he asked.

"Ja," she answered, "I am fine."

"Where have you been all this time?"

"Virgie and Richard's."

"All day?"

"Ja. They are nice people."

This was news. "Did they like your strudel?"

"They like it fine."

He fell into step beside her. "Want me to carry the basket for you? It looks heavy."

Her face, when she turned to him, was so filled with joy she practically glowed in the moonlight.

"Ja. It is heavy. You carry."

She very carefully handed him the basket, and he discovered that it was not weighted down with bricks or pastry after all. It was filled with the precious sleeping body of his son.

He felt the breath go out of him. "They gave him to you?"

"Ja."

"How in the world did you manage this, Ingrid?"

"I pray and pray all day at Virgie and Richard's. God listen. They give us Bertie."

"I thought I was going to have to fight my father-in-law to get my boy back."

"Richard not so strong," Ingrid scoffed. "You win—easy."

He handed the lantern to Ingrid and laid the basket on the ground so he could scoop the baby up into his arms. He reveled in the solid weight of the little boy who had grown since he had held him last. Virgie and Richard had taken good care of him.

The little girls were still waiting in the open doorway of his home, big-eyed and barefoot.

"Is it Bertie, Pa?" Agnes leaped off the porch and came running toward him.

"It is, indeed." He got down on one knee so the girls could cluster around. He pulled the blanket away from the baby's face, and Ingrid held the light up so they could all look their fill at their little brother.

"His cheeks are fat," Agnes said. "Grandma fed him good."

"Yes, she did," Joshua admitted.

"We get to keep him now?" Trudy asked.

"We do." He looked up at Ingrid. "Thanks to your new mother."

"Can we go see Grandma and Grandpa or are they still mad at us?" Agnes asked.

"They not mad at girls," Ingrid quickly interjected.

"Are they still mad at me?" Joshua asked.

"You." Ingrid gave a small shake of her head. "Maybe best you stay away."

"Is it working?" he asked.

"More food on me than in baby," Ingrid said.

It was true, her dress was splattered with the thin, milky gruel she was trying to feed Bertie with the little "pap boat" that Virgie had sent along with him. The device resembled a narrow gravy boat with a small spout that could be inserted into the baby's mouth. Keeping a trickle going, just enough for him to suck but not enough for him to choke on, was exceedingly difficult.

Joshua caressed his son's dark hair. "It must be possible," he said. "Virgie managed to use it."

"Virgie have not so much to do." Ingrid glanced around at the four girls. "Except feed baby."

It was the first time Joshua had heard Ingrid say anything resembling a complaint.

Bertie gagged, spit the milky gruel back out, and began to cry. Joshua grabbed the pap boat out of Ingrid's hand so she could sit the baby upright. Agnes brought a cloth to wipe his chin.

"It'll be all right, Bertie," Trudy said in a soothing voice. "We're gonna take good care of you."

Ellie waggled a little clothespin doll in front of him that Agnes had made for her just that morning. It was now Ellie's favorite toy.

Bertie stopped crying when he saw the girls. His eyes sparkled and he kicked his feet as he reached out for the clothespin doll.

"Don't give him that," Agnes chided Ellie. "He'll stick it in his mouth and the clothes'll come off and choke him."

Ellie immediately put it behind her back. Bertie stretched out his arms to her as though he thought she was playing a game with him, and gurgled happily.

"Did he manage to eat anything at all?" Joshua asked. He had never witnessed this process before. Diantha had experienced no trouble nursing their babies.

"He eat some." Ingrid placed the baby over her shoulder and rubbed his back. "Bertie need his bed. Bring down?"

Joshua went up to the loft and came back with the walnut cradle Richard had made for Agnes while Joshua was away at war, and which had also held all of their other children.

When he got it downstairs, Ingrid was holding the baby cradled in the crook of her arm, with four admiring little girls clustered around her.

"Can we hold him?"

"Tomorrow," Ingrid said. "Time for bed now."

"He sure is pretty," Agnes said. "Prettier than Ellie or Trudy. They were kinda funny-looking." She glanced down at her little sisters and ruffled their hair. "But they got over it."

Polly, evidently jealous of the attention Bertie was getting, tried to climb onto Ingrid's lap. Agnes held her back, and she started to wail.

"Joshua?" Ingrid said. "Take Bertie?"

He gladly plucked his baby boy out of her arms, and Ingrid opened her arms wide to Polly. The little girl climbed onto her lap.

"Polly my baby too," Ingrid crooned as she placed Polly in exactly the same position that she had held the baby. "Bertie not change that. I love Polly always."

Polly stuck the inevitable thumb in her mouth and settled back against Ingrid. As Ingrid hummed a tune, the little girl's eyes began to droop, and soon she was asleep.

"She is so tired. That why she cry," Ingrid said. "Now, girls go to bed."

"We wanna stay up and play with the baby," Trudy said with a pout.

"Bertie here in morning. You get much time now with baby."

"Come on." Agnes gave Ellie a light swat on the bottom. "Let's go to bed. You'll get tired of him soon enough, just like I got tired of you."

"You never got tired of me," Ellie said.

"You're right," Agnes said. "But I might if you don't hurry on to bed like I said."

The drama of getting Bertie here had seemed to placate Ingrid. She was a different woman than the one he had found chopping kindling at three in the morning.

While Ingrid rocked Polly to sleep, Joshua had a chance to get reacquainted with his son. Had it only been six months since Diantha had given birth to this little boy right here in their bed?

It seemed like a lifetime ago.

# 12

"Breakfast is ready." Ingrid had come to the barn to find him. "What you doing?"

"Building a bed."

"Who for?"

"For me. I'm tired of sleeping in the barn under a horse blanket."

"Aww. I sleep much good in *my* bed. Plenty room stretch out. Nice, clean, smell-good sheets."

She turned and went back inside the cabin while he quietly fumed. In his opinion, this thing between them over what had happened the night he had left her to sleep in the barn was getting a little ridiculous. He had apologized. He had even picked her a bouquet of spring flowers and apologized a second time. He had asked nicely for permission to sleep in his own bed again, but no matter what he said or did, no matter how well they got along during the day—come nightfall, she protected her space with a ferociousness that astonished him.

Women never forgot anything!

As he threaded the rope back and forth through the holes he had drilled, making a foundation for a mattress, he contemplated the differences between the two women he had married. Diantha went silent and brooded for weeks when she was hurt—and it took forever to find out what he had done wrong. In the meantime, the whole family would suffer. Ingrid spoke her mind, even if it meant giving him a tongue lashing in Swedish, since she tended to forget her English when she was upset. Then she would brighten up and be all cheerful again, often leaving him to wonder what had just happened. The nice thing was, her temper blew over quickly and supper would invariably still appear on the table.

But his rejection of her that one night? *That* she did not forget.

So he was building a bed.

A lot of families kept a bed in the sitting room of their cabin. It was handy when someone was ill or if there was a sleepover guest. For a family such as his, which didn't have money to purchase a sofa, the bed could be used for the same function.

He blew the last shavings away and put his tools back where they belonged. Then he carried the bed with him to the house. He hoped he wouldn't need to make his own mattress too—but that would depend on whatever mood Ingrid might be in. He would fold up some blankets and simply sleep on the rope webbing if he had to. He'd slept in worse places during the war. It hadn't exactly been a picnic in the barn with mice scampering over him.

"There." He positioned the bed in the corner of the sitting room.

Ingrid, holding baby Bertie on her hip with one hand and a wooden spoon in the other, came over to inspect it. "I make mattress."

Ah. She was in a good mood. "I appreciate that, Ingrid."

"Need nice heavy cotton ticking."

Ticking. He hadn't thought about that. "We could go into White Rock and see if George has some in stock."

"He have." She seemed pensive.

"Is there something wrong?" Joshua asked. "Do you not want to see him?"

"Who? George? He not problem." She dismissed George with a wave of her wooden spoon. "We maybe visit Susan?"

"Susan Cain?"

"Ja."

"That's right," he said. "She did invite us."

"Agnes and me have new dresses."

He vaguely remembered seeing her working with some pink flowered material.

"This afternoon, right after we've eaten dinner, we'll pack up the children, go into town for the ticking, and stop by the Cains' house to see if they're home. Would you enjoy that?" he asked.

"Ja!" She gave him the benefit of a sunny smile and immediately handed Bertie off to him. "You hold baby. I cook breakfast. Cinnamon rolls. And omelet."

Even though she wouldn't let him have his bed back, it was hard to remain upset with Ingrid for long. Her breakfasts alone were enough to turn a man into a slavering fool.

"I can't keep her anymore, Josh. I'm sorry, but Barbara's in the family way again, and she says it's your turn."

"Turn?" Ingrid asked.

Their family had just gotten back from the mercantile and from paying a short visit to the Cain family. It was their first venture out as a married couple, and she had enjoyed the outing tremendously. Susan had even expressed admiration for the dresses she had made for herself and Agnes. Susan's father had been quite interested in the principles of Pietism and had questioned her in detail. It had been a wonderful day.

But who was this man awaiting them in their front yard, and who was Barbara?

Joshua frowned. "We're kind of in a fix here ourselves, Zeb. I don't know . . ."

"What?" Ingrid looked from one man to the other. She saw a strong family resemblance, although Joshua was more striking. This Zeb had the same coloring and features, but he looked weaker.

"This is my brother, Zebulon," Joshua said. "Zeb, this is my new wife, Ingrid."

"Pleased to meet you, ma'am." The brother dipped his hat. "I wasn't aware that you had remarried, Josh."

"It was a bit sudden."

It wasn't hard for Ingrid to see that something was up besides a visit and pleasantries between two brothers. There was too much tension in the air.

"You could have written, given us some time to make plans," Josh said.

"You know how women get when they're . . . that way. Barb wouldn't let me. She was afraid you'd turn us down, and she said she was done."

"Done what?" Ingrid asked.

"Taking care of our mother," Zeb said. "She's on your porch. I have to be getting back now."

"You spend night?" Ingrid asked.

"No, no." Zebulon's eyes darted back and forth between them. "I'd best be heading back. Barb's close to delivering and it'll take me the best part of two days to get home."

And with that, Joshua's brother climbed back onto his wagon and drove out of their yard.

"Ain't Uncle Zeb stayin' to supper, Pa?" Agnes asked.

149

"No."

"What's he doing here, then?"

"Droppin' off your grandma."

"The one we don't see all that regular?"

"Yes. That one."

Joshua started toward the house, but Ingrid stopped him.

"What is this about mother?"

Joshua sighed. "Ingrid, you got a bad bargain when you married me."

"I know that," she said impatiently. "You tell me about mother."

"My father owned a good farm a couple days' ride south of here. When he died, my brother and I divided things up. He got the land, the house, the tools, the livestock, along with the responsibility of our mother."

"And you?"

"I got no land, no farm, no tools, no livestock—and no responsibilities. It seemed best at the time. I was headed off to war and didn't know if I would make it back alive. Zeb had a slight heart condition and had to stay home. It seemed the best thing to do."

"Your mother. Is she bad person?"

"No."

"Why this Barbara want her leave?"

"Barb was not happy about the decision Zeb had made. She did not want to move into her in-laws' place. Then she and Zeb started having children one after another. Last count I heard, they have ten with now an eleventh on the way. I'm guessing Mother is starting to feel like a burden to her—or perhaps she just needs the extra bedroom. Frankly, I never cared much for Barb."

"Ten children and one more come soon? Zeb's heart must not be so sick!"

As Zeb pulled away, Ingrid saw Joshua's mother sitting on the edge of the porch, a few bags grouped around her.

The poor woman was nearly comatose from the trip. Ingrid collected every extra blanket she had in the house to temporarily cushion the rope webbing of Joshua's bed so that the old lady would have a place to sleep. She decided that sewing up that mattress would be the first thing she would accomplish tomorrow after breakfast.

While Joshua fed Bertie, Ingrid fed his mother, helped her undress, and helped her slip into her makeshift bed. Somehow, some way, they got the children and baggage and beds sorted out until it was just him and Ingrid standing there, looking at his aged mother as she slept curled up like a child.

Joshua expected Ingrid to really let loose, to tell him off, to throw a fit over the unfairness of his brother dumping his mother off on them. Instead, she just stood there, saying nothing.

"I am so sorry, Ingrid," he said. "I had no idea this was going to happen."

Ingrid wasn't paying a bit of attention to him. Instead, her foot was tapping—a habit he had noticed whenever she was either upset or thinking hard.

"Are you angry?" He was fairly certain he knew the answer. That foot tapping was getting intense.

"Oh ja. Ingrid *very* angry."

He didn't blame her. If there was ever a woman who had the right to feel put upon, it was his new wife—and here was yet another load for her to bear.

"Ingrid, I—"

"Why they put old woman through this?" Tears glistened

in her eyes. "Treat her like garbage, dump off on porch!" That toe was tapping a mile a minute as she fought back tears.

"You see this?" She pointed at bruises on his mother's arm. "And this?" She touched what looked like the remnants of a slap mark upon his mother's cheek. "That woman be very mean to mother." Her eyes blazed, and she punched him on the shoulder. "What wrong with you—leave mother with those persons so long time?"

Then the tears came in earnest as she bent to gently smooth the gray hair away from his mother's forehead. "Look how thin! Hair is look like a *mus* nest. In morning I make good breakfast. I comb the hair. You see. Mother be fine."

He felt his throat close up in response to her words. Why *had* he allowed his mother to stay there for so long? He had known Barb was not particularly kind. He had known his brother Zeb was weak. His only excuse was that he hadn't realized Barb was *that* unkind, or Zeb *that* weak. No wonder his younger brother had been in such a hurry to leave. He had known that once Joshua got sight of his mother's bruises, he would get a thrashing himself.

The only thing he could say for his brother was at least Zeb had gotten their mother out of there before Barb could do any worse damage. Still, the trip itself had been hard on her.

Ingrid brushed away her tears and headed toward her bedroom.

"You. Sleep in here with me. You be ready if mother need help in night."

He was tired to the bone and enormously grateful not to have to sleep in the barn again. He pulled his shirt off over his head and climbed into his good bed for the first time in days.

The baby stirred in his cradle on Ingrid's side of the bed, and he heard her set the cradle rocking while she hummed a soft lullaby. He left the door of their bedroom open so he could hear if his mother got up in the middle of the night. He knew she would be disoriented and frightened.

Soon, little Bertie, calmed by the rocking of the cradle and Ingrid's lullaby, settled back down. There was not a peep from the girls upstairs. The only sound was that of crickets outside their windows.

Ingrid lay poised, with her arm draped over the side of the bed and her hand on Bertie's cradle, ready to set it in motion again if the baby started to stir.

Joshua turned on his side and put his arm around her waist, so grateful for her tenderness toward his mother and children that he could hardly speak.

"What?" She shoved his arm away. "You want be friendly? Now we have baby on one side and mother on other side?"

"No," he answered, putting his arm around her waist again. "I'm just grateful to have you here beside me."

Ingrid lay for a long time, staring into the darkness, with Joshua's arm heavy around her waist and his breath against her neck. He had fallen asleep quickly. She did not mistake his touch for the embrace of a loving husband. She knew that at this point she was not much more to him than Polly's rag doll was to her—something comforting to hang on to.

There was a very good chance that was all she would ever be to Joshua, nothing more than something to cling to when life got hard. This knowledge made her miss her twin brother terribly. There had never been a time when she had been without her brother's love and protection. That very fact was the thing that convinced her that he no longer lived. She knew him too well.

The day after the wedding, Hazel had promised to send Ingrid's new address to the boardinghouse where she was supposed to have met him, just in case he finally showed up—but there had been no word.

Sending the address was only a long shot anyway. If Hans were alive, nothing would have kept him from meeting her. They had made such good plans. Hans would be making a dollar and a quarter per day in the lumber camps. Timbered-over land was going for less than a dollar and a quarter per acre. One year's pay would buy them more land than they could ever dream of owning in Sweden. They had discussed the legacy they hoped to create for their families—two farms, close together. Maybe as much as three hundred acres between them. Even more if Hans spent another year in the lumber camp. They had planned for their children to grow up together as close as brothers and sisters.

Now, that good and decent dream was forever gone, and instead she had eight people to feed, dress, and clean up after—all crowded together in a two-room log cabin. Her responsibilities were growing. With the exception of this one glorious day when she and her new family had gone visiting, her marriage with Joshua had felt like they were two mules yoked together, pulling the same heavy load. She was a strong woman, but even she could only bear so much—especially when she knew that she was not loved.

At an emotional dead end, she carefully extricated herself from the bed and knelt beside it, her head bowed.

*How do I do this, Lord? How do I endure? How do I continue to serve and love this man and his family when I know that he may never view me as anything more than convenient household help? The work is hard, and the days are long. Now, with Joshua's mother here to care for, it is nearly overwhelming . . . how do I do this, Father?*

She rested her bowed head on her clasped hands, hoping for something that would give her the strength to go on.

There was no voice, no miraculous revelation. Her great fatigue made her want to forget about praying and simply climb back into bed and sink into oblivion—but then a glimmer of an idea began to form. An idea that was so simple and pure that she was amazed she had missed it.

As a married woman, she had focused her life entirely on what Joshua thought, if Joshua would be impressed with her management of his home and children . . . if Joshua would ever love her.

No more.

She could not spend her life trying to gain Joshua's approval. If she continued to base her happiness on the moods of this damaged man, she knew that someday there would be nothing left of her.

A long time ago, she had vowed to serve the Lord in everything she did, wherever he led. For a while she had lost sight of that vow. Now, she renewed it. No longer would she be serving only her husband and his family with the work of her hands.

Clothes would still get washed, meals would still appear on the table, the children would still be lovingly cared for. But the motive behind all her hard labor would change.

From now on, she wouldn't just be diapering Bertie, or scrubbing clothes, or washing sticky little hands and faces— she would be serving the Lord. Every meal she cooked, every bucket of water she lugged from the well—all of it would be in service to the Lord. Everything she did in caring for these precious children, this fragile mother, this damaged man—would be, in her heart, a sacrifice of love to Christ.

Her workload would be no lighter, her hunger to be loved by her husband no less, but she knew instinctively that her life would be infinitely easier if she could simply hold on to this one, noble premise—of quietly living every mundane detail of her life for God.

With that one resolution, everything changed and she went to sleep with renewed strength to face the challenges of the coming day.

## 13

Joshua awoke to find Ingrid standing over him with Bertie in her arms. Her toe was tapping furiously. "You change and feed baby," she said. "I need to help . . . what is mother's name?"

"Mary."

"I need to help Mary." She lay Bertie beside him in the bed and hurried out the door.

Joshua yawned and propped himself up on one elbow. "I guess it's just me and you, little fellow."

Bertie gurgled and kicked his strong little legs out of the baby blanket in which Ingrid had wrapped him.

"Oh, you want to play, do you?" Joshua captured a tiny toe. "This little piggy went to market . . ."

Bertie belly laughed, which made Joshua smile. Then the little boy quieted as he anticipated Joshua's next move. "This little piggy stayed home."

Another peal of belly laughter.

It was intoxicating, playing with his child. The need to head out the door and start his morning chores evaporated as he lost himself in the moment.

"This little piggy had roast beef." Another belly laugh.

"And this little piggy had none."

The door flew open and Ingrid stood there with her hands on her hips. "You change baby and feed baby. Not play with baby. Ja?"

He looked directly at her as he deliberately disobeyed and tweaked the littlest toe. "And this little piggy went wee, wee, wee, all the way home."

That one definitely hit Bertie's funny bone. He giggled so hard that neither Ingrid nor Joshua could keep from laughing with him.

"I know. I know." Joshua climbed out of the bed and lifted Bertie up into his arms. "Feed baby. Change baby."

"Breakfast is almost ready. Bertie's too."

Joshua saw his mother dressed and sitting quietly on the side of the makeshift bed.

"Mother?" he asked. "How are you feeling?"

His mother was in her early seventies, but she had failed so badly since the last time he saw her, she could have been mistaken for a ninety-year-old woman.

"It was a very long trip." Her voice quavered, whether from fatigue or emotion he couldn't tell.

"I know, Mother. I'm sorry."

"I don't want to go back." Her eyes looked haunted.

"You don't have to, Mother. You can stay with us."

"That woman over there . . ." Her voice sounded worried. "She's not Diantha."

"Her name is Ingrid. Diantha died."

"Diantha is dead?"

"Nearly three months ago. Remember? I wrote to you at Zeb and Barbara's?"

She grasped his hand and looked straight into his eyes. "I don't want to go back there."

He glanced up at Ingrid. She was standing by the stove, watching. Their eyes met, and there was a flash of understanding between them. Both wanted to wring Zeb and Barbara's necks.

Once Mary had been given breakfast, she seemed to grow a little stronger, both in mind and body. Agnes took over the job of brushing her grandmother's hair. Ellie and Trudy hovered around her. Polly kept bringing small items and laying them on her grandmother's lap as though she were trying to give her presents.

Little by little, Mary seemed to come out of her near-stupor. She began to notice the children and even pretended to examine the items Polly brought her, thanking her for each little gift.

"How in the world did your hair get in such a mess, Grandma?" Agnes said as she worked at untangling another snarl.

"I-I couldn't find a comb or brush for a very long time."

"But it would take weeks to get this many tangles."

"I used to have a beautiful brush and mirror set that your grandfather bought me. It was ceramic and had little violets painted on the back."

"What happened to it?" Agnes asked.

"Barbara gave it to her oldest daughter."

"Did you ask for it back?"

"I did, but Barbara said I was too old to have such pretty things."

Ingrid did a slow boil. What kind of a woman would do such a thing? If she ever met her sister-in-law, she was going to give her such a piece of her mind!

After setting some stew to simmering for dinner and washing the dishes, she spread out the new ticking on the table, measured the bed Joshua had made, and began to cut.

"I used to sew well." Mary's voice was tentative. "But I can barely thread a needle anymore."

"The girls thread for you—you want to help?" Ingrid asked.

"Oh." Mary acted startled. "I doubt I could do a good job."

"So what? Is only a mattress."

"I suppose I could maybe do some basting."

"That is big help."

She wondered what was going on inside Josh's mind. Why he was allowing her to carry the conversation with his mother. He had chosen to work inside this morning, which was unusual. At the moment he was standing near the stove, soldering a cooking pot that had developed a leak. It was not, however, a pot she particularly needed—it could have easily waited until winter when he would be forced to stay inside.

After Agnes finished brushing all the tangles out of her grandmother's hair, she parted it in the middle and braided it into one long braid.

The change in Mary's looks with her hair brushed and neatly braided was startling. Ingrid could now see where Joshua had gotten his good looks. In spite of the gray hair, Mary still had dark eyelashes and brows, which made her lovely blue eyes, Joshua's eyes, especially noticeable. Ingrid could see the shadow of the girl Mary had once been and decided that Joshua's mother had probably had her choice of beaus.

Mary ran her hands over her smooth braid. "Oh, that's such a relief. Thank you."

Ingrid pinned the edges of the mattress together, then handed Agnes a needle and thread. "Here, thread this for Grandmother."

No matter how badly Mary sewed, it could be redone later. For now, her mother-in-law needed the reassurance of doing some small task, but considering how weak Mary had been last night, Ingrid wasn't entirely sure she could even push a needle through the cloth.

"Come over here to table, Mary. I need help, please."

Mary sat staring at the material, the needle and thread in her hand.

"Is something wrong?" Ingrid asked.

"I need my spectacles."

"Agnes, find Grandmother's spectacles."

Agnes found them in one of the bundles, and Mary began to sew. At first, she was slow. Then she asked for a thimble, and after a few minutes, she seemed to find a rhythm, and the mattress began to take shape quickly. Ingrid stole a glance at her stitches and was impressed. They were as tight and even as her own.

"You are very good at the sewing," Ingrid said. "Maybe after we finish mattress, we cut new dresses for the girls? You want to help?"

"If you think what I'm doing is good enough."

"What you sew is very good. Big help." This time, Ingrid meant it.

"If we get new dresses made for the girls," Mary mused, "maybe we could go to church soon? Barbara and Zeb seldom went, and I've missed it terribly."

Then she glanced up, like a child who was afraid she had said something wrong. The look of fright on her face made Ingrid's heart ache with a mixture of pity and anger.

"Ja. We go to the church. *Eller hur?* Good idea, Joshua?"

Joshua appeared to be so deeply engrossed in his work that he didn't respond immediately.

"Joshua?"

"What? Oh, sure. That's fine."

"*Underbar!* We make the dresses. We go to the church."

"Ingrid?" Joshua asked. "Could I talk with you outside for a moment?"

His voice was so serious, and his frown so deep, it worried her. Had she done or said something wrong? The only thing she had done was tell Mary they could go to church. Maybe he didn't want to be seen at church with her. Then another thought struck. Maybe he didn't believe in going to church. Maybe he didn't even believe in God! Maybe his prayers at the table before each meal were nothing more than habit. The possibility of Joshua not being a believer had never crossed her mind. Well, she would take the children and Mary to church, even if he didn't want to go with them!

Joshua was so angry he could hardly trust himself to speak in front of his children and mother. He paced back and forth in his yard.

Ingrid came out and closed the door behind her. "What? You not want to go to church? You not believe in God? You not tell me? Why?"

Sometimes, for the life of him, he had no idea what the woman was talking about.

"I go to church, Ingrid, and I most definitely believe in God."

She seemed slightly mollified by that. "I do something wrong?"

How in the *world* had she come to the conclusion that she had done something wrong? All he'd done was ask to speak to her outside.

"You haven't done anything wrong. I just wanted to tell you that I'm leaving for a while."

"What! You leave me? With children and baby and mother to care for? You not dare run out on me, Joshua Hunter!"

"Who said anything about running out on you?"

"You! You say you leave me!"

Joshua decided he would think twice before he asked to speak to Ingrid alone again. Evidently, it had scared the girl silly.

"I have something I need to take care of. It will take me all day. I won't be back until very late. Probably not until morning."

"All day? All night?" Ingrid narrowed her eyes and contemplated his face. "I bet you go to the brother."

"That's right."

"Zeb say he on the road two days."

"That's because he drove a wagon with our mother in it, and he had to stay on passable roads. Cutting cross country, I can make it there and back in half the time. I've done it before."

"What do you do when you there?"

"I haven't decided yet."

"Hmm." Ingrid's toe began to tap, and he knew she was thinking things through. He waited. The toe tapping stopped. She had come to a conclusion.

"I pack you food for trip," Ingrid said. "I feel sorry for brother when he see you come . . . but not much sorry."

All day and all night passed and Joshua did not return. She had expected him in the middle of the night, but now she was getting worried. Then the sound of horse's hooves filtered through the logs. It was not yet daylight.

She hurriedly dressed and ran out to him, passing Mary, who was still asleep on her new mattress stuffed with fresh straw.

"You are home!" she said.

"Is everything all right here?"

"We are fine."

He dismounted, unbuttoned his shirt, and pulled out an object wrapped in cloth that he had been carrying next to his body. "Here." He handed it to her. "Be careful with it."

Ingrid unfolded the cloth and discovered a beautiful ceramic brush and mirror set, decorated with delicate, hand-painted violets, just like Mary had described. "This is mother's?"

"I thought she should have it back." He had that steely look in his eye that made her very glad it wasn't *her* with whom he was angry.

"You have much trouble to get it?"

His jaw clenched. "Nope."

He started to walk his horse to the barn.

"Joshua?"

He stopped. "Yes?"

"Do you hit brother?"

"Yep." He drew the word out as though it gave him a great deal of satisfaction.

"Much hit?"

"Once." He flexed his right hand, the knuckles of which were skinned and bruised. "But it felt real good."

While he tended to his horse, Ingrid ran back into the house with the lovely set he had ridden so far to retrieve. Mary had awakened and was sitting up. Her face lit up when she saw what Ingrid handed her.

"Joshua bring."

Mary traced the violets on the back of the mirror with one finger. "It was the last birthday present my husband gave me before he passed."

In her excitement, Ingrid blurted out, "Joshua hit Zeb." Then she put her hand over her mouth.

"Well, now. Josh shouldn't have done that." Then for the first time since she had arrived, Mary's eyes twinkled. "But I can't say that I much blame him."

## ~ 14 ~

Their arrival to worship with those who met in the Cains' sitting room caused quite a stir. Ingrid was proud of her new family. With the exception of Mary and Joshua, everyone was dressed in identical pink calico dresses. Even little Bertie—much too young to wear trousers—was dressed in pink calico.

Ingrid liked the idea of the children and her going to church all dressed alike her first time there. She wanted everyone in that village to know that she, Ingrid, was now the mother of these children. None of the little girls, including Agnes, seemed to mind. They were just happy to have a new dress to wear.

Thank goodness Hazel had chosen such pretty material, because Ingrid had decided she had seen enough pink calico to last her a lifetime. Mary, as she had gotten her strength back and some confidence, was becoming quite the seamstress again.

The first face Ingrid saw as they walked in was Susan, who was seated on a long wooden bench. When she saw Ingrid, she immediately scooted far to the side and motioned for the entire Hunter family to fill in the bench beside her.

Ingrid held her head high as she took her place beside

Susan. She had accomplished much in the past three weeks and had nothing to be ashamed of. A sprig of hair stuck up on Bertie's head and she licked her thumb and slicked it down. Her family was a handsome bunch, and she was proud of them.

"I'm happy to see you!" Susan whispered after Ingrid had settled down beside her.

"Ja!" Ingrid beamed. "I happy you see me too!"

The services began and Susan's father spoke about the young David fighting the giant and how there were many different kinds of giants in people's lives. Ingrid nodded with understanding. After these past two months, she knew a thing or two about giants. She believed she had fought her fair share of them. Today, with her sparkling-clean children grouped around her and a good dinner and clean house awaiting them at home—she felt like she'd won a few battles herself.

Joshua was enjoying his conversation with the other men after church so much that, for a moment, he didn't remember exactly how he had ended up with Bertie. He thought it came about when Ingrid had handed him off to Agnes, and Agnes handed him off to Mary, who handed him off to Hazel, who eventually handed the baby to him. He was a little bothered by the fact that his son was wearing a pink calico dress. All baby boys wore dresses, but he thought he might have a talk with Ingrid about making Bertie something a little more, well, a little more masculine before next Sunday rolled around.

He was fairly certain they would be coming back next Sunday. These past three weeks while they had gotten on their feet as a family, he had not even brought up the idea of going to church. Diantha had been indifferent; she attended with him, but it was never a priority for her. Ingrid, on the other hand, seemed to be practically thrilled to death to go—which pleased him enormously. The strength of his faith, tried and tested on the battlefield, was something he wanted to pass down to his children. Their mother had been less than lukewarm about it, and this had been a worry to him.

He was a little surprised to see Private Lyman at church. It was quite a ways for the man to ride.

"Your daughters seem to have really taken a shine to that little Swedish gal you married," Lyman said as they shook hands. "I'm glad it turned out so well for you and your family."

Joshua didn't think the word *little* described Ingrid, but she was definitely Swedish, and the girls had taken more than a shine to her. As he looked at his daughters right now, they were practically hanging on Ingrid while she chatted with Hazel and Susan. Trudy was leaning against her, and Polly was holding a wad of her skirt with one hand and sucking her thumb with the other. Agnes and Ellie were standing only inches away. Even though Ingrid was deep in conversation, one hand rested lightly on Ellie's head, as though to reassure herself that the little girl wasn't wandering off.

"She's been good for them," Joshua said truthfully. "What are you doing here today? It must be an hour's ride."

"An hour's ride goes by fast when a man's in love."

"You're in love?" Joshua was startled. "Who with?"

"The preacher's daughter." Lyman nodded toward the small clump of women near Ingrid. "She caught my eye the day me and the other men came to back you with the judge. I liked the way she jumped in to help that little wife of yours get herself a wedding. One of the nicest things I ever saw a woman do for another. I kind of thought if she was that kind, she might not mind too much being courted by a man with only one good arm. I've been coming down every Sunday since. Her and her mama have been nice enough to invite me to Sunday dinner each time."

"What about her father?"

"The preacher?" Lyman chuckled. "I'm not sure he notices I'm there. He's kinda distracted. Keeps making little notes on pieces of paper he keeps beside him during dinner. Susan says it's all the things he wishes he'd said in his sermon but forgot to."

Joshua took out his pocket watch and observed the time. Brother Cain had preached for over two hours. "He couldn't have left out much!"

"Well, now," Lyman said. "I would say you're probably right about that."

Joshua wondered how to broach the subject, especially in a house filled to the rafters with females. He weighed the odds of getting into deep trouble with his request and decided it was about fifty/fifty.

He waited until they had eaten Sunday dinner and the dishes had been washed. The girls were outside playing, and his mother was upstairs resting. She had gained enough strength in the past couple days that she had begun to go upstairs, where she now shared a bed with Polly and Agnes. She seemed to prefer the semi-privacy of the girls' loft to sleeping in the middle of the sitting room.

He cleared his throat and waded in, choosing to start with a compliment.

"Um, Ingrid, you and the girls looked wonderful today. I appreciate all the hard work you and Mother did on those dresses."

She looked up from her Bible, which he had noticed she was reading more and more these days—in fact, ever since the night his mother had come. "Thank you." Then her head went down again.

He cleared his throat. "Look, Ingrid. I appreciate you making clothes for the children, but could you make a dress that's a little less . . . feminine . . . for Bertie before next Sunday?"

He tensed, wondering if there would be a blow-up.

"Ja, sure. You buy little bit of boy material, and I sew that." She perused her Bible again.

"I just heard what you two were saying." His mother came downstairs. "I've been thinking. Before Barb got so mad at me, I used to try to send enough material to Diantha every Christmas to make dresses for her and the girls. Did she use all of it?"

"I don't think she used hardly any of it," Joshua said. "Her mother sewed most of the girls' clothing out of fabric she purchased herself. There should be plenty of it left."

"Where?" Ingrid asked. He suddenly had her full attention. "Where this material hide?"

"The last I saw, it was in Diantha's trunk."

"Where is trunk?" Ingrid asked. "In barn?"

"Beside the bed," Joshua said, "where the lamp is."

"That big box with long fancy cloth on it?"

"Diantha liked to keep it covered with a tablecloth her mother had embroidered—she said it made the trunk look like a table."

"We open, please?"

"It's probably locked," Joshua said.

"You have key?" Ingrid sounded hopeful.

"No." He shook his head. "I never knew where Diantha kept it. I had almost forgotten the trunk was there."

About that time, Agnes came inside.

"Do you know where your mother kept the key to her trunk?" he asked.

No," Agnes said. "But Ma was always real careful about that key. She had a special hiding place for it, and she made sure we never knew where it was."

"Why she lock up dress material?" Ingrid asked.

"She said she was afraid the girls would get into it and cut doll clothes out of it."

"Ja, I see that happen," Ingrid said. "You think of place for key, you let me know."

Ingrid closed her Bible. She was pleased that Mary was feeling so much better today. She was happy about getting to go to church. It felt good to have the family all around her now on this quiet Sabbath. Even Joshua was reading his *Michigan Farmer* magazine, content to take a day of rest. But Ingrid's mind was darting here and there, trying to figure out a good hiding place for that key. If there really was fabric in that trunk, she needed it to clothe her children, but there was also a part of her that couldn't help wondering if there was anything else she might find in that locked trunk.

Although the rest of the family seemed to take it as a matter of course, it seemed odd to her that Diantha would bother to lock up something as mundane as fabric—especially since she didn't even value it enough to use it. Sugar, yes. It was expensive. A small birthday present, yes. Children were nosy. But fabric? She didn't think so.

They heard a pitter-patter on the roof, and Ellie, Trudy, and Polly came tumbling inside. "It's raining!" Ellie shouted.

"Finally." Joshua looked up. "We need the rain. It's been such a dry spring."

"Maybe rain barrels fill up," Ingrid said. "Give us nice, soft water for washing hair and clothes."

"Pray that it continues, Ingrid. Our crops need it."

# ༺ 15 ༻

The two-day rain brought wildflowers—armloads of them seemed to spring up around their farm overnight.

"Ma always liked flowers," Agnes said, her nose pressed against the window.

"Maybe you take her some," Ingrid suggested.

"What do you mean?" Agnes asked.

"Go put flowers on mother's grave."

"You wouldn't mind?" Joshua asked.

"No. Why I mind?" Ingrid said. "Go." She made a shooing motion. "Take flowers for mother."

"If you're sure."

"I pack picnic. You stay long time. Talk with children about mother," Ingrid suggested. "Remember together."

"Thank you, Ingrid. That's very thoughtful of you," Joshua said. "I think that would be a good idea."

Although he looked at her a little suspiciously when she said "stay long time" and handed him a basket of sandwiches, he accepted the basket and headed out with the girls.

"Pick many flowers for mother," Ingrid called as they left.

She knew that Diantha's grave was in a family plot on top of a rise behind Virgie and Richard's house. With any luck, the walk, the picnic, the picking of flowers, the remembering would keep them away for an hour or two.

Ingrid hoped they would stay gone as long as possible. It would give her a chance to do something she had been itching to do—search the house over for that key.

"You and my mother will be all right alone here with Bertie?" Joshua asked.

"We fine." Ingrid fought back frustration with his slowness to leave. "Go. Have good time."

The minute the girls and he had left, she placed Bertie in his cradle and scooted it over near the rocking chair where Mary sat basting a new baby dress for him out of the navy blue material Joshua had brought from George's yesterday— in spite of having to make the trip in the rain. Joshua must *really* not want Bertie to wear the pink calico.

"You watch baby?" Ingrid asked.

"Of course." Mary peered at her over her glasses. "You're going to go looking for that key, aren't you?"

"Ja." Ingrid was impressed. Mary seemed to be getting more alert each day. "How you know?"

"What woman wouldn't want to know what a man's first wife was keeping locked away in a chest?" Mary said. "Diantha was always cordial to me, but she was a secretive little thing. Where are you going to look?"

"Upstairs in girls' loft?"

"No." Mary shook her head. "I already checked out all the hiding places up there."

"You do that?" Ingrid was even further impressed.

"I had to sacrifice to send that fabric each Christmas," Mary said. "Plus, Barb resented it. It bothers me that Diantha evidently never touched it. I'd like to see it put to use for what I intended it—clothing for the children."

"Where I look then?"

172

"I'd look in the bedroom—where it would be handy and where she could close the door so the girls couldn't see where she was hiding it."

"That make sense." Ingrid headed toward the bedroom.

"Except that Diantha was an outdoorsy woman. It could be in the barn or one of the sheds. Or even in a tree somewhere for all I know."

"I never find key!"

"Well, I would look in the bedroom first. Are some of Diantha's things still there?"

"Ja. Joshua angry when I try to sort things for Agnes. I not touch since long time."

"Where do you keep your things," Mary asked, "if Diantha's are still there?"

"I have not much." Ingrid shrugged. "Fits in box under bed."

"That's not fair," Mary said.

"Maybe. Maybe not," Ingrid said.

"I tell you what. I'll keep a lookout here at the window, and if I see them coming home—I'll tell you. You'll have plenty of time to put things away. And I'll have a talk with my son about you not having any place to put your things later. When you aren't around."

"That a good idea!"

Their bedroom was not large, but it was big enough to hold a bed, a dresser with a mirror, a chair, and the trunk. It was actually a long box made of solid white pine. The lock, she discovered, was turned toward the wall, which was the reason she had never noticed it.

Ingrid decided to concentrate on the dresser. She had only emptied one drawer when Josh had come home and found her before. The other drawers were still mysteries.

She ignored the top one—it was the one she had already

opened and which had held most of Diantha's dresses. She already knew there was no key hidden in there, and for all she knew, it still held remnants of that sickly sweet perfume Diantha had worn.

The second drawer, she discovered, was filled with Diantha's underthings and nightclothes. There were, in Ingrid's opinion, entirely too many nice things in there for a farm wife to own. Many appeared to be store-bought. How had Joshua afforded so many nice things for Diantha?

"You see Joshua?" she called to Mary.

"No. How are you getting along in there?"

"Diantha have many pretty things," Ingrid said. "How did Joshua buy?"

"Oh, don't let that bother you, honey," Mary said. "She brought them with her into the marriage. Diantha was Virgie and Richard's only surviving daughter and they spoiled her. That girl had more clothes in her trousseau than I probably owned my whole life."

That made Ingrid feel a little better. Still, the petite size of Diantha's things bothered her. A pair of Diantha's lacy pantalets would hardly fit on one of Ingrid's legs. But she couldn't help taking stock of the possibilities. These very pantalets should fit Agnes in a couple more years. If care was given, they could be handed down to Trudy, and possibly even Ellie. New ones would have to be made for Polly, of course, because Ellie would be sure to wear them out or rip them on a branch of whatever tree she was climbing.

No key in the undergarment and nightwear drawer. She packed everything back in as closely as possible to how it had been arranged, and opened the third drawer—the last one.

This drawer held four different pairs of Sunday-type button-up, high-top shoes with small heels, and they were lovely. The shoes, more than anything else she had found among Diantha's things, made her ache. Such delicate, feminine things! One pair of beautiful, light-color calfskin gloves lay beside the shoes. She picked up one glove and fitted it against the palm of her hand. The fingers were a full inch shorter than hers.

There were two parasols folded up inside the drawer. One that was elaborate, with fringe and cutwork, and one that was slightly plainer. She unfurled the fancier one and held it over her head—imagining how proud Joshua must have been to have Diantha on his arm. Diantha in her small, fancy shoes, her perfect gloves, her lovely parasol.

With a heavy heart, she started to close the drawer and then noticed something else in the far back, a small box. She reached in to draw it out. It was a pretty little box, but when she opened it, she saw that it was nothing more than body powder. Once again, she inhaled the heavy scent of roses.

She could hardly put the lid on quickly enough to mask that smell. What if Joshua came home and found her looking through his wife's things again? What if he smelled that scent again?

As she bent to place the box back where she had found it, she heard something inside of it shift and scrape. Something heavy was inside that scented talcum, something that should not be there.

Wrinkling her nose at the smell, she opened the lid once again and stuck an exploratory finger into the powder. There, at the bottom of the box, was something metal.

She dredged it out, and sure enough, there was the key.

Holding the key at arm's length, she went out to the kitchen.

"You found it!" Mary exclaimed.

"Ja." Ingrid walked to the dry sink, upon which sat a basin she kept filled for the family's hand washing, and dropped the key into the soapy water.

"Why on earth are you washing it?" Mary asked.

Ingrid didn't know how to explain except to say, "It smell like Diantha."

After allowing each child, including Polly, to gather a fistful of wildflowers, Joshua took the children the long way around through the woods to Diantha's grave. It would be faster and simpler to walk past Virgie and Richard's home, but he wanted to avoid a confrontation with them—especially when he had the children with him. There would come a time to try to sort things out and make amends, but that time was not yet and it was certainly not now.

The small cemetery held seven graves: Diantha's, still brown from dirt freshly dug, plus her two younger brothers who had died at birth, her younger sister, who died from diphtheria at age two, another younger sister who died from complications from appendicitis at age eight, and two younger brothers who survived to adulthood, but one had died fighting at Fredericksburg, the other had died from dysentery while encamped in Tennessee. His wife, the oldest child, had helped her mother and father bury six brothers and sisters. He had always wondered if this grisly experience had been a factor in her emotional struggles.

"Do you think Ma can see us?" Ellie asked. "Does she know we're bringing her flowers?"

"I don't know, sweetheart, but if she can, I know that she's loving those flowers."

Trudy added, "Ma always liked spring best, when the wild-flowers bloomed."

"Yes, she did."

Agnes was quiet, thoughtful. "You suppose we oughta plant a rosebush here sometime?"

"I think your mother would like that."

"It would make the grave look a little less . . . raw," Agnes said.

"Time will take care of the dirt," he said. "But a rosebush would be nice."

As he stood there, his mind was flooded with so many emotions, but mainly he was angry over the four years that the war had stolen. Neither he nor Diantha were the same people they had been after he came back from the war. He had demons to fight—memories of the battlefield he struggled to put behind him so he could build a life for his family. She had been quiet and withdrawn, wrestling with her own demons.

He had trained himself to think as little as possible about the battles he had fought. Instead, the only moment of the war he allowed himself to dwell on, the image on which he focused during the worst times, was a scene he and his men had come upon in Tennessee in the spring of 1862. They had been traveling fast, bent on a mission that was taking every ounce of their endurance. He was tired, disillusioned, hungry, and then suddenly, while riding through a remote Tennessee valley, they came upon a young mother walking with her little girl in a cherry orchard. The white cherry blossoms had been at their peak, their scent so pure and removed from the smells of the battlefield that it had seemed like the most peaceful, beautiful, gentle thing he had ever seen.

He and his men had not stopped. They had thundered past the young mother on that back road. He had tipped his hat to her as they sped by, and even though they were Union troops, she had gracefully dipped her head in return.

From that moment onward, he had vowed that if the Lord allowed him to make it back to Michigan, he would plant a cherry tree, and he wouldn't stop planting until he had acres of those trees with the white blossoms. He had envisioned his beautiful Diantha walking through that cherry orchard someday, and he imagined her feeling the same peace while strolling beneath those blossoms that he had felt those brief seconds his battle-weary eyes had feasted upon it.

Now, that would never happen.

A cherry crop was a good crop to invest in, and that's what he told people was his reason for planting and nurturing it. But the real reason, his secret reason, was that to him, an orchard represented peace and hope.

The girls carefully laid their little bouquets on their mother's grave.

"Should we say something, Pa?" Agnes asked. "I mean, we've put the flowers on Ma's grave. Now what?"

Now what, indeed?

"Do you girls *want* to say something?"

"Like what?" Agnes asked.

"I don't know. Maybe something nice you remember about her?"

"Ma didn't get mad at me for climbing trees," Ellie offered.

"That's true," Joshua said.

"And she made good flapjacks," Trudy added.

Everyone nodded in agreement.

"Ma . . ." Agnes shrugged. "Did the best she could."

That about summed it up. Diantha had done the best she could.

Polly had lost interest in flowers and was starting to tug on the picnic basket, which also had seen service as the strudel basket and Bertie's coming-home basket.

"Are you hungry, Polly?"

She nodded enthusiastically.

"Where would you girls like to have your picnic?"

"Let's head on over to that grassy place beside the spring,"

Agnes said. "That's the best place for a picnic. It's getting hot standing up here in the sun."

It struck Joshua how relieved the children seemed to be to walk away from the cemetery. Children were not built to grieve—that was for adults. Children were built to grow and live.

With Mary still keeping watch, Ingrid moved the trunk away from the wall, got down on her knees, and fit the key into the lock. It turned easily, as though it had been used frequently.

The lid creaked as she opened it.

"What do you see?" Mary asked.

Mary's hearing was much sharper than Ingrid realized, and she made a note to remember that.

"Purple material," Ingrid said. "With flowers."

"Oh, I sent that last Christmas. What's next?"

"Pretty yellow."

"Really? That was Christmas before last."

Layer by layer, Ingrid dug through the treasure chest of pristine material. Evidently Diantha had sewn nothing.

At the bottom, as though it had been deliberately tucked as far down as possible, were two things that had nothing at all to do with clothing. There was a small, flat, round box and some kind of a diary.

"Is Joshua coming?" she called.

"I don't see hide nor hair of him," Mary answered.

Ingrid opened the notebook. On the inside cover, Diantha had written her name. On the next page, Ingrid saw very odd handwriting. Even though the paper was lined, the sentences ran downward, practically dripping off the lines. There were many splotches and dabs of ink and crossovers as well. The handwriting alone gave her a bad feeling.

179

Ingrid debated what to do. She sincerely doubted that it held things that Diantha would want her family to know or she would not have taken such pains to hide it.

If this notebook was turned over to Joshua, she might never know what was in it, but if the notebook was left in the trunk, the knowledge of it being there would eat her alive. She glanced up at the clock. It had been exactly one half hour since the children and Joshua had left. At the very least, she and Mary should have another thirty minutes to safely examine the notebook and pillbox.

The problem was, she didn't know what was in the notebook. If Diantha had chosen to say bad things about her mother-in-law, it could very well break Mary's heart. Mary did not need or deserve that, and once she had read it, there would be no erasing it from her mind.

In the end, Ingrid chose to compromise. She unbuttoned the side seam of their straw mattress, shoved the notebook inside, and took the pillbox out to show Mary.

# 16

It was lovely at the spring.

"You want me to go get Ingrid, Pa?" Agnes asked. "She would enjoy being here with us."

"By the time she traipsed all the way here toting Bertie, we'd probably be finished with our picnic."

Polly was happily splatting barefooted in the shallow pool while Ellie and Trudy munched bacon sandwiches and made little leaf boats to blow across the smooth surface of the water.

"Can I ask you about something, Pa?" Agnes said in a voice low enough that her sisters couldn't hear her.

"Sure."

"There's something that's been bothering me, but you gotta promise not to get mad."

"You can ask me whatever you want."

"I haven't had a whole lot of experience with mothers. All I've ever known is Ma."

Joshua wondered what was coming next. With Agnes, he never knew. The girl could ask some of the most unexpected questions of any child he had ever known.

"What do you want to know?"

"Was Ma . . . normal?"

His heart lurched. "Why?"

Agnes concentrated all her attention on a small pebble that she tossed back and forth from one hand to the other. "I probably shouldn't ask."

"You can ask me anything you want," Joshua said. "I'll do my best to answer, but what do you mean when you ask if your mother was normal?"

"Because sometimes it feels like Ingrid loves us more than our own ma did," Agnes blurted out. "I know what you're gonna tell me—that I shouldn't say things like that."

Despite his promises to answer any question she asked, he did not know how to answer this one. The truth was, Diantha had reminded him of a ginger-colored barn cat he had owned that had given birth to a healthy litter but had walked away from the mewling kittens and had never gone back. They would have starved had not another mother cat who had given birth a few weeks earlier adopted them.

The ginger cat had gone feral soon after, stalking small prey in the woods, avoiding the other domestic animals in the barn. He had only caught rare glimpses of her from time to time as she had flitted from tree to tree—until she disappeared entirely.

In a way, that described Diantha's behavior too the past few years. It had been the strangest thing to watch this pretty, feminine woman slowly going feral.

He saw other women having child after child and caring for them like lionesses—but not Diantha. When she was in her darker moods, sometimes she went for walks and left the children, no matter how young, to fend for themselves.

Then she would come back, her pockets stuffed with hickory nuts, or wintergreen, or an apron full of blackberries. She would act as though she were slowly coming out of a fog when she arrived home, as though she had forgotten she even *had* a home, or children, and had somehow wandered into someone else's cabin by mistake.

He often feared that she would forget to come home entirely, that she would simply merge and blend into the shadows—like that feral cat—until he never saw her again.

On her good days, Diantha kept them fed and clothed. She even put up food and gardened, but her emotional detachment when they were hurt or sick was disconcerting.

How could he possibly explain this to his daughter when he didn't understand it himself? There was one thing he did understand—Agnes deserved and expected the truth, not some platitude.

"You were right back at the cemetery," he said. "Your ma did the best she could, but she had a greater struggle with being a mother than most women."

"That's kinda what I thought too." Agnes nodded her head. "Pa, I know the only reason you married Ingrid was because it was the only way that the judge would let you keep us—but there's something I think you need to know."

"What's that?"

"Ingrid always acts like she loves us—even when you aren't around to watch."

It was such a strange thing for a child to say, but then, Agnes had never really been a child. She had become a sort of surrogate parent long before her mother's death.

"The day after Ingrid came to live with us," Agnes said, "she told me that it was all right for me to be a little girl—and that I didn't have to do the laundry. She told me to just . . . go play."

Joshua felt a lump forming in his throat. "And did you?"

"Yeah, Pa. I did. And it felt real good."

"Did you find something?" Mary called.

Ingrid carried the pillbox out of the bedroom and handed the pills to Mary.

Mary adjusted her glasses, peered at the bottle label, and read out loud: "Graves Pills for Amenorrhea."

"What is this big word mean?"

"I have no idea." Mary began to read again. "These pills have been approved by the M.R.C.S. of London, Edinburgh, Dublin as a never-fail remedy for producing the monthly flow. Though perfectly harmless to the most delicate, ladies are earnestly requested not to mistake their condition, as miscarriage would certainly ensue."

"What all these words mean?" Ingrid asked.

"I've seen advertisements for this kind of medicine in the newspapers," Mary said. "Some say they are to be used to unblock menses."

"Unblock menses?" Ingrid said. "How menses get blocked?"

"The only way I know of is with a baby. I overheard two of Barb's friends talking about it. One said that she took something called 'Female Regulator Pills' every month just in case she and her husband had created another baby."

Ingrid was appalled. "Women do such a thing?"

"It appears so."

"What is in these pills?"

"Poisons of some kind. Roots. Herbs. They can cause a woman to lose her baby if it doesn't kill her first. They were advertising these things even back when I was a young woman, but it was never a temptation to me. I always wanted more children than the two boys I had."

"How you know all this?"

"That's why Barb began to hate me so much," Mary said. "I saw the pills. I knew what they were for and I told Zeb. They had a terrible fight about it. It's hard for young women

184

to have one baby after another . . . I know that." Mary stared down at the box she was holding. "But I couldn't stand by and keep quiet. My grandchild had already quickened within her. Barb was three months along."

Ingrid glanced out the window. "Quick. Give box. Joshua is coming!"

Mary handed it back to her. "Are you going to tell him what you found?"

"I not know."

"It could be the reason Diantha died."

"Diantha kill self, getting rid of baby? This hurt Joshua so bad, he cannot stand it. I think I need hide it."

Ingrid hurried into the bedroom and buried the pillbox deep within the straw along with the diary. Then she tugged the large trunk outside into the front room and opened the lid. When Joshua and the children came through the door, she had pulled one piece of fabric out and was measuring it on the table with Mary's rapt attention.

"You have nice picnic?" Ingrid asked, trying to look as innocent as possible.

When Joshua and the girls entered the cabin, the first thing he saw was that Ingrid had managed to open the trunk.

"You found the key. Where was it?"

"In drawer." She seemed distracted by some yellow material. "Mary, you hold this end, please?"

"Was there anything else in there?" he asked. "Besides all that fabric?"

She dug the last piece of material out of the trunk and brandished a hand over it. "All empty."

Agnes pounced on a length of lovely dark rose. "Could you make me a dress out of this one, Ingrid?"

"Ja. I make you fine dress soon."

He thought he caught a look of guilt on his mother's face, but dismissed it. His mother would certainly have nothing to feel guilty about.

Mary held some dark lavender material close to Ingrid's face. "This would be a lovely color on you."

"Very pretty! I like."

Pleased that his mother and Ingrid were getting along so well and obviously enjoying themselves, he grabbed his hat and headed out to the barn. He had spent most of the morning with his daughters, but it was time to get back to work. With Ingrid in charge of his home, he was getting more accomplished than ever before. He had finished planting all the corn and managed to get all his spring wheat planted. Today, he was hoping to start claiming another acre or two of virgin soil with his new John Deere plow.

Hopefully he would get it finished soon enough to have the time to smooth out the newly plowed acre with the metal teeth of his old spike-toothed harrow before starting to put up hay for the winter. He didn't have the money for more seed to plant the new ground now, but if this year's wheat, corn, and oat crop did well, next year he should have enough to plant every inch of his tilled land.

His head was filled with ideas for improving his land now that he was free to work without constantly worrying about and checking on the children. He had never dreamed that having Ingrid beneath his roof would give him so much freedom or heart for the future. As he hitched one of his horses to the plow, he was whistling.

Later that night, after the children and Mary were all in bed, Joshua went out to check on their cow that was ready to calf. Ingrid went into the bedroom, closed the door, and quickly changed into her nightgown. This gave her a few stolen minutes to examine Diantha's diary.

She sat on the floor on the far side of the bed and dug Diantha's diary out of the mattress. Beneath the oil light, she closely examined the unfamiliar handwriting. It was slanted so far to the left Ingrid had to cock her head to read it. The words started out with no preamble, nothing except a date and Diantha's stark words.

*December 2, 1870*

*The snow is high. Up to the windowsill. Too much snow for this early in December. Joshua has shoveled a path to the barn for me and suggests that I wrap up in something warm and come out with him for a breath of fresh air.*

*I don't want to go to the barn. I don't want to breathe frigid air. I want to stay in my bed forever. If it were not for these children, I would not have to stir, but they are greedy little things who demand to be fed. Sometimes I get up and cook just to make them be quiet.*

*I see Agnes looking at me with critical eyes when she has to fix breakfast for the other girls. I see Joshua trying to wash dishes, doing my work for me, because I no longer care if the dishes get washed or not.*

*His devotion sickens me. His constant determination to get me out of this "mood," as he calls it, irritates me. The "winter doldrums," he says, as though it is a disease that can be cured with the coming of spring.*

*Perhaps he is right, but it is a long time until spring, and there is yet another baby to birth before then. I don't mind the carrying of the baby—it gives me an excuse to stay in bed. And I don't mind the birthing of* the baby—that part is easy for me. But oh, how I hate the thought of taking care of it!

Joshua thinks it strange that I care so little for our children. He has not yet realized that it is foolish to care—that caring only makes things worse when you have to bury them—as Mama did, and as I will probably have to. We did everything we could to save the little ones, Mama and I, and nothing made any difference. Nor did we have any control over the deaths of my two brothers. It bothers Mama so that their graves are not graves—but pretend graves where their bodies should be, instead of where they are, moldering away in some Southern state. I am glad I don't care much for my own. It will make burying them, when the time comes, so much easier. I refuse to be like Mama and spend the rest of my life grieving.

I wish I had never laid eyes on Joshua and his never-ending expectations. I wish I never had to see disappointment in his eyes again. I look back and wonder who that girl was who married him. It certainly was not me. I cannot imagine ever having enough energy to care that much.

It is interesting to me that Mama gave me this diary book for my birthday. She said I could keep track of my children's accomplishments and funny things the little ones say. She says it will help me remember these sweet moments later in life.

I doubt she intended for me to use it as a way to drain the poison out of my brain. Someday, when this book is filled, I will bury it somewhere no one will ever find it—but for now, it is the only place I can say what I want without doing any more damage than I already am.

There was a polite knock on the door.

"Are you decent?" Joshua asked. "I need some clean rags. She's going to have that calf any time now."

"One little minute," Ingrid said.

She quickly stuffed the diary back into the straw and opened the door so that Joshua could get whatever it was he needed. She was shocked nearly speechless by what she had just read. What kind of a woman deliberately chose not to love her own children simply out of fear of losing them? What kind of woman, expecting a baby or not, allowed her twelve-year-old daughter to take over the cooking for the family and allowed her husband to take over the household chores when there was nothing physically wrong with her?

Ingrid could not imagine ever wanting to stay in bed all day when there were so many interesting things to do. Diantha could have used some of that beautiful fabric to make clothes for her children. She could have sung to them, played games with them, and enjoyed them. She could have spent time with Joshua, who adored her. The whole thing was incomprehensible, except for one thing she knew for sure: Joshua did not deserve to read these terrible things that his wife had written.

With a heavy heart, she went to find her husband an old towel with which to welcome the little calf when it came.

# 17

*December 5th, 1870*

*The babe is here. A boy. Joshua is ecstatic. The girls are thrilled. My mother—poor, besotted fool—can barely bring herself to lay the baby down.*

*And I feel nothing.*

*Joshua wants to name him Bert, after someone he knew in the war. I don't care what he calls it. I just want to be left alone, but the more I want to be left alone, the more everyone seems determined to talk to me. Joshua keeps bringing the baby in to me, wanting me to admire the little fingers and toes, etc.*

*And I continue to feel nothing. Except sleepy. Sometimes I feel like I could sleep for years. I will have no other children. I am finished. Joshua has his boy now. I will not give birth to one more thing I have to care for.*

Ingrid glanced at the clock. Joshua had been gone a long time. The cow must be having a difficult time.

So was she. It hurt to read these terrible things, and yet she could not stop. The diary drew her with an almost sick fascination. It also helped her better understand this family she had taken on. No wonder Agnes had talked and acted like a thirty-year-old woman when Ingrid first came! It also explained why the girls accepted her so quickly, even though she was a stranger and a stepmother. They were starved for a mother who would actually love and take care of them.

*March 11th, 1871*

*I went for a walk in the woods this afternoon. I know Joshua thought it was a good sign. He was thrilled that I had actually gotten dressed and left the cabin. He probably thinks my "mood" has taken a turn for the better. Little does he know that what I really want is to start walking and never stop. It was everything I could do to make myself return to this place. I stayed out until dusk, even though I knew the nighttime predators were already out hunting. I stood at the edge of the woods for a long time, trying to pull myself together enough to go back inside the house.*

*It appears that I have merely exchanged one obsession for another. Whereas I could hardly make myself leave the cavern of my bedroom this winter, now I can barely force myself to go back inside at all. It made me physically ill to see the lights in the windows and know that people I care nothing for are waiting for me to come in and take care of them. I am so tired—of Joshua, of the children, of the drudgery. Even though I rarely lift my hand anymore, the work is still there, nagging, nagging, nagging, like a bad toothache.*

*Today, my mother asked what was wrong. She is a timid soul around me these days and afraid of offending, especially now that I am her only living child. It took great courage for her to even ask me such a question.*

*I told her I thought all I needed was a spring tonic.*

*She was thrilled with that answer. Within the hour, she had dug and washed the fresh roots of a sassafras tree, steeped the thin orange-colored shavings into a pan of boiling water, and came to me bearing sugar-sweetened sassafras tea—my spring tonic—which will presumably fix me right up. The tea did, at least, taste good. I shall have to remember to pretend to be refreshed and happy the next time she visits.*

*The real answer to her question is that I know there is something wrong with me, but I don't know what it is. I don't know how to fix it. I know I'm not normal. I know I'm not a good wife or a good mother—but I don't know why.*

*I've tried to figure out how other women do it—how they manage to find pleasure in their lives, and I think I have finally figured it out. They are too stupid to know any better. They are like cows munching grass while their calves nurse—no thoughts in their heads except for the next mouthful of grass.*

*I have many thoughts in my head. Too many. Sometimes it almost feels as though there are voices in there too. This is new. These voices-that-are-not-voices call me from the dark woods around our home and tell me that it would be good to start walking and not stop.*

*I have tried not to obey these voices-that-are-not-voices, but they continue to call. Sometimes that call is louder than others. Sometimes I sit on the porch and strain to hear them. I get annoyed when Joshua talks to me. I would rather listen to the voices. I tried to ignore them at first, but lately, I find them much more compelling.*

*This is my secret. I have told no one. I know if anyone found out what is inside my brain, they would take me to the insane asylum in Kalamazoo and lock me up. So I am very careful around Joshua, since he is the most likely to realize that there is something wrong with me. He is the one most likely to sniff out my secret.*

*I force myself to smile and nod and pretend I'm listening to him even though I am not. Joshua sees what he wants to see—the lovely young girl he married. Men are so easy to fool. There is nothing he can say that interests me—but the voices have much to say that interests me . . .*

Ingrid slammed the diary shut and stuffed it deep beneath the mattress. She had never read such terrible words in her life. Diantha had not loved Joshua. She had not even loved her own children. She had preferred listening to her pretend voices rather than the sound of her own husband's voice, or her children's. It was obvious the woman was sick in the head—how could Joshua not have seen?

The answer came to her in a sudden flash of understanding. Joshua had not *wanted* to see. He had loved the young Diantha he had fallen in love with so much, he could not accept the reality of the sick woman she had become.

Ingrid did not know what to do with the diary. If she gave it to Joshua, it would break his heart. If one of the children ever read it, it would break theirs. And yet it did not seem right to destroy it.

She walked into the sitting room and listened. There were no sounds coming from the upstairs except Mary's snoring, so the girls were all asleep. Bertie was out for the night in his cradle here beside her bed. She had never seen such a good baby. How much Diantha had missed!

Ingrid wondered if Diantha could not help the way she was,

or if she had simply allowed herself to fall into that spiral of self-pity and detachment from everyone around her—until her mind began to play tricks on her.

Joshua was still out in the barn and the whole family was asleep around her. It was a rare opportunity for her to finish reading the cursed diary. She no longer *wanted* to read it, but she knew she *had* to—if only to have enough knowledge to protect her family from these terrible revelations.

She carefully closed the bedroom door behind her yet again, bent over the cradle, and smoothed a wisp of a curl back from little Bertie's forehead. She smiled over the little frown he always wore when he slept, his lips poked out, as though concentrating very hard at sleeping.

With a sigh of resignation, she pulled out the toxic book one more time, sat close to the lamp, and began to read.

*March 30th, 1871*

*I am "that way" again. The signs are unmistakable even though it is early. It is not Joshua's fault. I was the one who turned to him—the voices told me to do so. I do everything the voices tell me these days. It is so much easier to obey them than to fight them.*

*I do not want this new baby growing within me. I confided my problem to Millicent last week when I drove into town. She is the closest thing to a friend I have, and I told Joshua I wished to go visiting. The man was nearly beside himself with happiness that I was doing something so social, so normal. He readily agreed to watch the children while I was gone. He would not have been so happy had he known what I intended to do. This was no social call. I had heard whispers that there are preparations a woman can use that will take care of this problem. Since she and her husband own the store, I thought Millicent might know how to go about obtaining such a nostrum.*

*Millicent—it turns out—is a bit of an expert.*

*She tells me that in these modern times, there are several patented products on the market that are specifically created to "treat" my condition.*

*To my great relief, she said she had some pills that she would give me. She confided in me that this method is quite safe, and that she has used these pills on several occasions. Millicent worships her figure and chose many years ago to never mar it with bearing a child. She tells me that some women, in order to make it even more effective, drink tansy tea along with the pills. I told her that I know a place where tansy grows.*

*The label of this box says that it can safely be used by the most delicate of ladies, and since I'm not very far along, I'm not afraid to try it. I'm certain that the makers of these pills wouldn't be allowed to sell their medicine if it could hurt someone.*

*My only fear is that the medicine won't work, or will only partially work. I want no mistakes. I want to make absolutely certain about this, so tomorrow morning, when I take the medicine, I intend to double the amount. Then I intend to sit with Joshua at breakfast, smiling and drinking my special tea. It is amusing to me that he will have no idea that what I am drinking will help me get this over with as fast as possible.*

The diary ended. Ingrid quickly stuffed it back inside her mattress. Then she lay down upon her bed, absorbing the impact of Diantha's words. There was no way she would ever tell anyone about what she had read. Joshua could never know this terrible thing.

Thinking about Joshua made her long to be near him. She got up, put her work clothes back on, wrapped the still-sleeping Bertie in a blanket, and walked to the barn.

When she slipped through the door, Joshua and the poor, laboring cow were illuminated in a circle of lantern light. He didn't realize she was present until she came close enough to step into that circle of light.

His first reaction was concern. "Are the children all right?"

"Everything is fine. Children are good. Baby is good. Mother is good. All good in the house. I cannot sleep, and think, maybe Joshua like company while he wait for calf."

"I'm afraid this is going to be one long night. This isn't the first time this cow has calved. It always takes her a long time."

She settled herself on an upturned bucket. It felt good to simply be near him right now. "You want Ingrid talk or be quiet?"

"I've had more than enough quiet tonight. Maybe you could tell me something about your life in Sweden. It seems like we're always working, or the children are interrupting. I know very little about you except that you are the most competent woman I have ever met."

Ingrid could not have been happier or more surprised by the gift of his compliment than if he had handed her the crown jewels of Sweden. "What thing you want to know?"

"I'd like to hear more about your brother, Hans. I'd like to know about the farm you and he worked. I want to know about your parents—you must have had an extraordinary mother for you to be so wonderful with children."

"Ja. I have very good mother and father."

"Agnes told me today that you said she could go play because you were the mother now and she didn't have to be."

"Agnes too old for her age."

"She also told me that you act like you love them, even when I'm not around to watch."

"Agnes say that?"

"She did." He paused. "It feels disloyal to say this, Ingrid, but you've earned the right to know the truth—you are a better mother to my children than Diantha ever was."

Ingrid's heart positively sang with those words of praise. "I tell you about mother and father and farm and neighbor who teach me English and Hans and—"

She stopped midsentence. Joshua was listening with a look of amusement on his face while she went on and on.

"I talk too much?" she asked.

"Not one bit. I'm looking forward to hearing all your words, but would you mind bringing out a pot of coffee first? I think this might be a long night."

She whirled to leave, giddy with all the good things he had said to her. "I go get coffee now. Be right back. Do not go away."

He chuckled at her enthusiasm. "I won't move an inch."

## 18

"I believe you managed to somehow accidentally marry the 'virtuous woman,' son," his mother said as she sat in the upstairs room with a lapful of mending.

A drawer was sticking in the bureau they had designated for her, and he was repairing it. It was the first time since his mother had arrived that they were alone together. She was obviously planning to use the rare moment of privacy for a heart-to-heart talk. He didn't mind. He was grateful that she had recovered so well. There was no evidence of the haunted, disoriented woman Zeb had dropped on their doorstep.

"What do you mean, 'the virtuous woman'?"

"You know, the last proverb when it describes a woman who makes clothing for her children and keeps everyone well fed, and who makes everyone in her house feel safe and secure. The proverb says her price is far above rubies."

"Ingrid is that," he mused, "and more."

"But you don't love her." His mother picked up one of his socks that had developed a hole, inserted a wooden darning egg, and began to weave her needle back and forth.

"I'm grateful to her, and I have endless respect for her—but I'll never be able to love her as a husband should. I'm afraid that kind of love died with Diantha."

"Diantha was never the woman you thought her to be," his mother said. "You do realize that, don't you?"

"I know she struggled—I watched her struggle—but sometimes I think I loved her all the more because of it. She needed me."

"The heart is a strange animal. It will love whomever it wants to love—regardless of what the brain tells it to do. But sometimes"—she stopped darning and looked up at him—"if you treat someone with love—and you do that every day—the feelings will eventually follow."

"Do you know this firsthand, Mother? Did you have to learn to love my father?"

"No." She began to ply her needle once again. "But I watched my mother turn a marriage around by applying that principle. My parents had an arranged marriage; they barely knew each other when they immigrated to America. I was their firstborn, and I watched my mother being so kind to my father, and I watched him being good to her in return. It took several years, but I actually watched my mother and father falling in love."

"I will be grateful to Ingrid until the day I die, but I can't imagine that ever happening. She's just too . . . . different."

"You mean she's too different from Diantha."

"Yes."

"Perhaps things will change. We'll wait and see. I'm praying about it."

"Pray all you want to, Mother, but it would take a miracle for me to ever be physically attracted to that tall, rawboned woman down there in the kitchen—no matter how grateful I am to her."

"Supper is ready," Ingrid said from midway up the stairs.

He glanced down and saw, by the high color in her cheeks, that she had heard every word. Dear Lord, he wished he hadn't said what he did. He should be shot for those words, and he knew it.

She looked so pitiful standing there in her old work dress, still wearing George's cast-off boots because she had decided to save the new ones Hazel had purchased for Sundays. His heart broke for her. He wished he could take every syllable back.

"Ingrid, I—"

"Supper is ready." She turned on her heel and went back to the kitchen.

"You don't deserve her, son," Mary said. "I'm sorry, but you just don't."

"You're right," he said. "But I'm what she's stuck with."

"Then for goodness sake, son, at least buy the poor girl some decent shoes!"

Joshua's words stung worse than Millicent's whip. Ingrid had no idea what "rawboned" meant—but the contempt in his voice told her it wasn't good. And he said it would take a miracle for him to ever be attracted to her.

What was wrong with her?

It wasn't fair. Diantha had curled up like a cat and watched life go on about her, completely disengaged emotionally from her children and from him—and he had adored her. Ingrid had worked like a mule, loved his children so much that she would die for any one of them, and he felt nothing for her but gratitude? She had hoped, after those hours of easy companionship in the barn last night, that things were changing between them, but she had been wrong.

For two cents, she would hand Diantha's diary and the pills over to him and let him know everything—let him know that his wife had been nothing more than an insane, crafty little thing who had cared nothing for him.

After everyone came to the table, Joshua blessed the food, but Ingrid sat in silence, still digesting those terrible words he had said. Her food tasted like sawdust.

Mary made a stab at dinner conversation, but it didn't take. Neither Joshua nor Ingrid followed up on any of her comments. The children looked from one adult to the next, trying to figure out what was wrong, gave up, and simply ate their supper.

This was not the happy family Ingrid had tried to create. She was sorry, but this evening, she had had enough. If they weren't already legally married, she would walk away from him right now. The problem was—she would want to take the children with her. There was no way she was going to leave her children behind.

"I am not hungry." She pushed away from the table. "Trudy and Ellie, you help Grandmother with the dishes. Agnes, you take care of Bertie."

Everyone looked up at once.

"Aren't you feeling good?" Agnes asked. "Do you need to lay down? Mama always needed to lay down when she wasn't feeling good."

"No," Ingrid replied. "I'm going to take a long walk."

"Can I come?" Ellie asked.

"No," Ingrid said. "Not now."

She went into the bedroom to get her shawl and hesitated beside the bed. Was now a good time to show Joshua the diary and the pills? Was this a good time to show him how dark his precious Diantha's mind had been? Frankly, she was grateful that Diantha had died. Had she continued in the spiral she was in, it was likely that her unborn babe might not have been the only life she would have destroyed.

She pulled the diary and the pills out of the mattress and looked at them. Once it was done, it was done. There would be no taking it back.

Deep down she knew that, even though she was hurt and angry, if she handed him these two items, she would regret it the rest of her life.

She shoved them into her skirt pocket, grabbed her shawl, and headed out the front door.

"Where are you going?" Joshua asked.

She looked him straight in the eyes. "I do not know."

"Be careful," he mumbled just before she slammed the door.

There was still some daylight left, but not a lot. She decided not to go into the woods with darkness so close. Unlike Diantha, she did not enjoy the company of nighttime predators. Instead, she chose to climb the small rise that lay behind Virgie and Richard's house. Joshua had pointed it out to her as the family graveyard, but she had never felt the desire to see it.

She decided it was high time that she gave Diantha a piece of her mind.

If Joshua had thought that looking Ingrid in the face after what he said would be hard, he had not taken into account the impact of five pairs of angry female eyes.

"What did you do wrong this time, Pa?" Agnes asked.

He did not want to talk about this with his children. "What makes you think I did something wrong?"

"Because Ingrid's mad and none of us have misbehaved today." Agnes frowned. "In fact, it was a really good day. Ingrid even taught us a song in Swedish while she worked. She was happy all day—until she called you to supper. What did you do?"

"I said something stupid."

"What did you say?" Agnes said. "Maybe you can fix it."

"This is not your business."

Agnes turned to his mother. "What did he say to make Ingrid mad? It must have been something bad, 'cause Ingrid hardly ever gets mad at us."

"Ingrid overheard him saying something that made her feel"—Mary shot a glance at her son—"ugly."

"What would possess you to say something like that, Pa? Ingrid is *beautiful*!"

"I agree," Mary said. "And she gets more beautiful in my eyes every day I live here with her."

Joshua threw his napkin on the table. "I don't intend to discuss this."

He grabbed his hat and escaped outside, wondering why God had seen fit to bless him with a houseful of women. He felt bad enough about what he had said. He didn't need the children and his mother rubbing it in his face.

He started to go out to the barn, his sanctuary of choice when things crowded in on him, but then his eye caught a figure far away at the cemetery.

He supposed now was as good a time as ever to go apologize. At least he wouldn't have a house full of females listening through the keyhole.

As he got closer, he saw Ingrid drop to her knees. For a moment he thought she was praying, and then he saw that she was digging. Why would she be digging, with her hands, in the cemetery?

The closer he got, the more concerned he became. She appeared to be digging into the mound above where Diantha was buried!

Had she been so angry with him that she had decided to desecrate his wife's grave? He began to run.

"What do you think you're doing!" he shouted when he reached her.

Ingrid did not act the least bit guilty over what she was doing. Instead, she simply looked tired and resigned. "I try to protect you."

"Protect me from what?" He snatched out of her hand the stick that she had been digging with and threw it away, utterly disgusted with her. "My wife's grave? Are you that jealous of her? What kind of a woman *are* you?"

Her eyes did not register fear; instead, strangely enough, he saw pity. Then he saw something else—lying beside her was what appeared to be a small leather diary. It looked vaguely familiar. Hadn't Virgie given that to Diantha for her birthday? There was also a small round box.

"What are these?" He bent over and snatched both items away from her. "Where did you get them? Why did you bring them here?"

Ingrid got to her feet and backed away.

He opened the diary and recognized his wife's handwriting—although it was much more sloppy and blotched—unlike her usual neat penmanship. "Where did you get this?" he demanded.

"It was in the trunk, beneath the fabric."

"You told me there was nothing else in there."

"No, I told you it was empty. I never lied."

"I don't understand. Why would you be digging in her grave?"

"Only a few small inches. The book and the pills belong to her. I pray what to do about them. If to give them to you. When I stand here, I think I should give things back to Diantha. This the only way I know to do. I not want in house where children might see."

He was not only angry, he was confused. "Why not simply give them to me? Didn't you realize that I would treasure any sort of diary Diantha might have kept? The children should have this to keep. A treasure like this . . . I can't believe you were trying to keep it from us. So help me, I had no idea you were that selfish."

"I am try to protect you," she repeated. "But if you read it, read it here—not in front of children."

Ingrid's anger and hurt had somehow dissipated during her walk to the cemetery. She had prayed for wisdom. Instead, God had given her peace. She knew that if Joshua was here it was because God wanted him here, and for no other reason. The Lord had taken the decision of whether or not to let him have the diary completely out of her hands, and she was relieved to no longer carry that burden.

She walked over to a tree, sat down with her back against it, and waited.

Joshua did not sit down. He was so eager to read Diantha's words that he stood there, rapidly turning pages. He read much faster than she did.

She waited, studying his face. Watching him go from eager anticipation to a grim, frowning determination to finish.

She knew he was drawing close to the end when he glanced down at the pillbox in his hand and studied the label.

He closed the diary and swiped his shirtsleeve across his eyes, as though trying to wipe away the reality of what he had just read. Then he walked over to where she sat, dropped down beside her, and fell back onto the grass, staring at the darkening sky.

"I knew she wasn't happy, but this . . ." He tossed the diary a few feet away as though he could not bear to have it near him. "I had no idea. After Trudy's birth, it seemed like she went into one of those moods that women sometimes go into directly after childbirth—except it never went completely away and it seemed to deepen with Polly and Bertie's births. Thank God the children will never have to know how little their mother cared for them!

"And this!" He held the box out for her to see. "She was trying to get rid of our child. She was so determined to do so that she took double doses and drank that tea she made just to make absolutely certain. Ingrid, she sat there at the breakfast table with me that morning, sipping that poison, enjoying the fact that I did not know what she was doing." He glanced at the label once again. "She killed herself with this poison."

"I know."

"She cared nothing for any of us," Joshua said wonderingly. "What little she did was just an act to keep me from putting her away—which is something I would never have done."

"You not know how bad she get?" Ingrid asked.

"She would wander off sometimes, but she would always come back. It seemed to me that she spent a lot of time just staring into space, and it was hard to get her to focus on what I was saying sometimes. I thought she was thinking about something so deeply, she couldn't always hear me. Now I realize that she was listening to something or someone I knew nothing about. Voices! My wife was listening to voices that weren't there!

"Dear God"—he threw his wrist over his eyes—"what a fool I've been, grieving for a woman who cared so little for us that she managed to accidentally kill herself trying to get rid of my child. I'm lucky the voices didn't tell her to murder me in my sleep."

Ingrid decided that the pain he had caused her with his hurtful comment back at the cabin was small compared to the pain he must feel. At least what she and Joshua had, such as it was, was built on truth.

"It is as though Diantha bewitched me thirteen years ago, and I could never break free from the spell, even when all the signs were there that she wanted to be anyplace except with me. I'm sorry, Ingrid. I'm sorry about using you simply to keep my children. I'm sorry for jumping to conclusions about what you were doing here in the cemetery. I'm sorry about what I said about you to my mother. It wasn't fair and it wasn't true. I was aggravated with that stupid drawer and the fact that I couldn't make it slide in and out properly. I was aggravated that my mother was asking questions that I didn't want to answer. Sweetheart, you need to know that there are thousands of men out there who would give anything to have a woman like you."

He looked haggard and cold lying there on the ground.

"You need coat." She scooted closer to him and lifted his head onto her lap. He did not protest. She gently traced the contours of his face with her fingertips, in exactly the same way her mother had soothed her as a child. It was the most intimate thing she had ever done with a man.

"Ingrid, I am just so sorry—"

"Shhh." She touched his lips with her fingers. "We do best we know how." She pulled the maroon shawl off her own shoulders and placed it over him. "We do best we can."

He looked up at her. "The children can never know about this; they can never know how much their mother despised them."

"I not tell them. That hurt so bad."

"Millicent was the one who gave her that . . . medicine. She should have to pay for what she did. She *knew* what she did! That's why she was so adamant about pinning the blame on me. She was probably afraid that if the real reason for Diantha's death were to come out, George would find out what she had been doing all those years."

"Why he need to know? What good it do? It break his heart—just like this break yours."

"I'm going to show Richard and Virgie that diary—then they'll know what really happened to their daughter and quit blaming me."

"Virgie blame you anyway. Virgie say you cause daughter's mind problem."

"Then what am I going to do?"

"You do nothing," Ingrid said. "You are not important, Millicent is not important, George is not important. Richard and Virgie are not important. The only important persons is the children. There is things children no need hear."

He was silent as he considered her words. "You're right."

She continued to trace his face with her finger. The worry lines on his forehead had begun to ease away. He seemed in no hurry to go.

"Was Diantha always this person?"

"No . . . yes . . . I don't know. I met her at Michigan State Normal School in Ypsilanti when we were both training to be teachers. We were only nineteen. I was straight off the farm, shy and tongue-tied. The fact that someone like her would agree to marry me was a matter of wonder and amazement. She was different than anyone I had ever known, more beautiful than anyone I had ever seen, and I wanted to find a way to impress her."

"Did you find?"

"I thought I had. When war was declared, everyone was all in a fever to go to war. I signed up to ride with the Michigan First Cavalry." His voice was bitter. "It was all quite dramatic and romantic. We thought the war would be over in a few weeks, and we didn't want to miss out on the excitement. We were young and as ignorant as tree stumps—about life, and about war."

"Diantha impressed?"

"Far from it. Agnes was only a baby then, and Diantha was furious with me for volunteering. She went home to live with her parents while I was away. Michigan was a long way off from the battlefields I was on. I didn't see her again until the war ended, and by that time, we were complete strangers. I was a bitter man with too many bad memories. She had buried two brothers and lived too long with her parents' grief."

"You and Diantha," Ingrid asked, "you fall in love again?"

"I did. At least I thought I did. From what I just read, the woman I loved did not exist."

Those eyes that were the color of the ocean looked up at her. "You were trying to save me from knowing this. You were burying it so I wouldn't be hurt by knowing—even though I had wounded you by my words. You should be angry at me."

"My heart not hurt as bad as your heart." She laid the palm of her hand upon his chest. "We have healthy family, food, cabin, work, hope. Everything be all right someday."

# 19

"The trees, they need water," Ingrid pointed out after breakfast when she found him staring at the cherry orchard.

Her innocent comment irritated him. It was such an obvious thing to say. Did she think he couldn't see for himself that his trees were thirsty?

The early promise of the cherry crop had withered beneath the scorching sun of this year's strange weather. They had not had the cool, damp spring common to Michigan. Instead, the weather they were experiencing was an aberration, as though the lovely state in which he had placed all his hopes and dreams had been picked up and placed by a giant's hand in the middle of an area fast becoming a desert.

It was August and there had not been a drop of rain in two and a half months. They were in danger of losing the cherry trees entirely if they did not get water soon.

"I know," he said.

"You need to give them a drink," she said.

His annoyance increased. He was already worried sick about the cherry trees. What was wrong with the woman? Did she think he was blind?

The little creek from which the livestock drank was

disturbingly low. The barrels that caught the rain from their roof had been bone dry for weeks. Their well would give out soon.

There were only two dependable sources of water accessible to him. The lake, which was two miles away, over a rough road, and the spring that was about a half mile from their house.

Diantha had called it the Faraway Spring, and the name had stuck. It was a half mile from the cabin—close enough for a pleasant walk but far enough away to make everyday use a chore.

The spring, welling up from some deep, unfathomable source, never went dry, but it was surrounded by an old growth oak forest that the lumber men had ignored in their quest for white pine. It would be impossible to get a wagon into it without cutting down trees and blasting out stumps. As it was, creating a wagon trail to give him access to the spring was simply too much work to contemplate.

"Cherry trees need water," Ingrid pointed out once again.

"I know they need water!" He threw his hat on the ground in frustration. "What do you want me to do, woman? Carry it to them on my back?"

"Ja!" she shot back. "That what you do—carry on back."

"You're crazy."

"Ja," she agreed. "I crazy like fox!"

"I can't carry enough water to save them all."

"Maybe you save *some*."

She was right. It was time to start carrying water. He had gone to too much work and expense, purchasing the saplings, carefully transporting them from the Traverse City area. He could save some, possibly even all, but it would take the biggest part of every day to do so. Of course, it wouldn't be forever—they should get rain any day now.

"Garden need water too," she said, "or no food for winter."

"I'll see what I can do."

The first thing he did was load their two empty rain barrels into the wagon, then he fashioned a water yoke for himself out of light, sturdy poplar. By late afternoon, he had pulled the wagon as close to the spring as possible. Then with the help of the water yoke, he walked the water out, two bucketsful at a time, filling the barrels. When the barrels were full, he drove the wagon to the garden and orchard and reversed the process. It was tedious and time-consuming work, but there was nothing else he could think of to do. Allowing the garden and orchard to shrivel up and die was not an option—not if he wanted his family to survive.

Surely the rain would come soon.

It didn't rain that week or the next, and it felt like he had done nothing except carry water. The trees and garden were still alive, but doing the rest of his farm chores on top of this extra work was beginning to take a toll.

He finished his last watering trip for the evening, put the horses up, and went into the cabin. All he wanted to do was fall into bed and sleep. Every bone and muscle in his body ached.

As usual, the cabin smelled of good cooking, but he was almost too tired to eat. He sank down onto the sitting room bed and dozed while he waited for supper.

"So tired." Ingrid came over and put a palm against his cheek. "Work too hard."

"I have no choice."

"Make water yoke for me," Ingrid suggested.

"Don't be silly, Ingrid."

"Make water yoke for me."

Her request went all through him. A man did not allow his

wife to do his work unless completely incapacitated. "Thank you, Ingrid. But no. You are already doing too much."

"Make water yoke for me," Ingrid said. "Two persons cut water-carry time in *halvt*."

He absolutely hated the idea, but he knew that she wouldn't let up until he had made that yoke for her. The woman was more tenacious than a bulldog, and she was right, it *would* cut his carrying time in half.

The next day, he made the yoke, and carrying water became a family ritual. Every morning they went out together, with the children accompanying them. They would spend the next two hours trudging back and forth from the spring to the wagon and then to the garden and orchard. Until Ingrid began to help, it had taken him four hours both morning and night.

The sight of that woman trudging back and forth to help him keep his farm alive was a memory he knew he would never forget. She should not have to do the work of a pack mule, but that is what the drought and marrying him had done to her. He wondered how much more she could endure before she broke down completely.

And still the rain did not come. The days began to blur together as they trudged back and forth every morning and every evening carrying water to the trees and the garden.

How could a farmer make a living without rain? It was a desperate battle they waged, their only weapons buckets, strong backs, and the blessing of a deep underground spring.

Agnes took upon herself the job of waiting at the wagon. There she would unhook the buckets from the yokes and empty them into the barrels. Ellie and Trudy's job was to entertain Polly and Bertie. Mary, who was becoming progressively stronger each day, began to walk to the spring to help keep an eye on the little ones. They timed it so that there was always an adult at the spring when the children were there.

In town, rain had become the sole topic of conversation. All were praying. All were hoping. All were desperately waiting for the rain.

In this way, they made it into September, and still the rains did not come. The level of Lake Huron dropped an astonishing two feet. There were rumors of long-forgotten shipwrecks being discovered in the shallower depths left behind. The strange summer of 1871 took them into an unprecedented drought that descended on a peninsula surrounded by fresh water.

# ∾20∾

"Are you taking Ingrid to the harvest square dance over at the Andersons' barn tonight?" Lyman said as they shoveled out the barn together. "I'm taking Susan."

Lyman had found a paying job at the local sawmill. Joshua had given him permission to stay in the barn, which they fitted out with an old army cot. In return, he pitched in with the farm work each evening when he came home.

As long as Lyman could see Susan on a regular basis, he was a happy man. Joshua wondered if Susan's distracted circuit-riding father had noticed yet that there was an extra man frequently sitting at his table.

"With this drought, why bother to have a harvest dance?" Joshua said. "Even if we got a good rain tomorrow, it would be too late for anyone to have much of a harvest."

"Susan said that the Andersons had decided to have the dance anyway, just to raise everyone's spirits."

"That's nice of them, but I hadn't planned on going."

"Your wife wants to go."

"How do you know?"

"Because Susan told me. They were talking together after

215

church last Sunday. Susan said that Ingrid wants to go in the worst way and was hoping you would ask her."

Joshua leaned both arms on his shovel and gave it some thought. It seemed like a reasonable thing for a man to do—take his wife to a dance; but after all they had endured this summer, the last thing he felt like doing was going to a party.

However, considering the miles Ingrid had walked lugging those buckets of water—if anyone deserved to go to a party, it was her.

"Are you sure Susan heard right?"

"I'm dead sure. Susan gave me instructions to make certain you knew but without Ingrid finding out that you knew. Susan says it should sound like it was your idea."

Joshua liked Susan, and he could picture her black eyes snapping while she gave the besotted Lyman his instructions.

"I'll bring it up."

"You might want to bring it up now." Lyman nodded at a spot over Joshua's left shoulder. "The dance is tonight, and you probably ought to give her a bit of time to get ready."

Joshua glanced back and saw Ingrid approaching them.

"My stove is got problem," Ingrid said when she reached the two men. "I think something wrong with flue. Can you come fix, please?"

Joshua noticed Lyman sidling away. Ingrid noticed it too.

"I come at bad time?" she asked.

"Lyman and I were talking about that dance over at the Andersons' tonight," Joshua said. "I was telling him I thought I might like to go. Would you enjoy that?"

Her face, always so expressive, positively lit up. There was never any guessing about what was going on in Ingrid's mind. Her blue eyes grew wide. "I love to go!"

He smiled at her excitement. "You'd better hurry and get ready then."

Stove flue forgotten, she ran to the house.

She stopped midway and whirled around. "What about girls and Mary?"

"Do you want them to go?"

"I think yes!"

"Whatever you want, Ingrid. This is your night."

She ran the rest of the way to the cabin.

Lyman wandered back. "See what I mean?"

"That woman works so hard and asks for so little," Joshua said, looking after her. "Thanks for being a friend and letting me know. I had no idea it would mean so much to her."

"Might be a good idea if you spiffed up a bit too," Lyman said. "I don't think you're supposed to wear horse manure to a dance."

"Joshua says we can go to Andersons' party!" Ingrid burst into the cabin. "All of us."

"Well, he certainly didn't give us much time to get ready!" Mary exclaimed.

"No, but the girls' Sunday dresses is washed and ironed. Just need to clean faces and hands and put on clothes. I have many dry diapers for Bertie."

"You're awfully happy about this!" Mary said.

"Back in our village, I dance. I was just little girl, but was much fun. I want very much to go."

"Well, then," Mary said, "I have something you might be interested in."

"What?"

"Do you remember that lavender material that I thought would look so good on you?"

"Ja."

"Wait right here."

Mary went upstairs and came down with two boxes.

"What you have?" Ingrid asked.

"You'll see." Mary opened one box, shook out a lavender dress, and held it up.

Ingrid gasped. "It is beautiful!"

"I told you I used to be a pretty good seamstress," Mary said. "Thought I might see what I could still do if I really tried."

Ingrid touched the fabric. "When you do this?"

"I don't always sleep well at night. Instead of lying awake, I thought I might as well do something useful. I took the measurements off of your pink calico dress when you weren't looking and then added a few touches of my own. I think it'll fit well. The only person who knew I was making it was Josh—I sent him to pick out some buttons and lace at the mercantile."

"Joshua know about this?"

"He got you something else too—he had George send off for it special."

"Joshua get me present?"

"Go ahead and open the box. He told me to give these to you whenever I gave you the dress."

She pulled the top off of the second box and gasped. Nestled inside were a pair of lovely, lace-up, calfskin boots with a low heel. Real, honest-to-goodness lady shoes. Something so nice even Millicent would be proud of them.

Ingrid could feel her tears welling up. "How he afford this?"

"Remember that carpentry work he did for George over the summer? All those shelves George wanted him to build? He traded part of his time to buy you these shoes."

Now the tears came and she could not stop them. Ingrid sat down at the table, put her head on her arms, and just bawled.

"Oh, honey. I know." Mary patted her on the shoulder. "I know."

"I . . ."—Ingrid hiccuped—"am so happy."

"It's been a hard summer, especially for you. Nothing would make Josh and me happier than to see you have a nice time tonight."

Ingrid hugged Mary. "I have a very good time at dance in this pretty dress!"

While Mary went to get herself ready, Ingrid laid the precious dress and shoes on her bed and called the girls in from where they had been playing. After she had washed faces, tied bows, and packed a basket for the baby, she allowed herself to go into her own room and get ready. She could hardly wait.

She shed her work dress and slipped on the new one. The material was softer than she had ever worn before. Mary had made it in such a way that it fit her well on the top, then draped around her hips and fell in graceful folds to her feet.

There was no bustle, thank goodness. So far, Millicent was the only woman vain enough to wear that style in White Rock. It had amused Ingrid to see the woman fighting with her gigantic bustle the last time she had seen her riding beside George in his buggy.

The mirror in her bedroom wasn't full-length, but it was big enough to see how well the dress flattered her. There was a touch of white lace at her throat and also on her sleeves. Rows of matching buttons marched up the front.

Joshua had purchased the lace and the buttons; Joshua had chosen them. The thought made her want to cry again—but she resisted. She did not want blotchy skin tonight!

She turned sideways. The dress fit her like a glove. She had not realized it, but she had filled out some since moving here—probably from eating her own good cooking!

Around the farm, she had taken to wearing her hair in a simple braid halfway down her back, but tonight, she took pains to brush it out and braid it carefully into a coronet.

She had a slight curl to her hair, and loosened a few strands to frame her face.

The best moment of all was slipping on the shoes. They smelled of good leather and were as smooth as butter. Lacing them over her stockings was such a joy.

When she was finished, she pinched her cheeks for color. Mary had been right. The lavender did bring out the color of her eyes. What a sly, sweet woman Mary was. Imagine her staying up late at night, preparing such a gift. And that Joshua, working on shelving for George to get her shoes! Oh, she was a blessed woman.

When she opened the door of her bedroom, every member of the family was waiting for her.

"Oh, Ingrid," Agnes said. "That dress is beautiful on you!"

Mary was noticeably pleased with herself. "I guess I haven't completely lost my knack."

"Mama pretty!" Polly said.

"Thank you, sweetie, and look!" Ingrid held out her skirt to show off her new footwear. "Your father bought these for me!"

Ingrid's eyes sought out Joshua's, hoping to see approval there, but she could not read his expression. It seemed like there was an internal battle going on inside of him.

"You can throw George's shoes away now," he said.

Her face fell. He had given her no compliment, only a suggestion about what to do with her old shoes. But then he added, "You look stunning, Ingrid. Every man in the place will envy me."

Was he making fun? She checked his expression. No, he was not making fun. He was serious. He meant it.

"Thank you, thank you!" Her heart was filled to bursting with love for this man and their family. "We please go now?"

Joshua had taken Diantha to a few square dances during their marriage, but she had preferred sitting and watching. Usually she would ask to be taken home early. Because of that, he was used to being a quiet observer at affairs like this, but Ingrid was having the time of her life. He had excused himself for a few minutes to go check on the children and his mother, but as soon as this particular set was over, he intended to rejoin her on the dance floor. It was worth the effort just for the pleasure of watching her smiling up at him with such happiness . . .

"I do believe your wife is having a good time," Lyman said.

"I would say that is an understatement."

"Filled out a bit since the day I first laid eyes on her at the inquest," Lyman said. "Excuse me for saying so, but she was sort of pitiful-looking then. Now, well, you got yourself a looker, Josh."

Joshua had been thinking the same thing. He stood, arms crossed, leaning against an empty stall, watching her swing from one partner to another. She was no expert at square dancing, but her enthusiasm and laughter at her mistakes was infectious and added to everyone's enjoyment of the evening.

In the flickering light of dozens of lanterns, his Ingrid positively glowed. She reminded him of a tall candle, her blonde hair a beautiful bright flame as she danced to the homemade music. The lovely soft fabric of her dress emphasized the graceful curves of her body, and her smile lit up the whole room.

For the first time since he met her, it struck him that Ingrid had never been a pretty woman. As Agnes and his mother had pointed out—Ingrid was beautiful.

A man he had never seen before came over and introduced himself.

"The name is Downy. Jesse Downy. I just bought a farm a

few miles north of here. I was wondering if you gentlemen would mind pointing out the women who are spoken for and which ones are single. I'm in the market for a wife. A new farm isn't worth much without a woman to share it."

Lyman helpfully pointed out each single woman who had attended. Joshua was amused by the fact that Lyman studiously avoided mentioning Susan.

The newcomer didn't seem all that interested in any of the women Lyman indicated. Instead, he seemed distracted. Finally he asked, "Who is *that* beauty?"

"Which one?" Lyman said.

The man nodded toward the dancers. "That tall blonde with the big smile. I noticed her the instant I came through the door."

Lyman frowned and glanced worriedly at Joshua. "Are you talking about the woman in that purple-colored dress?"

"She's the one. I've not been able to tear my eyes away from her."

Joshua's voice was low and deadly. "That, sir, is my wife."

"Your wife?" The man gave a low whistle. "My sincere apologies. But you are one lucky son of a gun, if you don't mind me saying so."

The man tipped his hat and moved on. In a few moments, Joshua saw him talking to Susan. Lyman, who had stationed himself beside her, was looking distinctly uncomfortable.

"You don't know the half of it, mister," Joshua whispered to himself after the man was out of earshot. "You don't know the half of it."

He noticed that George and Millicent had just arrived. Millicent found her way over to a knot of women. Knowing what he knew, he could barely stand the sight of her, but with Millicent occupied, George gravitated over to him. "How's things going, Josh?"

"Things could be better. The drought has hit me hard."

"Everyone is suffering," George said. "I keep thinking that it has to rain soon—this can't go on forever."

"How are those shelves holding up?"

"Real good. I see Ingrid is enjoying her new boots."

"That she is."

Joshua had no problem with George. The man did the best he could . . . considering to whom he was married.

"Speaking of the drought, I've got some news you might be interested in, Josh."

"Oh?"

"A man came through today. Said Robert Foster is opening up a new section a couple days northwest of Saginaw. Foster is putting out the word he's hiring. Didn't you tell me you worked in a lumber camp a while back?"

"I was eighteen, it was right before the war," Joshua said. "I've heard of Foster. He runs a good camp."

"I've heard that Foster's wife and an old cook from up in Maine set a real fine table."

"When's he wanting a crew?"

"Soon as enough men get there. The man I was talking to wasn't losing any time. He said Foster's a fair man and the shanty boys trust him. He said he was going to try to get there before all the jobs are taken."

"What's he paying?"

"Standard. A dollar and a quarter a day."

"We could use the money."

"What with the drought and all the responsibilities you got—I figured so. Speaking of food—I think I need me some punch." George went off in search of refreshment.

Joshua continued to watch Ingrid as she laughed her way through an especially intricate dance step. The woman seemed to bring light with her everywhere she went.

As he looked around the room, to his great consternation, he saw that the newcomer was not the only man admiring his wife. Several male eyes were fastened upon her as she concentrated on keeping up with the movements of the dance. He also noticed that one of the men, during certain parts of the movements, was holding her a little closer than the dance warranted. A strong wave of possessiveness came over him, and he grew anxious for this song to end. He had checked on his mother and children, and they were fine. The moment this set was over, he intended to cut in and not leave the dance floor again until his wife was ready to go home.

The news that George had given him niggled at his mind. There would only be so many spots at that camp. The idea of coming home in the spring with a pocket full of greenbacks was a great temptation. He still had some cash from last year's crops and the carpentry work he had done for George—but he didn't have much. Come spring, he would need to buy seed, and . . . a paying job for the winter would be quite a welcome thing.

He hated to go, but if he was going to take the job, he needed to leave at once. He would talk to Ingrid about it later, when they were alone.

"You be gone how long?" she asked.

Josh had been sleeping on the bed in the sitting room ever since his mother had moved upstairs, but tonight, after the family was asleep, he went into the bedroom, closed the door, and sat on the bed beside where Ingrid lay. He wanted to talk in private with her before he allowed the rest of the family to weigh in on this decision.

"Eight months, maybe less. It depends on when the spring thaw comes."

224

"That is long time."

"I know."

A full moon was shining through the window, and he could see that she was chewing on her bottom lip, thinking hard.

"How much monies again?"

"A dollar and a quarter a day."

She frowned as she calculated in her head. "That is nearly three hundred dollars."

"I know."

"Do we have any monies left?"

"Not much. Barely enough to get the children and you through the winter."

"There is no monies from grain crops?"

"Not with the drought."

"Well, then." She gave a long, shuddering sigh. "I guess I take good care of family when you go away."

"I know you will take good care of them. That's the only reason I can go."

"When will you leave?" There was a catch in her voice.

"In the morning. Foster runs a good camp. Safer than most. The jobs will fill up fast. Lyman has promised to help you with the livestock, and I've gotten in a good store of wood. It should last you through the winter. The cherry trees should be dormant soon, so the burden of watering them every day will be over."

Her thick golden braid lay over her right shoulder, and she absently curled the end around and around her finger.

"I will miss you."

"And I will miss you." His voice softened. "You looked beautiful tonight, Ingrid."

"Ja?" She sounded surprised.

"I was proud to tell other men that you are my wife."

"Thank you for saying that kind thing," she said in a small voice.

"I'm not being kind." He lifted her hand to his lips and kissed it. "It is the simple truth. I found myself feeling sorry for every man there tonight who was not lucky enough to be married to you."

He braced himself with one hand on each side of her and leaned in to kiss her. She, who had rarely stopped smiling the entire night, was now deadly serious, watching him with wide eyes. He heard her quick intake of breath when she realized what he was intending. His own heart, to his surprise, pounded like a youth awkwardly trying to steal a first kiss from a sweetheart.

Then he saw that tears were starting to trickle down Ingrid's cheeks, and he pulled back, wondering if he had forever ruined his chances with this beautiful woman. Was she remembering all the mistakes he had made, all the hurtful things he had said? He wiped her tears away with his fingers.

"I couldn't see you, Ingrid. For a long time my grief was so dense I could barely see through it."

"Pa!" Agnes burst through the door with Polly on her hip. She stopped dead in her tracks. "Why is Ingrid crying?"

"That is none of your concern," Joshua said. "What do you want?"

"Tell me why Ingrid is crying!" Agnes frowned at him. "Have you hurt her feelings again?"

"I cry from happiness, my *dotter*." Ingrid gazed up at him, her eyes shining.

"Oh, well then." Agnes's voice was relieved. "That's all right."

He looked down at Ingrid's face, reading the love in her eyes, the miraculous love that was still there in spite of him. He smoothed a wayward curl away from her face and wished with all his heart that Agnes would leave.

"I'm really sorry to have to interrupt you two lovebirds, but Polly's sick."

As though to demonstrate, the little girl promptly threw up all over the floor.

"See?" Agnes said.

Joshua and Ingrid both leaped up at once. She grabbed the little girl and felt her forehead.

"No fever."

"Thank God for that," Joshua said.

Influenza had killed more than one small child.

"It could be all the cake and punch she ate," Agnes suggested.

"How much did she have?" Joshua asked.

"A lot."

"Why didn't you stop her?"

"Ingrid was busy dancing and you were talking to George. I didn't want her to start squalling and bother everyone, so I let her eat all she wanted. It kept her happy."

"Poor little girl," Ingrid crooned, sitting down on the bed and rocking her against her chest. "You feel better now? Get all bad stuff out?"

Polly nodded with her head tucked up against Ingrid's neck.

"Next time you be more careful, ja?"

Again Polly nodded.

"Can I go to bed now?" Agnes said. "I'm awful sleepy."

"Go ahead," Josh told her. "Thanks."

Agnes started toward the ladder, then turned around. "Can Polly sleep with you—just in case she starts puking again?"

"Yes." That was the last thing he had wanted to happen tonight.

"And it stinks up here," Agnes announced. "Do I have to clean it up?"

"I'll take care of it," Joshua said.

Ingrid threw him a grateful look as she carried Polly into the sitting room and sat down in the rocking chair. "Please ask Agnes to find Polly clean nightgown?"

"Of course."

"What's going on?" Mary came down the stairs and wandered over, wearing a voluminous white nightgown and cap. "What's all this commotion down here?"

"We think a little girl ate too much cake tonight," Ingrid said.

"That was good cake," Mary said. "I wouldn't have minded another piece myself. Is everything all right down here, then?"

"We are now."

"Talking about cake made me hungry. I think I'll fix myself some bread and butter," Mary said.

A half hour later, Joshua had finished scrubbing the floorboards upstairs and down with soft soap. Polly had been dressed in a clean nightgown and now lay sprawled and asleep in the middle of their bed. Bertie had awakened and needed to be changed and fed. Ellie and Trudy were awakened by all the activity going on around them, came downstairs, noticed that their grandmother was eating bread and butter—and wanted some too.

Once the family finally settled down, both Ingrid and Joshua fell exhausted into bed on either side of Polly.

"Just for your information, this is *not* what I had in mind for tonight," he said.

Her eyes sparkled. "You not like cleaning up cake and punch?"

"Not especially."

Ingrid started to giggle at the ridiculously complicated evening. Her giggle was so infectious that before long both of them were trying to smother their laughter so as not to awaken Bertie and Polly.

"Thank you for sticking with me and this crazy family," he said when they had finally sobered up. He reached over his daughter's sleeping body and grasped Ingrid's hand. "When I get home in the spring, we will start over, you and me. Things are going to be very different between us. I promise."

## 21

Joshua did his chores the next morning, gave Lyman some instructions, and then he packed up what the lumbermen called a "turkey," which was nothing more than a bag flung across his back. He wouldn't need much—just warm clothing and a couple of heavy blankets.

His family was sacrificing so that he could do this, and he would be one of the few who would not so much as step foot inside of a saloon come spring—no matter how glad he was to see civilization. He was determined to bring back every penny.

It was so much harder to leave them than he had expected.

"How far will you have to walk?" his mother asked.

"It should take me about four to five days."

"That is very far," Ingrid said.

"I'll be fine."

"Shouldn't you ride Buttons?" Agnes asked. "We could use one of the plow horses to pull the wagon."

"The foreman won't want to stable and feed my horse through the winter."

"Oh."

"I packed food," Ingrid said. "They will feed you good in the camp?"

"This particular camp is famous for its cooking."

"You have two blankets to keep you warm?"

"I'll be the envy of the bunkhouse, Ingrid."

"When will you be back, Pa?" Ellie asked.

"Come here, sweetheart." He got down on one knee and gave her a hug. "I'll be home in the spring. You girls be good to Ingrid while I'm gone."

"I'll keep an eye on 'em for you, Pa," Agnes said. "They won't give her any trouble."

Each girl got a kiss and a hug, and he held Bertie close for a moment, absorbing his smell and feel. His son and his daughters would change so much while he was away. It broke his heart that he would not be here to see it. He was afraid that he would seem like a complete stranger when he came back.

He kissed his mother on the cheek, and then he turned to Ingrid. They had not kissed since their hurried wedding. Now, with the family looking on, he gave her only a peck on the lips, but he wanted so much more.

When had the idea of leaving her become so hard?

Was it only when he saw her in her new dress, dancing with all male eyes fastened upon her?

Or was it when she had trudged beside him, day after day, lugging water to save his orchard?

Was it the evening he found her trying to bury Diantha's diary to save him the pain of knowing the truth?

Perhaps it had happened the night that she had taken in his mother without question and pulled her out of her near-coma of neglect and abuse. Because of Ingrid, his mother looked and acted like a woman twenty years younger than the one who had been left on his porch.

He couldn't pinpoint exactly when she had become necessary to his happiness, but he suspected it was simply the cumulative effect of months of sheer, unadulterated kindness.

It felt strange walking away from his family, knowing that he would be spending the next eight months without seeing them—but if that's what he had to do in order to care for them, then that is what he would do.

Mary took the smaller children back into the house.

"You coming?" Agnes asked.

"In a little minute," Ingrid said. "You go on inside."

"All right," Agnes said, "but watching him won't bring him back any faster."

"I know." Ingrid watched him walk away, the sack across his shoulders, headed off to a brutal and dangerous job to make a living for his family—and it was *such* a dangerous job! Had it been a lumber camp that had taken her brother? Would she ever know?

She knew that some women waited and watched for their husband to come home from the lumber camps, only to find out that he had been given a hurried burial beside the river where he had drowned—unable to reach the surface with tons of white pine closing over his head, his only headstone a pair of calked boots hanging on a lonely branch. There were also women who waited and watched, only to discover that the money they so desperately needed had been either stolen or used up in one wild, drunken spree in Bay City after the lumber camp broke up.

But she had no doubt that if he survived, Joshua would bring every penny back to his family. He was that kind of man.

There was nothing left to do except go back inside the cabin.

Mary looked up from her Bible when Ingrid came through the door. "So now we pray that he comes back safely."

"Yes," Ingrid said. "Now we pray."

It was seventy miles to Saginaw as the crow flew. When he got there, he would inquire about Foster's camp. His only fear was that Foster would already have all the men he needed. If so, Joshua would ask around to see if any other camps were hiring.

He figured he could get there in four to five days on foot. There were rumors that a railway line would be coming through soon—but he didn't put much stock in that. It was all still too raw and unsettled between White Rock and Saginaw.

There were a lot of hopes and dreams about railroads and such these days. With the war over, it seemed like every other man he met had some big idea on how to get rich. White pine was being cut as fast as possible, making wealthy men out of some, and breaking others. He had heard about those who had sunk every dime they had into copper mines in the cold Upper Peninsula only to lose it all on the difficulties of trying to take the ore out. There was a joke going around—probably started by the very ones who had tried mining copper—that a man needed to own a gold mine if he wanted to run a copper mine.

He didn't have the hunger to get rich. He just wanted enough to take care of his family.

There was no schoolhouse in White Rock yet, nor was there a schoolteacher. Each family taught their children as best they could. Joshua and Diantha had taught the girls what little book learning they knew so far. Now Mary, who had once taught school, was working with them. Ingrid was delighted. It gave Mary a chance to do something she had once loved, and it freed Ingrid to do both her and Joshua's chores.

It felt so strange not having Joshua around. Even though their marriage had been awkward at times, she missed him desperately.

As she looked out the window at the fall landscape, she wondered if it would ever rain again. It was now the first of October, and she counted back—June, July, August, September, four months without a drop of rain. If it weren't for the Faraway Spring, they would not even have water to drink.

She worried about food. There were seven mouths to feed, and sometimes eight when Lyman wasn't at Susan's. Their garden had not been abundant, but there had been enough to keep them fed so far. Ingrid had preserved everything they had not eaten.

There was a crock of cabbage pickling in brine in the cellar right now and another crock of pickled cucumbers. There were two apple trees that had fared better than the cherry trees. Joshua said it was because they were older and their roots went deeper. She had dried every last apple, even cutting the worms out of the misshapen ones to save every bite. Those dried apples garlanded the rafters of the cabin now and gave off a lovely scent. There were some potatoes, but not enough to see them through the winter. Joshua had gotten milled what little wheat had survived, and she thought she had enough flour. He had traded their bull calf to George for several bags of beans and rice.

They had not yet butchered the two hogs. Cold weather was needed for that. Lyman said he would help when the time came. After talking with and throwing scraps to the two pigs for months, she had gotten attached to the poor things, but there was no choice. Joshua had said that Richard had always sold them two piglets each spring from the litters he raised for market. She hoped that would hold true next year. The children would need every bit of fatty meat they could get this winter.

There were the chickens, but they were not laying well right now, which was a worry. Their cow, which Ingrid milked morning and night, was still producing enough milk, but there was always the chance that she would go dry before winter was over.

So far, none of the children had gotten sick, with the exception of Polly's memorable stomachache. Ingrid hoped they could make it through the winter without any major illnesses. She hoped to present Joshua with a happy, healthy family when he came home in the spring.

To do that, she needed good food and plenty of it.

She counted out the money Joshua had left with her. He had given her everything he had, and she would not spend it until she absolutely had to.

Agnes noticed that Ingrid was making a list of the food they had on hand. "Will we be all right?"

"We will be fine," Ingrid said. "When the cold comes, we will kill the pigs, and I will ask Lyman to kill wild animals for us. If a hen stops laying, we will make chicken soup. You children will not go hungry. I promise."

"It's nice having you here to look after us," Agnes said. Then she went back to working the arithmetic problems Mary had assigned her.

Ingrid went out to the garden, where she had left two heads of cabbage to eat fresh. She cut the crisp cabbage into pieces and put them into a kettle to steam. Then she cut up some scraps of ham and threw those in. There were two eggs today. Not enough to feed everyone—so she used the eggs and a few handfuls of flour to make into noodles to go with the cabbage. With salt, pepper, and butter, the noodles and the cabbage were a simple dish that the children and Mary enjoyed.

If it were God's will, and if she could remain healthy and

strong, they would survive the Michigan winter just fine. For the first time, she was grateful that she and Joshua had not truly lived as husband and wife. This particular winter would not be a good time to be with child.

She was just about to call the children to supper when she heard footsteps on the porch. She opened the door, and there stood Richard and Virgie. Richard carried a heavy cast-iron skillet with a lid, and Virgie held a basket covered with a towel. "We heard that Josh went to work at the lumber camps," Virgie said. "Is that true?"

"Yes," Ingrid said. "He will not be home until spring."

Although Josh had allowed Agnes, Trudy, and Ellie to walk the half mile to their grandparents' home several times this summer, Richard and Virgie had not yet taken her up on her invitation to come visit the children. Virgie meant it when she said she would not step foot in Josh's house while he was there.

"You want come in?" Ingrid asked.

Virgie stepped into the cabin, and Richard followed. Both looked around, as though reacquainting themselves with the room with which they had once been familiar. Ingrid knew it must be very hard for them, this first time back inside their daughter's home.

"You stay and eat with us?" she said. "Please?"

"I suppose we could," Virgie said. "If you really want us."

"Oh, we want. We have plenty food. Children be so happy to have grandparents here."

Just at that moment, Ellie looked down the steps and let out a screech. "Grandma Virgie and Grandpa!" Then she came barreling down and hugged both of them around their knees. Trudy and Polly followed right behind her.

"You'd better take this before one of them knocks me down." Virgie handed Ingrid the basket. Beneath the towel, Ingrid saw biscuits still steaming from the oven.

Richard sat the Dutch oven on the table and lifted the lid, releasing a delicious aroma. "Virgie and me killed a chicken and fried it up."

"I have cabbage and noodles!" Ingrid said. "We will have feast!"

Agnes came down the stairs, carrying the baby.

"Is that my little Bertie boy?" Virgie held out her arms. "Oh, he has grown!"

Ingrid rushed to set out extra dinner plates and then called everyone to the table. It was gratifying to listen and watch as the conversations swirled around her. She thought about the diary and poisonous pills that she and Joshua had buried beneath the tree at the cemetery. Many men would have rushed to show those items to their in-laws. Instead, Joshua had chosen to absorb their anger—not wanting to add that extra sadness to their lives.

Neither she nor Joshua knew if they had done the best thing, but they had chosen what they thought was the kindest thing. She often prayed for these two broken people, that the Lord would lift at least some of their terrible grief.

Although there was a bittersweetness to the evening for her, Ingrid knew that Joshua would approve. Nothing, in her opinion, could lift grief as quickly as being in a house filled with children. Loving Joshua's family had certainly helped her live with the grief she felt over her brother.

She had asked Joshua to inquire of every lumberman he saw if anyone knew what had happened to a big Swede named Hans Larsen, who had a triangle-shaped scar above his left eye and the sweetest disposition in the world.

It took Joshua three and a half days to get to Saginaw. By the time he arrived, he was convinced that if Michigan did not get rain soon, the whole state would dry up and blow away. It had been hard for him to find enough water to drink on the way here. This did not bode well for the lumber camps that depended on the rivers to move the logs to the lakes each spring.

He found a merchant on the outskirts of Saginaw who was able to give him the location of Foster's camp. It then took him a hard day's walk to get there. It was a new camp and neatly laid out. The cook shanty was well built and had fresh blue-checked curtains in the window. A woman's touch always boded well when it came to food.

He was foot sore, hungry, and weary when he walked into the cook shanty door. His spirits brightened when he smelled the aroma of bread baking.

"Welcome." A man who had been talking to a pretty red-haired woman enveloped in a cook's apron when he came in walked toward him with his hand extended. "I'm Robert Foster, owner of this camp. Are you looking for work?"

"I was hoping to get here before you filled up," Joshua said.

"What are you good at doing?"

"I spent one winter as part of a two-man axe team," Joshua said. "I didn't develop the knack for being a river hog. I can do a fair job on anything else, including carpentry."

Foster looked him up and down. "You hold yourself like a military man. Where did you serve?"

"I rode with the Michigan First Cavalry."

"Ah." Foster nodded. "Custer and his famous Wolverines! I saw him once at Gettysburg. I couldn't believe that young pup was a brigadier general."

"You were there?"

"I was one of the surgeons trying to patch men back together."

"I don't envy you having had that job."

"Nor I yours. How old was Custer back then?" Foster said. "Early twenties?"

"He was twenty-two when he became a general," Joshua said.

"From what I heard, he was a vain, pompous man who deserted his men to go visit his wife."

Joshua wondered why Foster was bothering to criticize his general. Was he trying to start a fight? If so, he would look for another camp to work at.

"General Custer had courage," Joshua said evenly. "He led the attacks instead of staying in the back. He had eleven horses shot out from under him. We overlooked his vanity and his fondness for his wife because we knew we could depend on him in battle. He saved more than one of our lives."

"You speak like an educated man." Foster abruptly changed the subject. "Are you?"

"One year at Michigan State Normal School is all, but my mother was a schoolteacher. Why do you ask?"

"I won't have any trouble getting together an axe crew," Foster said. "But I'm missing an ink slinger for the office. The man who worked for me in the past decided to stay home this winter and help his daughters build a beef cattle business."

"His daughters?"

"Seven of them. The oldest has turned into quite the manager. We used to rib him about how someday he would end up working for her, and that's what's happened. Are you good with figures?"

"I am."

"How would you feel about being ink slinger and storekeeper for the camp?"

"I'll work any job you want me to."

"Oh, and by the way," Foster said. "I have nothing at all against George Custer. I never met the man. I need someone

I can trust to keep my books and run the store. I liked the way you defended your general against me when I criticized him. I'm impressed with your loyalty. It shows integrity. Ink slinger is your job if you want it."

"Thank you, sir," Joshua said. "I'm grateful for the work."

His gamble in walking across the thumb of Michigan had just paid off.

Foster called out, "Katie, does this man have time to go drop his things off in the bunkhouse before you set out supper?"

"If he hurries." Katie sat a huge pone of corn bread on the table.

"When Katie says you'd better hurry," Foster said, "you had better hurry."

As Joshua was leaving the cookhouse, he heard a great clatter of tin dishes and an old man's voice cursing a blue streak.

"Jigger," he heard Katie say patiently, "I don't care if you did just drop a load of dishes. There's no call to use the Lord's name in vain. We have been through this before."

"Well, if I didn't have a dang woman in my way all the time, I wouldn't drop so many dishes."

It would be a long winter, Joshua thought, but an interesting one.

# ⷮ22ⷯ

Keeping the books and running the little store made a nice change. Joshua discovered that he greatly enjoyed visiting with the men as they came in for a new nose warmer—the small stubby pipe that the lumbermen preferred—or a new pocketknife, or perhaps a bar of laundry soap for clothes-washing Sundays, or maybe even a small sack of candy. The shanty boys, as the loggers called themselves, loved their hard candy.

Foster kept more stock on the shelves of his store than the owner Joshua had worked for in the past. He didn't know if that was in order to make more money or if it was simply Foster's way of making camp life a little less hard on the men. He'd even supplied a large pile of dime paperbacks and po-lice gazettes—the kind of reading material the men adored.

The only hard thing about his job was trying to sleep. The noise didn't bother him so bad, but the smell was awful. There were wet wool socks and sweaty boots perpetually drying out before the stove. Most of the men chewed tobacco, and many kept a tin can beside their bunks, which was not something a man wanted to stub his toe against. Some didn't bother with a can and simply aimed their streams of tobacco juice directly at the woodstove sitting in the middle on a thick layer of sand.

Most of them believed that tobacco juice sizzling on the stove would clear the air of any disease that might be floating around. Tobacco juice was believed to have other medicinal uses. Some used it as a dressing for small wounds.

The bunk beds, filled with sawdust, were only slightly more comfortable than sleeping on bare wood, and it was a challenge for him to sleep each night beneath the bunk of a French Canadian who snored like a steam engine, smelled like a wet dog, and occasionally cursed in two languages while asleep.

The camp filled up quickly with axe men, swampers, road monkeys, a blacksmith, a carpenter, and teamsters. The men had come from all over, and shanty boys were some of the biggest gossips in the world. Crammed together in a bunk-house, not seeing outside civilization for eight months at a time, and with little to occupy their time in the evenings, they had little with which to amuse themselves except the sharing of stories and the telling of tall tales.

He questioned each man who joined the camp, but none had run across a man matching Ingrid's description of her brother. He was beginning to doubt that Hans Larsen had ever stepped foot into the Saginaw Valley until a timber-looker—the loneliest profession in lumbering—came in after weeks of scouting for new stands of timber.

The man was unshaven and lean to the point of emaciation. He wore stained leather pants, which offered some protection against rattlesnakes and thorny brush, high-topped boots, a battered hat, and a wary expression.

"See anything interesting out there?" Joshua didn't expect the man to answer truthfully. Timber-lookers, if they were worth their salt, didn't reveal where they had been. Finding an undiscovered stand of white pine in the middle of millions of acres of almost shore-to-shore forest was akin to finding a gold mine, especially if it was anywhere near a river.

"Nothing to speak of."

In other words, he had no intention of talking about it.

"Looking to buy anything in particular in here?"

"I need a new knife. I broke the blade on mine."

Joshua brought out a selection of knives. The timber-looker tested a few blades on his thumb and then made his purchase.

He was almost out the door before Joshua thought to ask him if he had happened to run across a Swede matching Ingrid's brother's description.

The timber-looker stopped and slowly turned around to face him. "Why are you asking?"

Joshua closed the case of knives and put them away. "He's my wife's twin brother. She came all the way across the ocean to meet him, but he never showed up. No one seems to have seen or heard of him. She insists that he was working in a Saginaw Valley camp and was not the kind of man who would abandon her."

The timber-looker closed the door, and Joshua's pulse quickened. Did the man know something?

"How long have you been working in lumber camps, mister?"

"The name's Hunter," Joshua said. "I worked in the camps one winter a couple of years before the war."

"You were Union?"

"Michigan First Cavalry."

The man nodded. "You were one of the lucky ones who made it through Gettysburg."

"I was," Joshua said. "And you are?"

"Dyer Wright." A muscle in his jaw twitched. "I scouted for Sherman. Lost my taste for war and for people after serving with him through Georgia. Being a timber cruiser suits me fine. I leave everyone alone, they leave me alone."

Joshua wondered what this had to do with his wife's brother—if anything.

"There's a camp about ten miles north of here. Nice timber. Hard to get to. The owner of it lives in Detroit. He's a cripple, but he owns the right to more timber than he can keep track of. The foreman, Bart Mabry, is a hard man, and he runs the worst haywire camp I've ever seen. Drinks heavy. Feeds the men slop. Pockets the difference. Hungry men make mistakes. Dangerous ones. It didn't take long for the word to get out, and loggers stayed away. The foreman got desperate to keep his job. Desperate men do desperate things."

"What are you saying?"

"I leave people alone. I stop at a camp for a few hours to resupply, and then I head back into the timber. I do this job for a living—because frankly, I can't stand being around people for too long at a stretch, and I figure it's none of my business what happens in the camps."

Joshua gripped the edge of the counter, tense. This man knew something about his brother-in-law, and it wasn't good.

"A couple days ago, I saw where the foreman had set up camp and had been cutting into a stand of timber I own partial holdings to. I started to go have a little man-to-man chat with Mabry, but then I saw something that made me stay away—at least for now."

"What was that?"

"He's got some men working for him at gunpoint. I saw a big Swede like you described out working in the timber, with a guard over him and some other men. The guard was armed. I made my way over to the camp, and when I saw a padlock on the bunkhouse door, I figured I needed to get out of there. Been wondering what to do about it ever since."

Joshua was appalled. "They lock the men in at night?"

"Can't think of any other reason for that padlock to be there. Never saw a lumber camp bunkhouse with a padlock before."

"If the place caught fire, they couldn't get out."

"I doubt Mabry would care. Except for having to go to the trouble of kidnapping more timber cutters."

"Can you describe the Swede to me?"

"I was there long enough to see that he wasn't happy and was deliberately working as slow as he could get by with. The guard yelled at him several times. Called him Larsen. The man had a big scar over his left eye."

"That's him," Joshua said.

"What are you thinking of doing about it?"

"Go get him, of course," Joshua said. "I surely don't intend to let him stay there. Do you have any fight left in you?"

"No," Dyer Wright said, "but I'll lead you to them."

"Let me go talk to my boss and see if we can get some men together. Are you staying the night?"

"Katie Foster is the best cook in the Saginaw Valley. I walked five miles out of my way just to have supper at her table." For the first time since Wright had walked in, he grinned. "Of course I'm staying the night."

Joshua found Robert Foster in the cookhouse and told him what he had learned.

"I've heard of men being kidnapped to work in haywire camps before," Foster said. "It's a bad business. Ten miles, did you say?"

"Yes." Joshua waited. He would go by himself if he had to, but it would be better if Foster would lend him a couple of men to go with him.

"We'll need to leave just after midnight, then," Foster said. "I'm assuming it would be best to surprise them at dawn?"

"We?"

"You might need a good surgeon along, and we'll see which of my men are willing to go. One thing for sure, we aren't going to leave those men there."

Foster had not hesitated about freeing the men, and Joshua was impressed.

"Wright said he would lead us to them."

"Good. About half of the men in camp are veterans. I'm thinking we could muster at least a dozen ex-soldiers willing to go. I'll find out how many weapons we have. Many of the men carry a gun to camp with them in case they get a chance to put some fresh game on the table. I'll talk to everyone after supper."

Ten miles was no challenge for loggers. Most of them, like Joshua, had walked much longer distances to get to Foster's camp. They were all able-bodied and bent on their mission as they strode, single file, through a woods illuminated by a full moon.

"What's your plan?" Foster asked.

Although many of the men were veterans, Joshua was the only one who had strategic experience and who had led men into battle. He was the obvious choice to take charge of the rescue.

"I don't have a plan yet. I want to see the lay of the land first. I'm hoping the two sharpshooters will be good enough that the rest of the men won't have to fight."

It was no small thing to close down the work of the camp for an entire day to rescue the kidnapped loggers. Foster would lose money because of this. All of them would, but there wasn't one man who didn't want to go.

Even those who had not fought in the war had equipped themselves with axes and their long, spiked peaveys. There was nothing a shanty boy liked better than a good fight—it was almost a form of recreation for them—but tonight there was nothing but grim determination on their faces. Haywire camps—so named because they were reportedly held together by the wire left behind after the hay had been shaken out—were the scourge of lumbering.

The thought of fellow woodsmen being forced at gunpoint to do this dangerous job made their blood boil. Joshua wondered if the angry men would allow the kidnappers to live once the imprisoned men were rescued. It wouldn't be the first time a group of shanty boys dealt out their own form of shanty justice.

Katie's thirteen-year-old brother, Ned, and Robert's twelve-year-old son, Thomas, had begged to come along. They both had small jobs at the lumber camp and thought they were men—but their father had refused. Joshua was grateful. If things got ugly, he did not want two young boys along.

With Wright leading the way, they had set off in the middle of the night in order to get into position before the guards awakened. Surprise was always good.

Long before dawn, he had his small army in position, each man behind one of the many tree stumps left behind when the camp was cleared. The camp had been situated in a flat, low spot with a slight elevation all around it. The stumps plus the slight rise gave his men a distinct advantage. All were ready to attack when he gave the order. It was almost a perfect situation from which to fight, but he was hoping it would not be necessary.

Each man lay on his belly behind his own stump, waiting for the camp to awaken. The full moon illuminated the scene.

At five o'clock they saw lanterns being lit inside the cookhouse. A half hour later the man who, from the looks of his filthy apron, was apparently the cook, came out of the front door of the cookhouse and rang a triangle. He scratched his massive belly beneath his apron, passed wind loudly, and went back inside. Joshua's men did not move. It was not the cook they wanted.

A few moments later he saw a stocky man with a full beard emerge from a small cabin. He went over and pounded on the door of the padlocked bunkhouse.

"Get up, you lazy shanty boys. It's daylight in the swamp." There was sarcasm in the man's voice. Shanty boys all over the Saginaw would be awakening to the very same words. Even haywire camps kept some traditions.

Three other men emerged from the same cabin right behind him. Even though they were carrying weapons, it was easy to see that they were still half asleep. One was juggling his gun with one hand while trying to pull up his suspenders with the other. Another stumbled along, rubbing the sleep out of his eyes. The third seemed more awake. He looked up toward the line of hardwoods as though he sensed something.

Joshua decided it was time.

"Bart Mabry," he yelled into the still morning air. "Tell your men to put down their weapons. We have you surrounded."

Bart's head swung toward Joshua's voice, then lowered like a bull ready to charge. The man struggling with his suspenders tripped and fell. In trying to break his fall, he dropped his rifle and grappled in the dirt to grab it.

A sniper bullet zinged, and the gun jumped a foot away from him. His hands shot up over his head. "Don't shoot," he pleaded.

The guard who had been rubbing the sleep out of his eyes

dropped his weapon and also put his hands above his head. "This weren't my idea," he yelled.

The man who had sensed trouble had already ducked behind the cabin opposite from where the first sniper bullet had come. He probably thought he was momentarily safe, until the sniper Joshua had placed on the other side of the camp zinged a bullet into the cabin—directly above his head.

"I repeat," Joshua shouted. "You are surrounded. Lay down your weapons."

The last man came out from behind the cabin with his hands and rifle in the air. "I'm going to lay my gun down now," he said, and proceeded to slowly do so.

Joshua gave the signal for his men to rise. Bart's mouth hung open, and he wheeled around in a circle, seeing the shadowy forms of approximately thirty men materializing from behind the stumps—all armed with some sort of weapon.

"Men with firearms, stay in your position," Joshua called. "Cover us while we secure the guards and release the loggers."

Carefully, the other men and he moved toward Bart and his men. He motioned for three to go in and make sure the cook was not a potential danger. He saw two go in the back door of the cookhouse as one went in the front.

The loggers were not particularly gentle as they tied Bart's men's hands behind their backs with rope they had brought along for that purpose.

"Give me the key." Joshua held his hand out to Bart.

If Bart could have murdered him with his eyes, he would have done so, but with no other recourse, he fished the key out of his pocket and dropped it in his hand.

Joshua fit the key into the lock and opened the door.

It had begun to get light outside, but inside the bunkhouse it was a dark cave.

In a decently run camp, there would be at least one lantern

turned low and left burning through the night. Bunkhouses were built with no windows because the men got up before daylight and went to bed after dark. Windows served no practical purpose and would have let much-needed heat leak out in the harsh winters.

In this bunkhouse, there was no light at all, and it reeked.

Bunkhouses in lumber camps were famous for their rank smell. Too many unwashed bodies, too many unwashed woolen socks steaming on makeshift clotheslines, too much foul breath, too much smoke from stubby pipes.

But this bunkhouse smelled of urine and defecation from men locked in for long hours.

In his opinion, Bart Mabry and his men deserved to hang for what they had done.

"Somebody find me a lantern," he said. "You men in there, if you're able to, come on out. Your guards are unarmed and restrained. Men from Robert Foster's lumber camp have secured the camp. You're free."

The incarcerated lumbermen began to emerge. When all had crawled out of their beds of moldering straw, he counted twelve men altogether. Some of the older ones were weeping. It was a pitiful, ragtag crew Bart had assembled to take down those giant white pines.

An older man with a badly infected foot was the last to come out. He was supported as he limped by a tall, blond Swede.

"Are you Hans Larsen?" Joshua asked.

"Ja. How you know my name?"

"I'm your brother-in-law. Your sister is going to be very relieved to see you."

"You're not going to believe the pig slop they've been feeding these men." Disgust laced Foster's voice after he had inspected the kitchen. "It's a wonder they didn't come down with scurvy."

"This is *good* food for here," Hans said wryly. "The cook baked bread this morning."

"If you can call this bread." One of the snipers deliberately dropped a loaf on the floor. It was so heavy, it thudded like a rock. Bart and his men, including the cook, were led away, leaving Joshua and Foster to care for the four captives who were not strong enough to walk the ten miles back to camp.

"Horses are in the barn," Hans told Foster, who was tending to the man with the infected foot. "Bart care more for his horses than his men. Horses can carry the weak ones."

"Did he not realize he could get more work from men who were cared for properly?" Foster asked.

"Bart said we were . . ." Hans struggled to find the correct word. "Disposable."

"How did they capture you?" Joshua asked.

"Hans and friends work for Bart last winter. Got pay. On way to steamer to Detroit, four men jump me. Take back to Bart. He get our money. Work us all summer. Clear river. Set up camp."

"Mosquitoes and blackflies," Joshua said.

"Snakes too," Hans said. "How is my sister?"

"Ingrid is doing very well."

Hans gave a great sigh of relief. "I worry and worry about not meeting her."

"She did a good job of taking care of herself. She came to the Saginaw area to try to find you. She finally decided that you must be dead. She said that death was the only thing that would keep you from keeping your promise to her."

"That or a padlock and three guns." Hans cocked his eyebrow. "You and Ingrid, you have good life?"

"Yes," Joshua said with a certain amount of wonder. "We

251

do have a good life. I'm a widower with five children. Our family was broken, but Ingrid mended it. Your sister is an amazing woman."

"I'm ready to move these men out, now," Foster said as he tied off the bandage he had wrapped around the man's foot. "Could you two get the horses?"

"We have much time to talk, my brother." Hans clapped a hand on Joshua's back and nearly knocked him over. "Let us get these men back to your good camp."

Right before they left, Hans turned around and stood staring at the bunkhouse.

"I will come back and burn that building to the ground someday."

"You tell me when, and I'll help you," Joshua said.

As they began to walk toward Foster's camp, Hans's face lit up with a smile so familiar that it made Joshua's heart long to see Ingrid again. "Now—you tell all about children. I have nephews, nieces now?"

"When we get you back home," Joshua said, "you will have nephews and nieces coming out your ears."

## 23

There had been a smoky haze developing over the land for several days, and Ingrid was worried.

"Where is the smoke coming from?" Ingrid filled the teakettle with a half quart of precious water to make tea for Hazel, who had come for a visit.

"Don't worry," Hazel said. "There are always a few fires in Michigan this time of year. A lot of farmers burn their fields off in the fall. This is normal."

"But everything is very dry," Ingrid pointed out. "It is dangerous to start fires when it is no rain."

"True. I've lived here for a long time and I've never seen such weather." Hazel reached for a sugar cookie from the mounded plate in the middle of the table. "If you're worried, you can bring your family to my place until we get a good, soaking rain. I practically live on top of the lake. It might ease your mind."

"I like that very much." Ingrid lifted the tea canister off the top of the warming oven. "But I not want to leave Joshua's animals."

"It's just something to keep in mind," Hazel said. "By the way, did you know Susan and Lyman are getting married in the spring?"

"No! Lyman not tell me." Ingrid measured a small spoonful of tea into the chipped teapot. "I hope he not planning for Susan to live in my barn!"

"From what I understand, they'll be living with her parents."

Ingrid poured boiling water over the dried leaves. "Do her parents like this idea?"

"Emma's thrilled. Susan's father probably won't even notice. Last I heard, he had a crate of books shipped in from Boston. An old friend of his passed away, and his widow sent them to the Cains. Emma says he hasn't stopped reading since."

"Very much learning!" Ingrid clucked her tongue. "His head be too heavy to hold up."

"I hope not!" Hazel laughed. "Susan wants him to do the wedding ceremony."

"I have a good idea! I make Swedish wedding cookies for them," Ingrid said. "They melt in mouth."

"If they're anything like these sugar cookies, I imagine they will." Hazel bit into a second one. "Any word from Josh?"

"No. I hope he is all right." Ingrid poured the hot water into two cups.

"It's hard for the men to get letters out," Hazel said. "Spring will be here before you know it."

"You are right." Ingrid lifted the steaming cup to her lips.

Mary was upstairs working on lessons with the little girls. Bertie was napping on Agnes's lap, and Agnes was absorbed in an assignment her grandmother had given her. It was a rare luxury for Ingrid to be able to simply sit quietly and have tea with a good friend. She was savoring every second.

"How is your livestock faring?" Hazel asked.

"The creek has low places where some water is, but it will be dry soon."

"Me and She-Wolf are glad we live next to the lake." She ruffled fur on the dog's head. "Aren't we, girl?"

"Where do you find such fine animal?" Ingrid asked.

"I found her half-starved when she was small," Hazel said. "It was right after my husband passed. I needed that pup every bit as much as she needed me."

"God has a way of giving person what they need," Ingrid said. "Sometimes before they know they need it."

"I hope you are talking from experience?"

Ingrid blushed. "Joshua . . . he care for me now."

Hazel chuckled. "Well, it's about time!"

She-Wolf, who had been asleep, stood up, yawned, and stretched her back.

"I'll be leaving now," Hazel said. "She-Wolf wants to go home. She knows I have some nice venison waiting for her, and she's all excited about it."

At the word *venison*, She-Wolf trotted to the front door and stood there until Hazel opened it, and they walked out together.

Agnes looked up from her assignment at the closed door. "Hazel does know that She-Wolf can't really talk, right?"

"Maybe," Ingrid said, "but sometimes it seem that dog knows every word that comes out of Hazel's mouth."

"What I don't understand," Joshua said, "is what Bart thought he was going to do with you in the spring. He couldn't keep tabs on you once you men and the logs hit the water."

Joshua and Hans were lingering, absorbing the warmth and scents of Katie's cookhouse, their stomachs comfortably full. Joshua wished he could see Ingrid's face when Hans showed up.

"He kill us. He make plans for Indian river hogs to ride the logs."

Jigger, who had been helping Katie, took off his apron, came over to the table, and sat down on the bench beside them.

"I'm Jigger—the head cook of this camp." He looked over his shoulder at Katie and then raised his voice, as though wanting her to overhear. "There are some who make the mistake of thinking that that there red-headed woman is the head cook, but she ain't!"

Joshua glanced at Katie, who was most definitely in earshot. She seemed utterly unflustered by this comment. Without her hands pausing for an instant in kneading bread, she gave Joshua a big smile and a wink, as though letting him in on a secret. Evidently she had learned to deal with this ancient banty rooster by humoring him as much as possible.

"What happened to the men that kidnapped you?" Jigger asked.

"Loggers take them to Bay City to jail."

"Them men are lucky they didn't get strung up on the spot. Loggers can be terrible rough. One camp I worked for, the men found a couple of river pirates while they was on the spring drive. The pirates had a little tributary off to the side where they was doing their dirty work. They was snagging other camps' logs, cutting off the ends where they was branded with the other camp's sign—and then putting their own brand on it."

"What happen?" Hans asked.

"It was up in Maine and it had been a hard winter." Jigger put both elbows on the table and leaned forward. "The conditions had been terrible. They never got a good, hard freeze where they could sled the logs out easy. Everything had to be dragged through mud. We'd only gotten out about half of the timber the foreman had hoped for. None of us were sure we'd even get our full pay. Without a good snow, the river was low that year and the drive was hard. And then, while they was trying to get the logs they *did* have down the river, they found those two weasly river pirates stealing their hard-earned lumber. The men strung them up on the spot. It weren't pretty."

"I'm sure it wasn't," Joshua said.

"Men who steal other men's logs, and those who kidnap because they run such bad camps no one wants to work for them—they deserve what they get." Jigger spat on the floor with contempt and then sheepishly ducked his head and looked around at Katie.

"You can clean that up later, Jigger," Katie said calmly. "Go ahead and enjoy your conversation."

Jigger looked relieved.

Katie dusted the flour off her hands and took something that smelled wonderful out of the oven. "I just baked some fresh molasses cookies," she called. "Would any of you gentlemen like some?"

Joshua saw Hans's eyes light up. "Ja!"

"I guess I'd better get back to work now," Jigger said without moving. "That woman can't cook worth spit without my help."

Katie brought a platter of molasses cookies to the table. They were the size of small dinner plates. Then she brought all three of them mugs of strong, hot green tea.

"This and some good 'chaw' will pert' near cure anything that ails you, boys." Jigger took a big slurp of the green tea. "I made an awful mistake a few years back. Took a job cooking for that health sanitarium down in Battle Creek. Thought I might teach them people a thing or three. I felt sorry for the poor things. Let me tell you something, boys. Them people are pitiful. No meat. No liquor. No tobacco. No tea. I give it my best shot, but after two weeks I had to hightail it out of there. Eatin' that food just about kilt me."

Joshua tried not to smile. It was obvious that Jigger's sojourn among the health-food enthusiasts had left him a haunted man.

"But you're back where you're needed now, Jigger," Katie said. "Can you show me again how to get these beans ready? I've got a good batch of coals built in the hole the boys dug, but I can't seem to get this Dutch oven cover on just right."

"You gotta seal it with bread dough, woman. To hold the steam in. I've told you a hundred times." Jigger shook his head as he stood, as though unable to believe her foolishness. "See what I mean? For some reason, people get it into their heads that Katie is head cook—but they're wrong. She can't do nothin' without my help."

The efficient and competent Katie humbly stood back and allowed Jigger to seal the cast-iron bean pot. It was the most Joshua had seen the fragile old cook do so far except blow the Gabriel horn to call the men to meals. It occurred to him that Robert Foster's wife was an exceedingly kind and wise woman.

Foster entered the cookhouse. "Well, that's good riddance to bad rubbish."

"The bad men are gone?" Katie set the kettle for more hot water.

"The bad men are gone, sweetheart." He went over and kissed her cheek.

"I heard that the law in Bay City is pretty lax," Joshua said. "Do you really think that they'll do anything to them?"

"Sure they will," Foster said with a smile. "The ones in charge don't want anyone taking the loggers' money except themselves."

"Is it still smoky outside?" Katie asked.

"It is," Foster said. "I think it might be getting a little worse."

"Do you think the camp is in any danger?"

"I don't think so," Foster said. "Those fires are still pretty far off. It's probably just some farmers burning off their fields."

"Awful dry to be burning off fields," Jigger said. "I'd hate to go through what we did back in '67. That was too close for comfort."

"What happened in '67?" Joshua asked.

"We got hit with a wildfire," Foster said. "It was touch-and-go. If you've never been in one, you have no idea how fast a forest fire can spread."

"You keeping all them loggers you freed?" Jigger asked. "It's gonna be a mite crowded in the bunkhouse if'n you do."

"Most of them want to go home after the ordeal they've been through and let their families know they're alive. What about you, Hans?" Foster asked. "Do you want to go home or would you rather stay and work?"

"Now that I know my sister is safe, I will stay and work." He dug a playful elbow into Joshua's side. "Me and my new brother will make much money, take it home, and give it all to my sister. Our Ingrid can turn a penny into a dollar."

"Find a bunk and get anything else you need out of the store. Josh will put it on the books for you."

As Joshua and Hans walked to the store, it seemed to Joshua that the smell of smoke was getting stronger.

# 24

"I hate to leave you and the children, ma'am," Lyman said. "I appreciate you and the captain giving me a place to stay, but my boss says he'll pay me extra if I sleep at the sawmill and make sure no fires start. There's a snug little shanty there he says I can winter in."

"I understand," she said. "I can take care of things here."

"I don't know if you been out to the creek in the past few days," Lyman said. "It's completely dry now, but I did a trick my daddy told me about once. I dug a hole in the creek big enough to settle a barrel down into. There's enough water still underneath the creek bed to keep those barrels full so the livestock will have something to drink, but you'll probably need to check it every day."

"Thank you, Lyman."

"If the barrels dry up, about the only thing you can do is let the livestock go find water on their own."

"It will rain soon."

He looked around at the tinder-dry leaves and the parched earth. "Some of the old people are saying that this is the worst drought they've ever seen."

"Hazel offered we go stay with her," Ingrid said. "Is it good idea, you think?"

"None of the other farmers have started bringing their families into town. If I was you, I'd wait a bit longer. Those fires are still pretty far away, and rain should come any day now. It always rains the first part of October. Just keep a sharp eye out. If you see a glow on the horizon, put the children in the wagon and get out of here. I'll come and check on you a couple times a week to see if you need help with anything."

"Take care," Ingrid said. "You been big blessing to us."

"It was the least I could do. If it weren't for Josh, I'd have never found my Susan."

As soon as Lyman left, Ingrid went out into the yard and turned her eyes westward. The land was so flat it was hard to find a vantage point.

There was a maple tree near the house with low-lying branches that Ellie liked to climb. With no man around to see her shinnying up a tree, Ingrid hiked up her skirts and climbed as far as the limbs could hold her. To her relief, there was no red glow on the horizon.

As she climbed down, she saw the strangest sight. A dozen or so domestic cats were running through her nearest field as though they were wolves running in a pack. Never in her life had she seen anything like that. Perhaps that was what cats did here. There was much about America that was new and strange, but still, it gave her a bad feeling.

She went to check the barrels that Lyman had buried in the creek. His trick had worked. They were nearly full. The livestock would be all right—at least for today.

"Lyman is leave us," Ingrid said when she went back inside. "He will stay at the sawmill."

"It is just as well," Mary said. "There's little he can do here now. And it is one less mouth to feed. Not having a full-grown man eating a meal with us every day will make the food last longer."

Even though it should not yet be dark, she noticed that Mary had lit a lantern to see by. The haze of smoke had begun to block out the sun.

"Is the smoke ever going away, Ingrid?" Agnes said. "I can still breathe all right, but it's hitting Trudy hard."

Ingrid didn't need Agnes to tell her that Trudy was struggling. The child had developed a dry, hacking cough that was a worry to her.

"The rains will come soon." Ingrid gave them the reassurance that Lyman had given her. "I will find something to help Trudy."

Joshua had four white handkerchiefs in his drawer. She whipstitched two ribbons onto one of them so that Trudy could wear it over her nose and mouth. Before she tied it onto the little girl, she dampened it—to make it more efficient at keeping the smoke out of Trudy's lungs.

She then wet a large dish towel and draped it over Bertie's cradle. She could at least keep him from breathing in smoke while he was sleeping.

"You watch children, Mary?" she asked. "I want to go see Richard and Virgie and ask what they think. They live here long time and know more."

Virgie was sweeping off her front porch when Ingrid arrived. Richard was just coming in from the barn.

"Is something the matter with the children?" Virgie asked.

"No, children all right. I wonder what you do if smoke get worse. You maybe go to town to stay until it rain?"

"No," Richard said. "There's no call for that."

Virgie and Richard had a dog that was so old, it had pretty much lost interest in the world around it and spent most of its time napping on their front porch.

Right at that moment, it raised its head and began to howl.

Virgie nudged it gently with her broom. "Now, you hush!" She glanced at Ingrid. "He's been doing that for the past two days. Just lifts his nose into the air and starts howling. I don't know what to make of it."

"I see strange thing this morning," Ingrid said. "Many cats run across my field like pack of wolves. I never see anything like it. That thing happen here?"

Virgie shook her head. "I've never seen anything like that in my life, but I've been seeing a lot of wildlife crossing our property."

"I keep thinking it'll rain soon," Richard said.

"If you think it is time to take children to town, you will tell me? Hazel say we can stay with her."

"I'll come tell you if I think you're in any danger," Richard said.

As she walked back home, she saw a sea of rabbits moving toward her, as though they were being pulled toward the lake by an unseen force. They parted at her feet and moved past her, showing not the least bit of fear at being so near to her. They seemed dazed as they went east.

Everything within her said to pack up the children and leave, but the few people she had questioned made her doubt her instincts. Everyone seemed to think that they were safe.

Then she saw a shadowy, huge shape in the semi-darkness and she froze. It was too big to be anything but a bear, and it was coming directly toward her. She knew it wasn't wise to run, and so she stood as still as possible. She soon discovered that the bear, like the rabbits, seemed not to be conscious of her presence. It, too, looked half-dazed as it moved toward the lake.

As soon as it was gone, she ran to her door and slammed it shut behind her. The strange behavior of the animals was far more frightening to her than the smoke.

She considered her options. Tomorrow was Sunday. She would be taking her entire family to the village for church. Unless there was less smoke tomorrow morning than there had been today, she would move her family to Hazel's, cramped conditions or not.

On Sunday morning, had it not been for the clock, Ingrid would not have known it was daylight. The morning sun was completely obliterated by the smoke.

"Time to get ready for church, girls," she called up the stairs. "Breakfast is ready."

As she changed Bertie into his Sunday clothes, she went back and forth in her mind, trying to decide what to do. Sweden did not have forests like this, at least not where she lived. Hans and she had grown up with well-ordered fields, every possible inch cultivated. Here, it was a hodgepodge of small spots of civilization in the midst of nearly endless forests—or the tangled aftermath the loggers left behind. With all her heart, she wished Joshua was here.

She tried to think like Joshua. What would he want her to do? Stay here? Care for his livestock? His possessions? His house? Or take his children and mother where she knew they would be safe—even if everyone else thought she was overreacting?

Looking at it through Joshua's eyes clarified everything. If she had good reason to doubt their safety—and she believed the smoke thick enough to block out the sun was a good enough reason—he would tell her to get Mary and the children out of there and keep them safe no matter what.

She made up her mind. She was taking them to Hazel's.

While Mary and the children ate their breakfast and washed the dishes, she lugged her straw mattress off the bed and dragged it to the wagon. It would make a decent pallet where she and the girls could sleep on Hazel's floor. She grabbed diapers, the bread she had baked yesterday, a change of clothes for the children, and an armload of wool blankets she had stored away for the winter.

That huge body of water beckoned to her.

Her cow had gone dry several days earlier. She didn't know if it was because of the strange weather, or if the cow was simply having too much trouble accessing water. In any case, the poor thing did not need to be milked. The chickens, the last time she had gone out to check, were up in the lower tree limbs with their heads tucked beneath their wings. They were confused by the constant darkness. Evidently they thought they were supposed to be asleep. Their two pigs had been fed late last night after supper. She didn't know what to do about letting their livestock loose. If the fire never came, she would hate to tell Joshua that she lost all of his animals because she panicked. How would he ever get the farm plowed without his plow horses? How would she feed the children without the cow and hogs?

By lantern light, she hitched Buttons to the wagon, then went to check the barrels Lyman had sunk into the creek bed. The water in them was lower. As she harnessed their horse to the wagon, she tried to think if there was anything else she should do except get her family out of there. Once again, she wondered what to do about Joshua's animals. Let them run free and the fire maybe miss their farm entirely? Joshua would be so upset! Without the fatty pig meat, the children would go hungry this winter.

"It is time!" she called. No one hesitated or hung back. Like the animals, they all felt drawn to the water—where it would be safe.

Normally, the girls would have thought it great fun to have

both the mattress and the blankets in the wagon, but not today. The air felt strange—charged—as though lightning had struck, even though there had been no lightning.

As she passed Virgie and Richard's house, the two of them were throwing buckets of water all over their roof and the outside of their house. Unlike Ingrid and Joshua's, their well was deeper and spring-fed.

"Do you want to ride into town with us?" Ingrid called. "There is room."

"We ain't leaving. This place is all we got." Virgie's expression was grim. "If a fire comes, we aim to fight."

"I take children to Hazel's where it safe."

Virgie's face softened. "You need to get the children out of here, but me and Richard—we have no children left to worry about."

Ingrid noticed something missing on their porch. "Your dog is gone."

Virgie looked troubled. "He abandoned us in the night. The poor old thing is as crippled with arthritis as an old man—but he up and took off. Guess he's going to the lake too—although I'm not sure he can make it."

"Promise if fire comes, you go to the lake. Don't try to fight fire all by yourself."

"I won't be by myself. I'll have Richard here with me. We built this place together, and we'll fight to save it together. You go on to church now and don't worry about us. Richard has been plowing for the past three days—on the west side of the farm—ever since the smoke started. Fire can't burn when there's nothing but dirt to burn. We'll be fine . . . but I sure wouldn't mind getting a couple hugs from my grandchildren before you go."

Ingrid held Buttons steady while Virgie hugged and kissed each of the children. Last of all, she took Bertie from Mary's arms and held him tight against her heart. "He always was such a good baby," she said and handed Bertie back to his other grandmother. "Now, get these children out of here!"

As they rode toward town, down the old lumber road, wildlife accompanied them on either side. The haze of smoke made it difficult to see very far, but there were so many shadowy figures, it felt as though an army of animals were walking through the woods alongside of them.

"I've lived in Michigan my whole life," Mary said. "But I never knew animals would do this. They don't even seem to be in a rush. They're all just moving toward the lake."

A magnificent buck with a rack nearly as wide as the wagon stepped in front of them. He seemed confused. As they drew nearer, he shook his head as though to clear it, and proceeded to walk a few steps in front of Buttons, as though leading them.

"I'm getting really scared," Trudy said through her handkerchief.

"Only one more mile and we'll be at Hazel's house."

"But what if the fire comes?"

"Then we'll go into the lake until it passes."

"But I can't swim."

"We will be careful not to go out so far that the water is too deep. The fire, if it comes, will not come any further than the beach."

Mollified, Trudy curled up on the soft blankets while Ingrid wondered if Mary and the little ones could survive the cold of Lake Huron in October.

When they got to White Rock, she saw that many deer had come to the village, presumably for safety. A bear walked right down the main street, looking neither to the left nor to the right, just simply lumbering along. The thing that concerned her the most, though, was the exhausted flocks of birds that were taking refuge in the village. They were everywhere, upon everything, and in such shock from whatever inferno they had escaped that they didn't move or even attempt to fly away when approached by a human.

Before going to Hazel's, they stopped to see if there would be worship services at the Cains'. Only a handful of people were there when they entered. She discovered that most of the people from the surrounding farms were making the same stand that Virgie and Richard were—trying to protect their homes.

"Have you heard anything?" she asked Susan when they entered the Cains' house.

"One of the steamboat captains stopped yesterday and told my father that the smoke is making it impossible to see anything out on the lake—even land. He said several ships have already wrecked because they couldn't see where they were going."

"We will go to stay at Hazel's," Ingrid said.

"I think that's wise," Susan said. "I'm afraid this is going to get bad."

# ∽25∾

"I don't like the looks of things," Foster said loud enough for everyone in the cook shanty to hear. It was Sunday morning and they were all eating breakfast. "There's too much smoke, and everything is too dry. I think the camp might be in danger."

All chewing stopped, and the men turned to look at him. Forks were poised in midair, hands reaching for bread were snatched back, and even Katie and Jigger, who were busy in the kitchen, paused.

There was one rule that was never broken in any camp, especially one where Jigger was the cook—no talking at the table. The men were supposed to eat in silence, as quickly as possible, so that the cooks could immediately begin the process of clearing, washing up, and resetting the table.

The rule was so ironclad that even for the owner of the camp to speak out was breaking serious protocol. Jigger had been known to smack men upside the head for something as simple as complimenting him for a good meal.

When they saw that Jigger wasn't going to hit anybody, one of the men ventured a comment. "We seen some animals acting real strange out there in the woods," he said. "A herd of deer passed within a few feet of us, and they didn't seem to be the least bit afraid—they was so bent on heading toward the bay it seemed like they didn't even see us."

"What are you thinking we oughta do, son?" Jigger's voice was solemn.

Foster stood up from the table and put his hands in his pockets. "Four years ago the camp I was running found itself directly in the path of a wildfire. It came in the middle of the night, faster than anything I ever imagined. There wasn't enough time to make it all the way back to the bay. Instead, there was an inland lake we ran to. The Lord saw fit to send a rain that saved most of my camp, and all of our lives. I vowed then that if I ever had an inkling my camp could be in danger, I would not wait around until it was too late."

There was a general sound of approval and nodding of heads.

"As you know," Foster continued, "I just got back last night from Bay City. There is so much smoke out on the lake that boats are coming in and hunkering down for fear of wrecking. That's never happened before. In my opinion, everything is so dry after this drought I think the whole state is in serious danger. I've decided that we should break camp and go to Bay City until it rains or the fires burn themselves out."

"What about our pay?" one of the men asked. "I came here flat broke. I can't even feed myself in Bay City."

"You can all go by the office and Josh will write you out scrip for the days you've worked, minus your purchases. I've made arrangements for you to get your money at my bank. As soon as we can get packed up, I want everyone to clear out and head toward safety. If the camp is spared, I would take it as a great personal favor if you men would come back."

"It ain't no personal favor for us to head back here—not with Katie's cooking," one of the men said as an attempt at a small joke.

There was a smattering of laughter, but when the men resumed eating, there was a somberness that had not been there before. Joshua left the table to get a head start on tallying the books and writing out the scrip. As he left he passed Katie and Foster standing close together near the door.

"You are paying all these men," Katie said, "even though we might lose this whole season and not make a dime this year? We are not wealthy people, Robert."

"I can't let the men go without something to live on."

"You are no businessman, Robert Foster." Katie put both hands on her husband's shoulders and gazed into his eyes. "But I love you for it. We'll survive."

Joshua decided that Foster was a lucky man to have such a wife as Katie, but he felt no envy. Ingrid was waiting for him at home, as lionhearted as any woman he had ever known.

It took awhile to total everything and write out a scrip for each man. He suggested that they not blow their wages on booze and broads in Bay City, especially after Foster had sacrificed out of his own pocket. The men listened—rough as they were. They'd seen Foster shut down the camp to rescue the kidnapped men. They'd eaten the good food he had provided. They'd been treated fairly, and to a man, they vowed to come back as soon as the rains came—if the camp was still standing.

The men loaded the wagons with the food supplies and as much equipment as they could carry. The teamsters cracked their whips over the mules, and then everyone followed the wagons on foot—except for Jigger—who rode beside one of the teamsters on the wagon seat. Katie expertly rode Foster's horse with their daughter, Betsy, riding behind. Katie's young brother, Ned, and their son, Thomas, walked alongside the men as they all set out on foot for Bay City.

The church service was brief. Everyone, including the preacher, was distracted by what was going on outside. Lanterns had to be brought from houses, and even then the haze was such that it was difficult to see the words in the hymnal. The smoke hurt their throats when they tried to sing.

No one commented on Trudy's mask—many were already holding handkerchiefs up to their mouths and noses. There was much coughing.

As soon as the last amen was said, instead of standing around and visiting, everyone hurried away, each to their own home.

Hazel sought her out as everyone else was leaving. "I hope you had enough sense to bring what you needed so you can stay with me until this is over."

"Ja. I bring enough."

"Good. Let's head on over there now before it gets any darker. I put some stew on—I thought you might be coming—I half-expected you last night."

The afternoon passed slowly in Hazel's house. The children, much like the confused chickens, became sleepyheaded because of the continual darkness. Normally at this time of day, they would be chasing each other all over the house.

Mary, complaining of a headache from the smoke, climbed the stairs and lay down. Even Bertie seemed listless. Ingrid couldn't help worrying about the poor animals she'd left penned up back at the cabin. What would Joshua have wanted her to do?

She-Wolf kept pacing the floor, looking at the door, until Hazel gave up and let her out. The minute the dog was outside, she raised her head and gave the most mournful, eerie howl into the darkness that Ingrid had ever heard. It was followed by every other dog in town and it went on and on until she wanted to scream.

"Did you see Virgie and Richard?" Hazel asked.

"They say they are staying. Richard plow up land all around their cabin to keep the fire away. They are putting water on house. They say they stay and fight."

"They still got water, do they?"

"Joshua say their well very deep and good spring at bottom."

"Water or not, if a wildfire comes, they won't make it through," Hazel said. "All these little farmers staying out there are crazy if they think they can fight a real wildfire. A little bitty bit of plowed ground and a damp roof won't even make it slow down."

"They make up minds to stay. They say house and farm is everything they have."

"People put way too much stock in their houses." Hazel shook her head. "But you can't reason with Virgie and Richard—I seen that when they turned against Josh." She sighed. "These old bones are tired, do you mind if I lay down for a bit?"

"Of course not," Ingrid told her. "Go get some rest."

All four girls were curled up together on the mattress, sound asleep. She lay Bertie down beside Ellie, and then she sat in the rocking chair, watching over all of them, looking out the window from time to time to see if anything had changed. She could see nothing but the unnatural darkness.

She must have dozed in the chair, because she jerked upright and looked around in the semi-darkness, wondering what it was that had awakened her. Then she saw that Agnes was missing. The first thing she did was look upstairs, but Agnes was not there. The next possibility was the outhouse, which she hurriedly checked. Then she heard She-Wolf barking incessantly around front. Hazel had once told her that the animal never barked unless it was something truly important.

She went to investigate and discovered that Agnes had managed to hitch Buttons back to the wagon, had the reins in her hand, and was not at all pleased to see Ingrid.

The minute their eyes met, Agnes yelled at the horse and slapped the reins on its back, but Ingrid was faster. She jumped onto the wagon before it could gain any speed and pulled back on the reins, shouting, "Whoa!"

Not once had she felt any real anger toward any of the children, but right now, she was furious. "What do you think you doing!"

The girl's lower lip began to quiver. The unshakable Agnes was on the verge of tears.

"I heard what Hazel said to you when she thought I was asleep. I heard her say that if the fire came, there would be no way Grandma and Grandpa could survive. I'm gonna go get them."

"Already we talk to them, Agnes. They will not leave."

"*You* talked to them. I didn't." Tears were running down Agnes's face. "I didn't know how dangerous staying there was going to be until I heard Hazel talking. They'll leave if I ask them to."

"Why did you not tell me you go do this?"

"Because you would have stopped me—just like you're trying to stop me now!"

"You see wild animals go to water? You see smoke? Too dangerous!"

"No, it isn't. See?" Agnes pointed. "There's no red glow on the horizon."

"You cannot see horizon. Too much smoke!"

"If they were *your* grandparents, *you* would go after them!" Agnes shouted.

Hazel came out onto the porch. "What's all the yelling about?"

"Agnes trying to go get grandparents," Ingrid said.

"They won't come, sweetheart," Hazel told the girl. "I've known Richard forever. He's as stubborn as a mule."

"I have to try!" Agnes was sobbing now. "Don't you understand? I have to *try*!"

Ingrid realized in that moment that her relationship with Agnes would forever hinge on what she did in the next few seconds, and she decided to not allow fear to come between her and her oldest daughter.

"Hah!" she shouted, slapping the reins hard against Buttons's rump. "Hah!"

It all happened so fast, Agnes barely had time to grab hold of the seat. Her expression of surprise and gratitude was something Ingrid knew she would remember for the rest of her life—if she had a life left after today.

The last place Buttons wanted to go was westward on the logging road toward their farm. Like the wild animals, his instincts were to go in the opposite direction. Ingrid had never used her whip on him before, but she did now—and with much eye-rolling, jerking of the head, and rattling of harnesses, he began to gallop.

"It's only two miles," Agnes said apologetically.

A strange, hot wind had begun to blow against them, and Ingrid had little doubt now that the fire was coming. There was a good chance they would all be standing knee deep in Lake Huron soon. No longer did she have doubts about whether or not to let their animals loose. It would be inhumane to keep any living thing penned up. She wished she had not dithered earlier. It had become clear to her that there would be no last-minute reprieve. No miraculous rainstorm. Nothing that would stop this terrible, burning monster that was eating up the land. She and her family would never live in Joshua's cabin again.

"You talk to grandparents," Ingrid said. "I will go home and free animals. When I come back, I stop for one minute. No more. You get on wagon. If Virgie and Richard want, they come with us. If they stay, you make promise to me you leave them. You make promise?"

"What if they won't come?"

"You have fifteen minutes before I come back. You stand beside road and wait for me. You hear me? You understand?"

"Yes."

"Promise me."

"I don't . . ."

They were approaching Richard and Virgie's cabin. She did not have time to be nice. She grabbed Agnes by her pigtail and turned the child's tear-streaked face toward hers.

"Promise!"

"I promise."

Agnes leaped off and ran into the darkness, calling out for her grandparents even before the wagon came to a full stop. Yet again Buttons began to rear and fight. What Ingrid was asking of him was against everything he knew. Once again she had to do something she despised other people for doing: scream and apply the whip. If she didn't hurry, she was afraid they both would be feeling more pain than the momentary sting.

She ran the wagon straight for the barn, leaped off, and jerked the reins into a secure knot. She knew that if the reins didn't hold, Buttons would bolt. She could see the muscles beneath his coat rippling with nerves.

Some women might have tried to run into the house to salvage something precious to them, but there was not one thing that mattered to her at this moment except freeing the livestock and getting Agnes back to the lake. She ran to the fence and opened the gate so their animals could escape. She jerked slats out of the hogs' pen, then slapped the silly things to get them to move out. The chickens and rooster, to her dismay, were all lying on the ground, dead, presumably from the smoke. She understood why; her own throat felt raw and sore from breathing it.

She ran back to the wagon, jerked the reins out of their knot, and maneuvered it around until Buttons was facing toward town. As she did so, she saw a terrifying sight. Even through the smoke, she could tell that there was a red glow on the horizon—and it was growing fast.

This time, the horse did not have to be encouraged. They were headed toward the lake. Buttons took off like a cannon. She prayed desperately that Agnes would obey her—and be waiting at the side of the road. There was not a moment to lose.

Agnes was, indeed, waiting by the road. She saw her small figure up ahead, and the little girl was alone. As she sawed on the reins, she realized that his fear was so great, she was not strong enough to get Buttons to stop. The most she could hope for was to get the horse to slow down. It became a tug of war between her and the terrified horse—but he slowed down just enough for her to scoot to the far left of the wagon seat, brace herself with her feet, and lean out sideways.

"Agnes!" she shouted. "You have to jump! Grab my hand!"

The horse did break stride, the wagon slowed momentarily, and Agnes was ready. The instant Ingrid's hand touched hers, the little girl leaped. There was a moment when all Agnes had was a toe hold on the wagon and a grip on Ingrid's hand, then as agile and quick as a monkey, she caught her balance and scrambled onto the seat.

She-Wolf had stopped howling. She pawed at the outside of the door until Hazel opened it. Then the dog grabbed the old woman's sleeve in her teeth and started tugging.

"What in tarnation . . ." Hazel tried to shake off She-Wolf, but the dog's eyes were pleading with her. Then, she realized that all the other dogs had stopped howling. Instead, there was an eerie stillness, as though every living thing was crouched down, carefully listening.

Then, in the distance, she heard the sound of crackling limbs and falling trees.

"Mary!" she shouted, scooping Bertie from the mattress and snatching the wool blankets under which the girls had been sleeping. "We have to get these children into the boat!"

Ingrid had never known that fire could whip through a forest so quickly. Buttons was running flat out, and she was doing nothing to slow the horse down, even though she was terrified that the wagon would hit a bump and flip over. It was a chance she had to take. To slow down would mean a death sentence by fire.

She glanced back. There was a wall of flame bearing down on them. She estimated that it was about two miles behind them, eating up the distance faster than a horse could run. They were about a mile from the village when fiery debris began to fall around them. A flaming wooden plank fell—straight from the sky—directly in front of Buttons. He reared in fright, and those few moments of getting him back under control and avoiding the flames that had fallen in front of them took time she could ill afford.

"The wagon is on fire!" Agnes screamed.

Ingrid looked back. A piece of burning punk had landed on the back of the farm wagon. The wagon was old and bone dry. It could easily burn right out from under them before they could get to the water. The terrible roar and howl of the flames and wind had become deafening.

278

"Take the reins!" she shouted.

Agnes didn't hesitate.

The wall of fire was pushing massive amounts of air ahead of it, creating a gale that she had to lean into and fight against as she climbed over the wagon seat.

There were some empty burlap feed sacks Josh had left lying in the back. She grabbed one and began beating out the flames. She found that not only was it nearly impossible to put out the fire that was consuming the wagon, she had to do so while trying to keep her balance and fight against the scalding wind.

"I can see the lake!" Agnes cried. "What do I do?"

Firebrands had been blown against and onto the roofs of White Rock houses. Ingrid saw that the villagers had formed a bucket brigade and were dousing the fires out. She knew that what they were trying to do was hopeless with the fire she had seen bearing down on all of them.

"Do not stop! Do not slow down! Run horse into lake!"

She dropped to her knees and scrabbled beneath the seat. There was a wooden box there where Joshua kept a few tools and odds and ends. Praying that she would find what she needed, her hands closed upon a hunting knife just as the wagon hit the water.

# 26

Many years earlier, Hazel's husband had purchased a twenty-foot dory, which they named *Wind Dancer* in honor of a medicine man who had befriended them when they made their way into Michigan fifty years ago. They had found it to be the perfect rowboat for fishing and traveling upon the rough open waters of Lake Huron. It had a flat bottom, high sides, and the capacity to carry several weeks' worth of supplies. It could also be powered by one strong person with a set of oars. She estimated it could hold no more than eight full-sized adults in an emergency, but since their group of nine consisted of three adults, four children, a baby, and a dog—they would still be within the limits.

Never knowing when she and She-Wolf might get the itch to go fishing, she always kept the dory in the water right beside her cabin, tied to a deep stake her husband had set. As she and Mary hustled the children to the boat, she thanked God for her proximity to the lake. She was afraid that wading out into the water while the fire burned itself out was not going to be enough—not with what she saw looming in the distance.

"I don't think I can do this," Mary said. "The sides of the boat are too high."

"You don't have a choice. Pretend you're fifteen again and climb in."

Standing knee deep in water, Hazel held Bertie with one arm and the dory as steady as she could with the other, trying to make it stationary enough for Mary to climb in. It occurred to her that she was entirely too old for this, but like Mary, she had no choice. They all had a better chance of surviving in the boat than in the water. It was October, and the waves lapping at her knees were cold.

The moment Mary got seated, Hazel handed the baby to her and then lifted the girls in one by one. She-Wolf, already a veteran of boat trips, hopped in with one giant leap.

"I want Ingrid." Ellie started to cry. "I want my Aggie."

"They'll be here soon, pumpkin." Hazel hoped with all her heart she wasn't lying to the child. The baby, upset by Ellie's sobs, began to wail. Polly looked like she was teetering on the verge of tears.

If only Ingrid would get back! Hazel could see the glow in the distance, and she knew that the fire was coming this way. She wanted to wring Richard and Virgie's necks for being so hardheaded. If it weren't for their stubbornness, they would all be on the boat by now and a half mile out into the lake!

The cold water lapping at her legs reminded her that even in the boat, they might get chilled. It was only a few feet to her back door. Now that Mary and the children were safely in the boat, she realized she might be able to grab a few supplies. She had no idea how long they would have to be out there on the water.

"I'll be right back," she shouted. The wind she had to struggle against made her grateful that she had a good anchor on board.

Inside the cabin, she grabbed a tin pail for bailing if the water got rough, dumped a sack of windfall apples into it, wrapped four loaves of bread that Ingrid had brought into a square of oilcloth, grabbed all the wool blankets Ingrid had brought, and hightailed it out of there. The wind had picked up even more in just those few seconds. It was so strong that it nearly lifted her from her feet.

The bulk of the townspeople, hearing the wind, had rushed outside. Some, looking toward the west, were in such shock at what was coming toward them they seemed paralyzed—rooted where they stood. Others hurriedly organized a bucket brigade to quench the flames that were suddenly blazing up on the cedar-shingled roofs as fire dropped, literally, from the sky.

Hazel saw a woman in an emerald dressing gown running toward them. As she drew near, she realized that it was Millicent, with her hair loose and whipping wildly about her face and shoulders.

"Oh, thank God you have this boat!" Millicent cried. She was carrying a small chest, which appeared to be very heavy. Before Hazel could stop her, she heaved it into the boat and then tried to climb in after it.

"We barely have room for *you*, Millicent!" Hazel shouted against the howling wind. "We do not have room for whatever it is that you have in that chest."

"Then make that dirty animal get out," Millicent yelled. "It weighs more than my mama's table silver."

She-Wolf bared her fangs and growled.

Hazel was stunned when Joshua's gentle mother calmly handed Bertie to Trudy, picked up an oar from the bottom of the boat, and held it poised in the air.

"If you don't take that box out of this boat right this instant, I'll brain you!" she said. "Ingrid and Agnes are coming, and no chest of your mama's silver is going to take their place. Do you understand me?"

"I have to save it!" Millicent wailed. "It's all I have left of home!"

"Then I suggest you teach it how to tread water!" Hazel grabbed the chest and dropped it into Millicent's arms. "For once in your life, why don't you worry about something that actually lives and breathes instead of your *things*, you silly goose!"

Millicent backed away, her eyes wide with fear and shock as she clutched the heavy box. She looked down at it, as though seeing it clearly for the first time.

"You're right." She shocked Hazel by dropping the chest straight into the water.

Hazel noticed that she was taking short, pant-like breaths of the smoke-filled air. "Are you all right, Millicent?"

"I have to get a knife!" Millicent hurried off with both hands clutched to her stomach.

"A knife?" Hazel asked Mary. "What is that woman talking about?"

"My best guess is she needs to cut the strings on her nighttime corset so she can breathe," Mary said. Then she pointed. "There they are! Oh, dear Father in heaven, help them!"

Hazel whirled around just in time to see Agnes at the reins, half-standing, leaning over, cracking the whip over the horse's head as it galloped wildly toward the lake with foam flying from its mouth. Ingrid was standing in the back, feet braced, balancing herself against the violent rocking of the wagon as she frantically beat at a fire that was gnawing away at the back end of the wagon. Ingrid was fighting a losing battle, and Hazel could only pray that Buttons would make it into the lake before the flames from the wagon engulfed them.

Agnes did not slow down. Screaming at the horse at the top of her lungs, she drove it straight into the water, plunging in with a violent splash. In a flash, Ingrid leaped out of the wagon into waist-deep water.

They all watched as she fought her way through the water

to the front of the wagon, where the terrified horse pawed and fought to get free.

"Over here!" Hazel screamed against the roar of the wind. She untied the boat and stood on shore with the rope in her hands, ready to leave the minute Agnes and Ingrid came.

She saw Ingrid say something to Agnes, who nodded in understanding and then took off like a shot toward the boat while Ingrid frantically sawed at the traces, trying to set the frightened horse free. Hazel held her breath . . . and practically wilted with relief when she saw Buttons lunge away from the wagon. Then she saw Ingrid running toward them. Her long legs ate up the distance so quickly that she overtook Agnes, scooped the skinny little girl up in her arms, and ran carrying her until she splashed into the water beside Hazel and deposited Agnes in the boat.

"Quick!" Ingrid panted. "Get in. Very big fire!"

To Hazel's surprise, Ingrid practically lifted her into the boat as she scrambled in. Then Ingrid leaped in, grabbed the two oars, fitted them into the oarlocks, and dug them deep into the water, pulling away from the beach with all of her strength.

Hazel was grateful for that strength. She did not think she could have made the dory move through the churning waters with all the extra weight it carried.

Suddenly, she heard a loud cry as the townspeople caught a glimpse of a horrific sight. A solid sheet of fire, over one hundred feet high, was racing straight toward them.

Those men who had been doggedly helping with the bucket brigade stopped everything and ran for their lives, diving straight into the water. Women with children in their arms fought their way through waves that seemed determined to fling them back onto the shore.

It took every ounce of Ingrid's strength to shove the oars through the rough water, propelling the dory farther and farther away from the shore. At first, she fought waves that tried to throw them back onto the shore. Then, as the hurricane-force winds brought on by the advancing one-hundred-foot wall of flame hit them full force, she reversed and rowed into the wind, trying to keep them from being blown into the smoky darkness. It was a hard balance to keep—far enough away to endure the heat, close enough to keep land in sight. She battled to keep the boat steady, praying with each breath that they would not capsize.

She was grateful for every inch of her height and her strong arms. She was grateful for every muscle and sinew in her body—even though it seemed as though each one was screaming out for her to stop fighting. She thanked God for the amazing little dory that rode the waves like a buoyant cork. She also thanked God for the boat's flat bottom, upon which the children now lay, shielded somewhat from the intense heat by the sides of the boat.

She saw Ellie start to peek over the boat's high sides.

"Stay down!" Hazel ordered. "All of you children keep your heads down!"

None of them wanted the children to see the holocaust taking place on land.

Illuminated as clear as day by the leaping flames, the scene near shore was a vision straight from hell. Men, women, and children huddled in the water, as far out as they could go without drowning. Mothers held their hands over their children's noses and mouths, taking them down into the water, holding them under as long as possible before coming up gasping for air. This they had to do to keep their skin from blistering, trying to keep themselves alive by taking themselves and their children beneath the waves, over and over. Children were screaming, crying, choking, and spluttering. Mothers and fathers fought to keep their balance in the turbulence of the lake's waters, all the while grasping one or more children. Some lost their footing and were thrown back toward the shore by the angry waves. From Ingrid's vantage point from within the boat, the heat was nearly unbearable. For those nearer, it was deadly.

Some of the people standing in the lake who initially had been trying to put out the roof fires had held onto their buckets, most of which were made out of wood. Now these wet, oaken buckets were brought into service as a sort of protective helmet by those fortunate enough to have one.

Ingrid could hardly believe her eyes at what she saw next. The heat was so intense, even several yards out into the lake, those water-soaked buckets were catching fire while still on top of people's heads.

"Are we going to die?" Trudy said.

"No." Ingrid did not look at the little girl. She kept her eyes on the shore, terrified of allowing them to get lost in this swirling, smoky madness. "I will not let you die."

They were far enough away that their boat was somewhat protected from the flaming debris that was raining down upon the people in the water. Ingrid could hardly bear to watch the desperate plight of the villagers. In addition to having to stay underwater as long as possible to keep their very hair from catching fire, they had to watch out for clumps of burning debris that kept falling out of the sky.

How naïve she and everyone else had been, thinking that they were safe, that if the fire came, all they needed to do was wade out into the water. This fire was not like anything they had ever seen. It was a living monster devouring everything in its path. She, who dealt with small, domestic fires on a daily basis, coaxing flames out of kindling inside her stove box and fireplace, could never have imagined a fire so intense, so huge, so all-encompassing that it could reach right out into the water and grab the fragile lives trying to flee.

How long could it rage with this kind of intensity? How long could she fight against the hurricane winds the wildfire produced?

"I'm going to throw out the anchor now," Hazel shouted against the howling wind, carefully feeding the weight and rope into the water. "We can't risk going out any farther."

Ingrid was grateful that the boat had an anchor. Hazel had told her that there was rarely a season in which a ship did not disappear. How much easier it would be for a small boat to be swallowed in this terrible darkness?

She-Wolf lay low and steady on the bottom of the boat, her weight distributed evenly in the middle. Agnes was lying curled around Bertie, both of them somewhat cushioned by the blankets Hazel had thrown in the boat. Ingrid could see that the baby was crying, but she could barely hear him, his cries blending in with the eerie wail of the wind. Ellie, Trudy, and Polly were a tangle of arms and legs, and they held tightly on to one another beside their grandmother's feet. Every so often, Mary would bend down and pet them, trying to be reassuring, but Ingrid could see the terror in her eyes.

She continued to be staggered with the immensity of the fire. Not only was there a wall of flame at least a hundred feet high, that wall blazed for miles along the shoreline—as far as she could see in either direction. It seemed as though the whole world was on fire, and she wondered if the end of the world had come.

As the waves tossed her boat about, as the wind howled like a living thing, as her shoulder and arm muscles began to give out, she wondered—despite her brave words to Trudy—if any of them would get out alive.

The anchor turned out to be useless. The rope was old and rotted from years of disuse.

It snapped within minutes of Hazel throwing it overboard. As strong as she was, Ingrid did not have the strength to fight against the wind forever. When her muscles began to tremble and her arms went numb and she could no longer grasp the oars, she bowed her head in defeat.

"I cannot do it," she said. "I am so sorry."

There was nothing that could be done except to allow themselves to be blown off into the vast darkness. With no fire for illumination and smoke like a blanket of fog all about them, their visibility was practically zero. Joshua had once told her that Lake Huron was over two hundred miles long and nearly two hundred miles wide. Without being able to see the shore or the sun for direction, there was a strong possibility that they could be out here for days—assuming that they did not capsize first.

"We need to stay on a sharp lookout for ships," Hazel said.

"Do you think they might rescue us?" Mary's voice was hopeful.

"No," Hazel said. "I'm afraid they'll run over us. They can't see any better than we can."

Ingrid's back muscles felt as though they were on fire. She had temporarily lost the ability to even lift her arms.

*I tried to save them, Joshua. I tried so hard to save your family. I did everything I could do.*

If they drowned out here, he would never know what happened to them. He would never know how hard she had tried. She wished she could see him just one more time. Then a terrible thought struck—something that had not occurred to her during the crisis of escaping the fire. She did not know exactly where the Foster lumber camp was in relation to the forest fire. For all she knew, the entire state of Michigan was burning. There was no guarantee that Joshua was even still alive.

"I'm cold," Ellie said.

From the chilliness that was beginning to develop, Ingrid guessed that they had now been blown several miles out toward the middle of the lake.

"We're all starting to get cold," Hazel said, "except for She-Wolf, who is wearing a warm fur coat. Why don't you girls snuggle up against her?"

"Will she let me?" Ellie asked.

"She-Wolf!" Hazel said.

The dog lifted her head and looked at her.

"Let the little girls lie beside of you."

Ellie scooted over and carefully snuggled up against She-Wolf. Trudy and Polly followed suit.

Hazel threw a blanket over all of them. "Better?"

"Better," Ellie answered.

She-Wolf licked the top of Ellie's head as though giving her a reassuring kiss, and then lay still once more, allowing her body heat to warm the children.

Hazel handed the remaining blankets to Agnes, Ingrid, and Mary.

Ingrid's dress had gotten completely soaked while she was cutting the horse loose. Now, with things cooling down, she started to shiver. The dry blanket was the single most comforting thing she had ever been given.

"This might be a very good time to pray, Mother," Ingrid said as warmth seeped back into her body.

"Oh goodness, child," Mary said. "I've never stopped."

# 27

It normally took the best part of two days to go from the camp to Bay City, especially for the teamsters, who were limited by how long their mules could pull the wagons without giving out. It was common to stop and camp out halfway there, but a healthy man in his prime could walk it in one very long day. A man alone on horseback could make it in less.

Many of the younger loggers simply melted into the woods and kept going. Joshua was torn. Part of him wanted to abandon the group and go straight home. On the other hand, he had confidence that Ingrid would have the wisdom to get their family to safety if it became necessary. Hans and he discussed it and decided that it would not be wise to travel all that distance, when it might rain within a few days. The chances were that while they were gone, the camp would roar back into operation without them. Neither man wanted to jeopardize his job.

Hans, having lost a year's wages, was not anxious to lose another day. He needed money to help fuel his dream of creating a fine farm. He said he would write Ingrid a letter as soon as he got to Bay City, letting her know he was alive and well. He had every intention of purchasing land nearby, where they would spend their lives in and out of one another's homes. Nothing would be gained by leaving at this point.

As they hiked along the logging trail, he and Hans enjoyed talking about what a reunion it was going to be come spring! His brother-in-law asked about each child, memorizing their names and little details about them—practicing to be a good uncle, he said.

Although it was customary for the wagons to stop for the night, the feeling of urgency was so great that they all kept going, pushing through, only stopping at intervals to allow the mules to rest.

It was the hardest on Jigger. The old cook clung to the wooden seat, wincing with every bump. At times, he would get out and walk alongside the wagon until his strength gave out and then he would climb back on and endure another few miles.

Bay City was a welcome sight. Katie and the children accompanied the teamsters on to her house, where she would direct them where to put the supplies. Hans went with them to help unload. Jigger, she insisted against the old man's halfhearted protestations, would stay in her and Foster's extra room.

While Katie and the teamsters went one direction, Foster stopped on the street to talk to a middle-aged woman dressed in a blue silk dress and enormous hat. This did not seem like a random meeting. She had apparently been alerted that they had arrived in town and had come specifically to talk to Foster.

"If you ever want to make money in this business, Foster"— she placed both hands on her ample hips—"bringing your men out of the woods six months early is a very stupid move."

Based on her age and her familiarity with his boss, Joshua jumped to the conclusion that this must be Robert Foster's mother or a bossy aunt. He was wrong.

"This is Delia, my business partner," Foster said. "Delia, this is my bookkeeper whom I told you about, Joshua Hunter. He'll go over all the records with you." He slapped his hat against his knee, knocking the dust off. "I know it wasn't a wise business decision, but you weren't there in the woods with us in '67. You don't know how fast a forest fire can move. Frankly, I'd rather live in a leaky tent with a clear conscience the rest of my life than a mansion with the knowledge that I gambled my family's and my men's lives just to dig more money out of the woods."

"And that"—Delia's voice softened—"is the very reason I wanted to be your business partner. You might just be the only lumberman in the Saginaw Valley who values his men's lives over the almighty dollar."

To Joshua's surprise, she then tucked her gloved hand into the crook of his arm. "Come with me, sweetie," she purred. "We'll have us a nice cup of tea, something good to eat, and then we'll go over those books together and see if there's any way we can keep this fine man from bankrupting himself . . . and me."

Her voice grew suddenly businesslike. "Robert, have one of your men bring over your records and logbook as soon as you get home."

It was disorienting to come straight out of the forest and find himself suddenly on a plank sidewalk, strolling along with a woman he did not know on his arm, a woman who made him distinctly uncomfortable. Delia was quite a force. How in the world had she and Foster gotten to be business partners?

They entered a large, ornate house, the front of which was almost directly on the sidewalk. Inside, it was like entering a different world. Every inch was covered with bric-a-brac. Layers of expensive-looking carpeting cushioned the sound of his boots. Velvet-covered upholstered chairs sat near an ornate fireplace where a small fire was laid out against the chill of an October day.

"Please have a seat, Joshua." Delia picked up a small bell and rang it. A young woman wearing a dark, long-sleeved dress appeared in the doorway.

"Yes, ma'am?" the young woman said.

"Mr. Hunter has just arrived from a long trek through the forest. I'm certain he is famished. Would you please assemble a tray of sandwiches for him?"

Delia was a study in contradictions. He placed her in her late fifties, but her face beneath the makeup had deeper grooves around her mouth and eyes than what he judged her age to warrant. He was surprised to see what appeared to be a knife scar on the left side of her cheek, cleverly disguised but visible when viewed close up. She was dressed in the kind of clothes that Millicent might have chosen if she were Delia's age and size, but in her eyes, he did not see a shallow woman. Instead, Delia had the seasoned, wary look of certain veterans he knew who had experienced the deadliest battles. He would wager a guess that there was at least one weapon on her person.

"Tell me about yourself, Mr. Hunter." She settled herself on the comfortable-looking chair directly across from him, extracted a wicked-looking hat pin from her hat, lifted the hat from her head, and gently placed it on the side table at her elbow. Her dark brown hair was streaked with gray.

"I have a strong suspicion, ma'am, that your own life would be infinitely more interesting than mine."

"You would be correct in that assumption, but I have no intention of getting into that discussion today. I don't get many visitors these days, Mr. Hunter," she said, "and I live a very quiet life. I would very much enjoy knowing where you come from and a little about you."

"There isn't much to tell." His hat, which he had been holding in his hand, he now sat on the floor. "I'm a farmer working in a lumber camp to make enough cash for spring planting. It's a common story."

"The story is common, but you are not, are you, Mr. Hunter?"

The young housemaid arrived at that moment and sat a small tea tray upon the table. "I'll be back with the sandwiches soon."

"Thank you, Lizzy," Delia said.

She busied herself pouring the tea, making certain that he had the right amount of sugar and milk. Then she settled back with her own cup, took a sip, and regarded him over the rim. She reminded him of She-Wolf the one time he had seen her lying on the porch, tracking with her eyes a field mouse scurrying across Hazel's yard. He could almost read the dog's mind as she debated whether or not it was worth her time to pounce.

Delia decided to pounce. "It has been my experience that if you dig deeply enough, people are almost always more interesting than they appear. I'm certain there is more to you than a farmer who found his way to a lumber camp." She took another sip. "Perhaps you would like for me to tell you your story." She smiled sweetly, but her eyes had narrowed. "I'm rather good at telling other people's stories."

"Please," he said. "Go ahead."

"You are a military man," she said.

"True, but that is a fairly safe guess these days," he said evenly. "Most men my age have seen service."

"Cavalry, I believe?"

"Yes."

"More tea, Mr. Hunter?"

"No, thank you," he said. "Were you guessing?"

"I almost never guess, Mr. Hunter. You hold yourself like someone who has spent a large portion of his life in the military. Cavalry from your boots, which have seen better days. Your speech is more educated than most, so I would think that you were an officer."

"I'm impressed."

"Then let me impress you even further." She put another dollop of cream into her tea. "You live approximately two miles west of White Rock, although that is not where you grew up. You moved there because of your wife's family—with whom, through no fault of your own, you are no longer on speaking terms. You were widowed in the early spring, and there is still some cloud of suspicion amongst some members of the community that you may have poisoned your wife. You remarried a woman you do not love. You have five children, a mother whom you and your new wife recently took in, and you have expended enormous energies trying to create a cherry orchard. Your farm is paid for, primarily with your military pay, and although you barely make enough money on your farm to keep body and soul together, you have a reputation in the community as someone who pays his bills and is scrupulously honest in all his financial dealings."

"You had me investigated," he said. "Why would you even bother?"

"Ah." She held up a finger. "Now that is an interesting question. Robert Foster took me on as a business partner when no other decent person in this town would speak to me. I ran a bordello, Mr. Hunter, and I ran it well—but I prayed daily for a way to get out. Robert gave me a chance when I hit bottom. He saw potential in my ability to read men and run a profitable business. He is one of the very few truly decent men I have ever known. He does not and will never know how carefully I watch over him and his family. When he told me that he had impulsively hired you to be his bookkeeper, I sent someone to White Rock to ask some questions."

She set her teacup down on the small table that sat between them. "By the way, a woman there by the name of Millicent truly despises you—even more so than your mother-in-law."

"That is not a surprise."

"You will be happy to know," she said, "that your family was fine one week ago. I'll make a final decision about your character after I inspect the ledger that Robert will be sending over. I order the supplies for that camp," she said. "And I know every single item in that store. If there is so much as an ounce of chewing tobacco missing, I'll know."

"Some people might think that you are joking." He studied her face. "But you are dead serious about this."

"I lost my sense of humor a long time ago, Mr. Hunter, when I was twelve."

"What happened when you were twelve?"

"My stepfather sold me."

Those four words hit him like a physical blow. Agnes was twelve, and he would gladly kill any man who touched her. "I am so sorry."

"So am I, Mr. Hunter. So am I. That is why I value the few men I have known who have integrity. I hope you are one of those men."

He had no doubt that she knew every item in Foster's camp. He also knew that he had been meticulously honest in all of his work. There was nothing to hide.

There was a knock at the front door, and the maid answered it. She arrived a few seconds later carrying two ledger books, one for the store and one for the men's hours and wages. "Mr. Foster sent this," she said.

"Thank you." Delia reached for the books. He saw the

young woman lean over and whisper something into her ear. Delia nodded. "How are those sandwiches coming, Lizzy?"

"They're ready. I'll bring them in now."

Delia had lost interest in him. She carried the ledger over to a small round table covered with a fringed brocade cloth. It was one of the few surfaces in the room that was devoid of knickknacks.

He watched as she took a pair of wire-rimmed eyeglasses from her pocket, placed them firmly upon her nose, opened the first book, and began to peruse the numbers.

The maid brought the sandwiches. Without even glancing at him, Delia waved her hand. "Go ahead and eat, Mr. Hunter," she said. "And please don't try to be polite. You may have the whole tray if you wish. I know how hungry men can be when they come in from the camps."

He bit into a delicate sandwich made of butter and cucumber. He would have preferred two thick pieces of Ingrid's bread and a slab of roast beef, but this would do. The next sandwich contained some sort of cheese. Next to the sandwiches, there was what looked like a fourth of a chocolate layer cake. He took Delia at her word, and as she pored over his figures in the second ledger, he finished every crumb.

Finally, she took off her glasses and slid them into her pocket. She closed the ledger. "It is in perfect order," she said, "but you knew that, didn't you?"

"Yes, ma'am. I did."

"Now that that is over, and you have rested and eaten, I'm afraid that I have some very bad news."

A chill went through him. She had said his family was fine as of a week ago.

Many things could happen to a family in a week.

"I received word via telegraph, a few minutes before you and Robert arrived, that both Holland and Manistee have been destroyed by a great forest fire. Hundreds of lives have been lost. Nothing is standing."

He was genuinely sorry to hear of such devastation but selfishly grateful that it had occurred on the western coast of Michigan. Far, far away from his family.

"Has that fire been the source of all this smoke?"

"Partially."

The way she was looking at him made him think that there was more—something she was reluctant to say.

"What is it?" he asked. "What are you holding back?"

"The wildfire did not limit itself to the western coast."

"My family." His heart felt like it would pound out of his chest. "Have you heard word of my family?"

"I know nothing about your family at this time. The information is spotty, but from what little we can gather, it is believed that White Rock, like Holland and Manistee, was completely destroyed by fire yesterday."

He had to get out of here. He had to act. He had to find his family. He jumped to his feet, crammed his hat on his head, and turned toward the door.

"Stop," Delia commanded.

He had already opened the door and was halfway out.

"Please stop, Joshua," she said. "I have not yet told you everything. There have been reports that there are survivors— I don't know how many. There is a very good chance that your family escaped."

He should have never left them, never have gone into the camps. They could have survived without the logging camp income. His stomach twisted as he thought of Ingrid, alone in that cabin with all those children and an elderly mother. Ingrid might be able to save herself, but how could she escape with all of those people?

Had she been wise enough to get out early?

Just then, there was a crack of lightning and a volley of thunder. And then it sounded as though the heavens opened and poured every drop of water they had been saving up all these months upon their parched and dying land. The rain that they had been hoping and praying for had finally come— one day too late to save the towns and forests and people.

He started, once again, to leave, but Delia grabbed his arm with a firm grip.

"You don't know where you're going or what you're going to do when you get there. Unless I miss my guess, you have not slept, except in snatches, for more than two days. If you have any sense at all, you will wait out the storm. You will go upstairs to one of my spare bedrooms and get some rest until the storm wears itself out. You cannot help your family if you get struck by lightning while you're hunting for them."

"Begging your pardon, ma'am, but whatever made you think that I have any sense? I'll figure things out along the way."

"And your family will have no help at all if you get struck by lightning. Go upstairs, choose any bedroom except mine, and at least try to rest. I'll wake you when the storm is over."

"Do you think I can rest with my family out there trying to survive in this?" He flung his hand out toward the heavy rain. "Where's the nearest livery stable?"

"Men never, ever listen to reason!" Delia sighed. "That's why I waited until you had eaten before I told you."

"The livery stable, ma'am?"

"You don't need a livery stable. I was fairly certain what you would say. While we were chatting, Lizzy looked into the possibilities of getting you on a steamboat headed toward White Rock. Under normal circumstances, the trip would be simple. Board the steamboat at our dock and step off onto the wharf at White Rock. But from what we can tell, practically all the steamboats and ships have stopped running."

He could not keep the impatience out of his voice. "Then what do you suggest I do?"

"I've had one of my strongest horses saddled for you. She is young and has the most endurance. While you were eating, Lizzy packed provisions and basic medical supplies. Although there will probably be no opportunity to use it, I also put a small pouch of money in there."

He was speechless. This was not a woman he would have expected to show such kindness. He would have assumed that her years of working in a bordello would have hardened her.

"Why are you doing this for me?"

"I am not doing this for you, Mr. Hunter," she said. "I have a soft spot for children. If yours are still alive, they desperately need their father."

"I am in your debt, ma'am."

"Just go find your family, Mr. Hunter," she said. "Your horse is right outside the back door."

Delia's maid was waiting beside the kitchen door holding a large, black raincoat.

"This old macintosh belongs to our handyman," Lizzy said, "but you need it worse than him right now. He said you could have it. We'll get him another one."

"Good thinking, Lizzy," Delia said.

He shrugged into the macintosh, grateful for its protection. Was his family out in this storm with no shelter? Could they survive if they were?

If he lost his family, he would no longer want to live.

He noticed that the tempo of the storm had changed. It sounded as though the thunder and lightning had rolled further out over the bay, leaving behind a heavy, steady rain. He could only wonder why God had not seen fit to send this yesterday.

The horse Delia was lending him was a young, black Arabian

mare. He ran his hands over her. She was well-conditioned and sound. He was impressed with Delia's choice.

"The employee I sent to White Rock to investigate you rode this horse." Delia was watching from the porch with Lizzy hovering nearby. "He said that if you pace yourself, fight the urge to race all the way there, and give her a break now and then, she should be able to carry you the whole seventy miles in about twenty-four hours."

He slung his leg over the horse and settled into the saddle.

"If you find your family," Delia said, "they are welcome here until you can find a better solution. My house has many empty bedrooms and I would not mind in the slightest if they were filled with children."

He closed his eyes at the impact of her words. From the moment he had heard that White Rock had burned, his mind had been searching for a place where he could shelter his family. With the rain pouring down upon him, he tipped his hat to the two women standing on the porch.

"I will never forget this."

"We shall be praying for you and your family," Delia said. "Godspeed."

Joshua's horse trotted through the solid sheet of rain as they headed out of town. As a cavalry officer, he was accustomed to riding through inclement weather. He buttoned the top of his macintosh and tugged the brim of his hat lower to keep the rain out of his eyes.

"You are leaving without me?" His brother-in-law, astride a large palomino, blocked his way.

# 28

He had forgotten about Hans.

"The only thing in my head was getting to my family."

"What is in my head is to find my sister. You know the way?" Hans asked. "In the dark?"

"Yes."

"We ride to White Rock." Hans fell in beside him.

"Whose horse?" Joshua asked.

"Foster's."

"Ah."

As they headed eastward in a loose, swinging trot, Joshua—not knowing what hazards the burned-over landscape might have—wondered if the horses would be able to make it through. If not, he would send Hans back with the horses, and he would continue on foot.

The rain seemed to have settled in—which was a blessing. Hopefully every burning coal and ember would be quenched. As they entered the blackened areas south of them where the fire had been, he despaired of finding grass for their horses on their way there—but they soon discovered a strange thing. The fire had been capricious—in some places it had bypassed whole houses and sections of farms, while completely obliterating the surrounding countryside for miles.

Several hours into the trip, at daybreak, they saw a neat,

302

white-frame house that had been miraculously left intact—a small oasis in the middle of a blackened land.

A girl-child, about the age of his Trudy, sat on the porch. She was rocking back and forth, hugging herself, her face streaked with smoke and tears.

"Are you all right, child?" he asked.

She did not acknowledge his presence. She just kept rocking.

While Hans held the reins of both horses as they rested and cropped grass in the rain, Joshua knocked on the front door, hoping an adult was alive in there. If not, he would have to take responsibility for the silent child—a time expenditure he could ill afford. One by one, a father, mother, and three more children wandered out—showing no surprise or even much interest in him. The mother's face was expressionless and her eyes were dull.

All of them seemed listless. He had seen the same behavior and lack of facial expression in some soldiers.

"Is your family all right, sir?" he asked.

"We climbed into the well." The father stared off into the distance. "But the heat was nearly unbearable. We stayed down there for hours. My oldest child"—he glanced down at the little girl Joshua had first seen—"has not spoken since."

"I am so sorry," Joshua said.

"That was my brother's house." The father pointed at a desolate field where nothing but black debris remained. "It's gone now. He had a wife and six children. We could hear them screaming—and I could do nothing to help."

"Is there anything we can do to help you before we go?"

"No," the father said, a small flicker of life coming back into his eyes. "But I thank you kindly for asking."

Without saying another word, the family wandered back into the house and shut the door. The little girl on the porch continued to rock back and forth.

This only intensified his desire to run Delia's horse flat-out, as fast as it could go, all the way to White Rock, but not only would it be inhumane to their horses, it was impossible. Their journey was greatly complicated by the fact that not everything had been burned into ash. In one area, giant trees, acres of them, looked as though they had all been felled by a giant mowing scythe. The force of the wind had laid them down, all falling in the same direction.

In other places, trees were tangled, lying this way and that, as though a giant hand had played the child's game of pickup sticks. The old nursery rhyme "five, six, pick up sticks—seven, eight, lay them straight" got caught in his mind and played over and over to the rhythm of his horse's hoofs, nearly driving him mad when he began to hear it being sung singsong in his girls' voices.

They made their way past a partially burned farm where they saw the farmer dead, lying beside his horses, as though he was trying to rescue them at the moment they were over-taken with fire.

They did not stop to bury the dead. There was too much urgency within him to find the living. They continued east through a forty-mile swath the fire had burned, passing farm after farm where people had lived and loved and hoped—their lives snuffed out in an instant.

Hans was thoughtful and subdued. Joshua was grimly determined. Neither of them had any appetite. The food Delia had packed for him went untouched. Ironically, they had plenty of water because the rain had never completely ceased—all he had to do was hold out his cupped hands to have water to drink.

They were surprised when they came upon a middle-aged man, unharmed, digging in the remains of a house.

"Do you need help?" Hans asked.

"No." The man turned to them, his eyes swollen and red. "This is my job to do alone—I want no one's help."

"What are you doing?" Joshua asked.

The man gave a shuddering sigh and wiped the back of his hand over his eyes. "My wife developed a hankering for a mess of fried fish. Wouldn't let up till I rode over to the lake and tried to catch her some. I had other things to do and was half-aggravated at the woman. We had words right before I left." He picked up a bucket sitting on the ground and cradled it in his arms. "This is all that is left of her."

The man's words hit Joshua like a fist and doubled him over. For a few moments he could not breathe.

Hans, beside him, grabbed his arm as though to steady him.

"Were you fishing anywhere near White Rock when the fire came?" Joshua asked.

"I was."

"My family was living on a farm right outside of it."

"Then I pity you, sir," the man said and went back to his digging.

As they neared the lake, Joshua recognized his home, but only because of the configuration of the land and creek. The barn, the fences, the cabin itself were piles of ash. The fire had incinerated everything he owned, everything he had worked for—except for the very earth itself.

His hope for the future—the cherry orchard—was a field of blackened twigs and twisted stumps. He was surprised how little its loss meant to him. The goal that carried him through the second half of the war, the image of Diantha strolling beneath the white blossoms of his own cherry orchard, had been nothing but a young man's daydream, a place in his head where he could retreat while the memories of battles and bodies piled up in his mind. As he stared at the burnt and broken orchard, that daydream dried up and blew away just like the white blossoms had withered and died during the dry, hot spring.

What mattered—the reality, not the fantasy—was the vivid memory of his precious wife trudging along beside him, day after day, week after week, carrying those heavy buckets of water to keep his orchard alive—and doing it without a word of complaint.

She had healed all of them, bringing peace and order into their lives, building a life in which his children could grow and blossom. He remembered the night she had brought little Bertie home—and how from that moment on, she had cared for the baby as tenderly as if she had given birth to him.

How he had railed at her the evening he had discovered her trying to "give back" the diary and pills by burying them beneath the surface of Diantha's grave. Then, in spite of his cruel words, she had held and comforted him as the full impact of what Diantha had done, and who Diantha was, had hit him.

So many memories packed into such a short space of time. The night she had taken in his mother without a moment's hesitation. How she had brought health and happiness back into his mother's life.

How much she had loved them all—this incomparable woman—and how little he had given back.

The thought that caused him the most pain and shame was remembering the night she had prepared herself for him—how she had tried to make herself pretty. How she had been sitting up, waiting for him, in the new nightgown that Hazel had bought, her golden hair spilling over her shoulders. The light of hope and love and welcome in her eyes.

He had extinguished that light with four words, "I can't do this," and turned away because he was still in love with his deceased wife, because Ingrid was different from what he was used to, because she could look him straight in the eye and match him step for step in endurance. Because—God help him—all she had to wear when he first met her were two worn-out dresses and an old pair of men's shoes.

If by some miracle he found her alive, he would spend the rest of his life cherishing her.

As he looked around at the ruined farm, he could not imagine mustering enough enthusiasm to ever rebuild it. All he saw when he looked at the burnt acreage was what a waste the terrible struggle they had gone through during these past unending months had been. No longer did he care about his farm, his crops, or his vanished livestock. He cared even less for his own life unless he could find his family.

"This is yours?" Hans glanced around at the devastation.

"Yes."

"You have a wagon?"

"A small one."

"Where is it?"

Joshua looked around him. Although in ashes, the shapes of everything were still discernible. He even saw two grease spots near the pigpen that he surmised was all that was left of his pigs, but there was nothing resembling a wagon. He knew that even if the wagon was ashes, the metal would be left. He studied the ground closely. No such thing littered his yard.

Ingrid had taken the farm wagon and had gotten his family out of there!

Oh, dear Lord, how he loved that valiant woman!

"It's only two miles farther—let's go," he said.

He had not slept in three days. He had rarely been out of the saddle in the past twenty-four hours, except when he needed to lead his horse through a particularly tangled mess. Both he and Hans had eaten little except a handful or two of jerky, had drunk nothing but rainwater. He should be completely exhausted—but this new reason to hope gave him strength. He no longer had the discipline to hold back. They took the last two miles to White Rock at a dead run.

He slowed momentarily at Richard and Virgie's. Here, too, there was little left except ashes, but those ashes included the remains of their wagon. Unless they had ridden with Ingrid, they were gone. He saw where Richard had plowed all around the house and barn, trying to protect his property from encroaching fire. If he knew those two people at all, he would wager that they had stubbornly tried to hold their own.

A few moments later, they saw the lake. A steamboat had stopped and it appeared that the people were trying to re-build a portion of the long wharf where the boats had always unloaded supplies in the past.

The first person he recognized was George, who was car-rying a toddler in his arms.

"Have you seen my wife?" Joshua dismounted and grabbed the man by the shoulders. "Is my family safe?"

George looked as though he had aged twenty years in the short time since Joshua had seen him.

"I don't know, Josh. Everything happened so fast. One minute I was in the middle of a bucket brigade, and the next minute we were all running for our lives." The man's eyes were red-rimmed. "It took eight hours before the fire died down enough that we could go back on shore. I didn't see any of your family the whole time I was in the water."

Joshua, who had felt a great hope when he saw that his wagon was gone, felt that hope crushed. Had Ingrid waited too long? Had they perished back there in the woods—and in his haste, he didn't see?

"You have shelter?" Hans asked.

"No, not yet."

"I'm surprised that steamboat is here," Joshua said. "I

was told the ships had all stopped running because of the poor visibility."

"Not the *Moffat*. Captain James Moffat is a brave man and an experienced skipper. I hear he's been using every trick he knows to find his way up and down this coastline without wrecking. He's been dropping off provisions for those who are able-bodied, and taking those who are badly burned to Port Austin."

"How many are having to be transported?"

"Hundreds. I heard that there's a Dr. Johnson on board who has been working nonstop since yesterday trying to care for the burn victims. When those who need medical attention have all been taken care of, Captain Moffat says he'll come back for us."

Joshua did not recognize the small child who was clinging to George.

"Who is this little fellow?"

"None of us know," George said. "Millicent saw him sitting on the shore all alone, crying and scared while the rest of us were running for our lives into the water. She grabbed him up and carried him out into the water with her. Saved the child's life. Some think he's the only survivor of some farm family that came in—but we don't know for sure where he came from."

"What are you going to do with him?"

George looked into the child's innocent, trusting face and smiled. "I thought I might keep him—unless someone shows up who has an awful good claim."

"Will Millicent be okay with that?"

"Millicent didn't make it," George said flatly. "A lot of people didn't make it. One minute she was beside me, holding on to the child, and then she told me she was tired and handed him to me, and the next thing I knew, she was gone. The water was terrible rough and she was a delicate little thing."

"I'm so sorry, George," Joshua said.

"Can you imagine, Josh? That wife of mine could have just kept going straight on into the water, but instead, she grabbed up this little boy and brought him out to me." Joshua saw the pride in George's eyes. "She saved his life. You know—my Millicent always was such a sweethearted woman."

Without another word, the shopkeeper plodded off. Joshua heard him talking to the child as he walked away. "Let's see if we can find you something to eat, little fella. Don't you worry none, George is going to take care of you. George will always take real good care of you."

And then he saw Susan. She was as bedraggled and exhausted as the rest of the survivors.

"Hello, Josh," she said, and swayed as though she was about to fall. He caught her and seated her on a charred stump.

"Have you eaten?" he asked.

"None of us have—but soon. They say there are cheese and crackers and tea in those barrels they're carrying onto the shore right now. People can be so kind."

In addition to being weak, she was shivering. He took his macintosh off, sat down beside her, and put it around her.

"Thank you," she said. "That's better. I need to tell you something. I saw Ingrid, Hazel, Mary, She-Wolf, and the children all go off in Hazel's fishing boat just about the time the fire hit the shore."

He closed his eyes while he absorbed this great news. "Do you know where they are?"

"That's just it—I don't. All I know is I caught a glimpse of Ingrid rowing, trying to get away just about the time the fire came down on us. I never saw them again."

Susan and he both knew that whole ships were sometimes swallowed up by Lake Huron, with no trace. A heavily laden rowboat had little chance. He was well acquainted with Hazel's fishing boat, but he had no idea how seaworthy it would be in rough water.

Lyman had already unearthed a blanket from one of the barrels delivered by Moffat's crew. "I'll take care of her now," he said. He handed Joshua's raincoat back, wrapped the blanket around Susan, helped her to her feet, and walked her to where villagers were opening barrels and passing out emergency food.

"Now what?" Hans asked.

"The only thing I know to do is search for them along the shore," Joshua said. It sounded so ineffective and weak. "Do you have a better idea?"

Hans shook his head. "No."

"We can cover more territory if we split up. I'll go south. You go north. Let's meet back here one day from now. If neither of us has found out anything, we'll move further on. I won't rest until I've scoured every inch of this shoreline."

Without saying another word, Hans swung into his saddle and headed north.

Feeling more alone than ever before in his life, Joshua headed south.

# 29

Before the rain came, Hazel had torn off chunks of the unsliced bread and handed them around to everyone—including a piece for She-Wolf. Even little Bertie had been able to gum some bread. There were two apples apiece for everyone. With Hazel's pocketknife, Ingrid had pared an apple until it was sauced enough for Bertie to swallow.

Had it not been for Hazel's quick thinking in grabbing the blankets and food, they would have been even more miserable than they were, although it was hard to imagine feeling any worse. If she had any idea which direction shore was, she would row toward it—with rest, the feeling had returned to her arms—but she did not want to expend the energy when there was a strong possibility that she might be rowing in circles.

After they ate, Mary and Hazel, their old bones chilled and aching, managed to lower themselves down and curl up next to where the dog and children lay. Ingrid kept one blanket for herself, then layered the other blankets over her precious passengers as they shared their body warmth the best they could.

"Can you stand it?" Ingrid asked.

"This floor is hard and miserable, but at least I'm warm," Hazel said.

"I has to pee-pee." Ellie sat straight up, dragging the blankets off of everyone.

"Bucket," Hazel said, "over there. It's the main reason I brought it—that and to bail with if necessary."

Ingrid helped Ellie relieve herself and had just gotten her tucked back beneath the covers when Trudy had to go, and then Polly.

When she thought things could not get any worse, she heard a crack of thunder, saw a streak of lightning, and the rain came. Hard, heavy rain.

Ingrid grabbed the bucket, and for more hours than she could count, bailed water faster than it could pour in. She turned into a machine, dipping and pouring, dipping and pouring, while Hazel, Mary, and the children huddled beneath the sopping wet blankets. The children were all so miserable, they were practically lying on top of She-Wolf now—and yet that amazing dog continued to allow them to draw warmth from her.

"Aren't *you* cold, dear?" Mary asked at one point when the rain had eased slightly.

"I'm fine," Ingrid lied. She was not fine, of course—but cold she was not—not with all the exertion of keeping the dory from sinking.

"Let me help." Ingrid felt Agnes's hand on her back. "I can bail for a while. You rest."

The child wrapped her own blanket around Ingrid and then, kneeling on the floor in front of her, began to dip and pour, dip and pour.

Ingrid had refused to allow Hazel to spell her because the two older women were at even greater risk when it came to cold and exposure than the children, but Agnes was a tough little nut—quick at filling that pail and throwing the water overboard. Ingrid was grateful for the rest.

And then, after several hours, the rain ceased.

Agnes went back to her place beside her sisters. Ingrid, utterly exhausted, knelt beside her seat, thanking God for the respite from the rain, thanking God that they were all still alive.

She rested her head in her folded arms for a moment and must have dozed, because a sound brought her jerking upright. What had she heard? Had they gotten close enough to land to hear voices?

Then she heard it again, a distant clang. Metal on metal. She could not determine from which direction it was coming. She hurriedly grasped the oars once again. If it was a steamboat or sailing vessel, she had to be ready to get out of its path.

There it was again—clang . . . clunk. It was getting louder. Yes, it was a ship.

Hazel sat up. "Do you hear that?"

"Can you tell where it is coming from?" Ingrid had barely gotten the words out when her jaw dropped, and for a split second she could do nothing but gape.

A foghorn blared, and a great, gray shape loomed out of the smoky fog, almost on top of them.

Mary screamed.

"Stay down!" Ingrid shouted, digging the oars into the water. "Everyone—hold on!"

The ship was so huge it could cut their boat in two without ever knowing what happened.

The foghorn sounded again. She-Wolf started to rise, thought better of it, and hunkered down once again—her eyes fastened on Ingrid as though willing her to have the strength to save them.

It was close. So very close. At one point she could have touched the side of the ship with her oar. Mary and Hazel were yelling and waving, trying to get someone's—anyone's—attention, but the ship plowed on through the water, an impersonal, unfeeling gray hulk that nearly swamped the little fishing boat in its wake.

Water splashed over all of them. Agnes, by far the calmest person on the boat, once again began bailing.

Ingrid had no idea how long they had been out here. She couldn't discern if it had been hours or days. There was no sun, no moon, no stars. No way to tell time. All she knew was that it felt like they had been bobbing around on this treacherous, dark, miserable water for an eternity.

As Joshua rode south, he discovered that Forestville had also burned to the ground. He passed refugees huddling beneath whatever shelter they could find, waiting to be rescued by the brave steamship crews that were plying the shore, picking up survivors. Sometimes he was in the water, sometimes he was out of it. Sometimes he had to skirt around burnt buildings or rough landscape, but he always kept himself within sight of the shore, where somewhere, someplace—if he just kept moving—he prayed he would somehow find his family.

His practical, analytical, rational mind told him that there was no way his family could have survived out in that vast, churning lake, in nothing more than a rowboat. And then he reminded himself that he had seen stranger, more miraculous things happen during the war. That thought kept him going.

Along the shoreline, he saw domestic animals wandering aimlessly without homes or owners. He was almost upon it before he saw a familiar-looking horse, its head down drinking from the lake. At first, he could only see the shadow of it, but when he dismounted and walked closer, he saw that it was Buttons.

The formerly frisky horse did not jerk away when Joshua grabbed hold of his mane. Instead, Buttons seemed as dispirited as the gray landscape. Joshua ran his hands over the good horse, comforting it, wishing the animal could tell him what had happened to his family.

"What happened, boy?" he asked. "How did you end up here?"

The last time he had seen Buttons, the horse had been a sleek young animal with no scars or blemishes. Now, the once-glossy coat was dull and covered with a damp ash. Joshua gasped with surprise when his hands encountered something he had never felt on one of his animals before. There were welts on Buttons's back. Two of them, several inches long.

His knees grew weak at the picture these welts conjured. Ingrid, his compassionate, loving Ingrid—a woman who had treated his animals with as much kindness as she did their family—had put those scars on Buttons's back for one reason only: to save the life of his children.

He could see it so clearly. She had waited too long. There had been a last-minute desperate flight to the lake. Buttons had carried his family toward the shore—running for all he was worth. Joshua could picture Ingrid looking back over her shoulder at the encroaching flames, plying the whip to force Buttons to go faster, faster.

He ached at the terror his family must have felt, trying to outrun the fire. Thanks to this good horse, they had made it to the lake and into Hazel's boat—but where were they now? He fished an apple out of the saddlebag and fed it to Buttons. Then he fashioned a makeshift bridle out of a roll of bandages Lizzy had packed, and rode on, leading Buttons behind him.

Feeding the apple to Buttons reminded him that he had not eaten in quite some time. He wasn't sure how long it had been. He forced himself to chew on a biscuit, swallowing mechanically because he knew he should—not because he was hungry. He could not imagine ever having an appetite again.

As the rocking motion of Delia's horse made his eyelids droop, he fought to stay awake. He knew he had to stay alert for fear of missing some small sign of his family—even if it was nothing more than a piece of *Wind Dancer*—Hazel's little dory.

South of Forestville, he saw something—something brightly colored caught in some rocks. As he drew closer, it reminded him of Ellie's little red cloak. He dismounted and dug it out of the sand and muck.

It *was* a red cloak, but whether or not it was Ellie's, he did not know. He thought it might be too small, but he had never been good at judging his girls' sizes. They all just seemed . . . little to him.

He remembered the first time Ellie had worn the red cloak. His mother had made it for her right before fall weather. The little imp had turned this way and that, standing on her tiptoes, prancing around the room, sparkling with happiness.

This was not Ellie's cloak. It could not be Ellie's cloak. He tossed it back on the ground with contempt. There was no way this sodden, bedraggled scrap of material had ever graced his daughter's body. He would not allow the possibility to even enter his mind.

Suddenly, the overwhelming smell of smoke and ruin, the loneliness, the desperation, the exhaustion, the sleep deprivation, took its toll and drove him to his knees in the sand. He grabbed the little cloak again, so very like the one that Ellie had worn, and cradled it in his arms.

"Why did you allow this, Father!" He stared up at the gray,

silent sky. "Where were you! How could you bring the rain one day too late to save our homes and our families! You who created rain and fire—would it have killed you, Lord, to bring the rain a few hours earlier?"

There was no one around to hear him in this desolate place. As far as he could tell, not even God was listening. "Can you hear me, Lord?" he screamed. "Are you listening to me? Why didn't you take me, Lord, instead of them. They were all so innocent. I was the sinner. I'm the one who took others' lives in battle, and I would rather *die* than live without my family! Where were you, God, when my family needed you?"

Silence.

He stood up and spat in contempt of a Creator who had not bothered to help his family, who had not drowned the deadly fires with a downpour before the wildfire reached the village of White Rock. If lightning struck him dead for what he had said, so be it. He would welcome it.

Then he mounted and began the slow, fruitless ride down the ravaged east coast of Michigan, for no other reason than he had no idea what else to do.

With no landmark to mark their progress, Ingrid could not tell, at first, that they were moving. Now, she realized that they were being pulled along by the wake of that huge ship. They had somehow been caught by it and were being gently eased along. The only way she could tell that they were getting closer to shore was that there was a marked difference in the temperature.

She didn't know how long this effortless ride would last, but she was careful to keep their boat's nose pointed toward the rear of the steamship as their little fishing boat accidentally caught a piggyback ride.

At one point their boat got slightly sideways of the wake and nearly capsized. In fighting to keep from being swamped, she lost the pull of the wake. With rising hope, she thought they might be getting close enough to shore to find a place to land—if she knew in which direction it was. The only thing she knew for sure was that her passengers had stopped shivering.

And then the strangest thing happened. She-Wolf, who had remained steadfastly in the bottom of the boat for so many hours, shook the children off, rose to her feet, and stared off into the distance. Her ears pricked forward as though she heard something.

"What is it, girl?" Hazel asked.

She-Wolf whined and did a nervous little dance step, her ears cocked forward, carefully listening for something they could not hear.

"Could we be getting closer to land?" Hazel asked. "Is it possible that we might not have to spend the rest of our lives in this boat?"

"Maybe closer. Maybe not. I have no idea where to row."

"I believe She-Wolf knows and is trying to tell you."

As though in answer, She-Wolf gave three short barks and then whined again, and glanced over her shoulder to see if Hazel was paying attention.

Ingrid used the direction that She-Wolf was facing as a compass as she began to row in earnest.

At first, Joshua was annoyed when Buttons balked. He tugged on the cloth bridle, but Buttons did not move. At first he thought the horse merely needed a rest, and he dismounted and led both horses over to the water's edge.

As the Arabian drank, Joshua noticed that Buttons was

uninterested in the water. Instead, his head was high and his ears were pricked forward as though he was listening to something.

Joshua could hear nothing over the lapping of the waves.

He was about ready to mount and ride on when he thought he heard a dog's bark. This would not be notable except it sounded as though it was coming from out on the lake—which was impossible.

It couldn't be.

Susan had said that She-Wolf had been in the fishing boat as they were being blown away from shore . . . but it couldn't be. The lake was too big. The coincidence too great. It was obvious that he was so desperate to believe his family was alive that he was beginning to imagine sounds that were not there.

Just to be sure, he stood very still and listened. Once again there was no sound except the waves of the lake.

One foot was in the stirrup and he was ready to mount, when he thought he heard something again. He stopped. Listened. Nothing.

And then he heard it. He knew he heard it. Three short, staccato barks—and they were definitely coming from the darkness of the lake.

"Who's there?" he shouted.

No one answered.

Then suddenly, there came the unmistakable howl of She-Wolf—a dog with a sound like no other dog he had ever known. She began to bark again, and this time she didn't stop. His heart leaped up as he heard the barks coming closer and closer.

"Over here!" he yelled at the top of his lungs, waving the red cloak above his head. "Over here! Row toward my voice! Ingrid, sweetheart, row toward my voice!"

She-Wolf was getting even more agitated as Ingrid rowed in the direction the dog was facing. The dog's body wouldn't quit trembling. She kept looking back over her shoulder at Hazel and Ingrid as though making certain they understood what she was telling them. She kept laying back her ears, giving short, staccato barks, then she would quit, prick her ears forward, and listen. At one point, She-Wolf raised her voice in a primal howl that sent chills down Ingrid's spine. That dog heard something—but none of them had any idea what it was.

She prayed that there was a beach where they were headed, instead of boulders to crash against. It would be a terrible thing to go through this ordeal only to lose their lives battered against sharp rocks.

Then Agnes said, "I think I hear a man's voice."

Everyone leaned forward, straining to hear over the rhythmic splashing of Ingrid's oars.

She felt as though her arms would fall off, but they could just fall off—she intended to get her family to shore if it killed her.

Then she heard it too. A man's voice, shouting, screaming. She-Wolf was now answering his shouts with almost nonstop barking.

The dog was so eager, Ingrid worried that she might jump overboard. There was a possibility that the boat would capsize if she did.

"Easy, girl," Hazel said. "We're doing what you want us to do. We'll be there soon."

Then Ingrid heard something that convinced her that the lack of food and sleep was causing her to hallucinate. She stopped rowing.

"Shhh—everyone."

Even She-Wolf ceased barking.

She had *not* been hallucinating! There was a man's voice in the darkness, and he was shouting her name.

"Over here," the voice shouted. "Ingrid! Sweetheart! Keep rowing. You're getting closer. Keep rowing. The beach is sandy here. There are no rocks, just come straight toward my voice!"

This was not possible. It was simply not possible. And yet everyone heard the same thing. The children started calling out to their father. Bertie, upset by the commotion, began to cry. Mary wept with relief that not only were they going to live but that her son was safe.

Hazel did not shout, did not call out. All she did was stroke She-Wolf's coat, saying, "Good girl, good girl!" over and over.

Every muscle in Ingrid's body was screaming in protest. Her mind knew absolutely that she could not do this. It was too far. The water was still too rough. The boat was too heavy. She had not eaten in so long. She was so very, very tired.

And then, as though carried on the very surface of the water, a familiar refrain began to play in her mind—right along with the rhythm of the oars.

*Love bears all things.*

Dip. Pull.

*Love believes all things.*

Dip. Strain. Pull.

*Hopes all things.*

She gritted her teeth and grunted with the effort of pulling the heavy boat through the swells. She was growing weaker.

Dip. Pull.

*Endures all things.*

She could not do this, but she *had* to do this!

Dip. Pull.

*Love never fails.*

Dip. PULL!

Ingrid finished those final yards on sheer grit alone. The

moment the boat touched sand, the instant she knew her family was safe, she dropped the oars and collapsed.

Barely conscious, she felt someone dragging the boat onto shore, and then Joshua was lifting her from the amazing little fishing boat that had saved their lives.

She had never heard a grown man break down before, but Joshua sank to the ground still cradling her in his arms, clutching her to his chest, rocking back and forth, half-laughing, half-sobbing, saying love words to her over and over.

"Pa," she heard Agnes say, "it's all right. We're all safe. It's all right. You don't have to cry anymore."

# Epilogue

"Hans wants to buy the farm from us." Joshua was lying beside her, on the softest bed Ingrid had ever laid in, in one of Delia's opulent guest rooms.

Ingrid felt a great well of happiness at the mere mention of her brother's name. The day She-Wolf had led them to shore, the day of miracles, there had been one more—the news that her beloved brother was alive and well and they never had to be separated again.

"Our farm is for the sale?" Ingrid lay facing him, twisting a small curl of Joshua's thick hair around one finger. Her husband needed a haircut. He had been at the lumber camp a full two months this time.

"I wanted to see what you thought before I agreed to anything."

Selling the farm was not something she had ever considered. She had assumed they would leave Delia's, go back home, and rebuild.

"Where we go if we sell to Hans?"

Nothing prepared her for what came out of his mouth next.

"Bart and his men, the man-catchers who kidnapped your brother, were released from jail recently. They are free men."

"How can this be?" She sat up, shocked. "They keep my brother locked up like animal! How can they be free?"

"Bart had connections and money," Joshua said. "He paid off the right people. There are some honest citizens here in Bay City who are trying to change things—but there is still much dishonesty among the powers-that-be."

She could not believe it. "The man who took my brother is free man? He not pay for his crime?"

"Only the bit of time he spent in jail. From what I understand, even there he got special consideration."

"This I cannot believe!"

"It's true." He looked at her, as serious as she had ever seen. "Ingrid, do you trust me?"

"You, I trust with my life!" she said. "Why do you ask such thing?"

"Do you mind if we don't go back? Would you mind if I didn't try to rebuild the farm?"

"Hmmph! I do not care if we live on moon as long as our family is all together!" She gave thought to the implications of his words. "Where will we go?"

"Delia has quite a few connections of her own." He was looking at her so intently, she knew there was something very important coming. "She is part of the group of people who are trying to turn Bay City into a more law-abiding town."

Ingrid frowned. "What does this have to do with Hans and farm?"

"Both Delia and my boss, Robert Foster, were favorably impressed with how I managed to help apprehend the kidnappers without any bloodshed."

"I am impressed too. What does this have to do with Hans and farm?"

"Delia also knows a lot of men in high places who don't ever want her knowledge about them to get out to the general public."

"She—how do you say this—black mark them?"

"The word is *blackmail*, sweetheart. Delia never used that word, but I believe she did make a couple of prominent men very nervous recently."

Ingrid was utterly confused. "Why Delia want to make men nervous?"

"Because these men have the ear of the president."

"The president?" Ingrid let out a huff. "You tell me what you are talking about, Joshua Hunter! Right now!"

"Delia and Robert informed me that based on the recommendations he has recently received, President Grant has appointed me U.S. Marshal for this area. I don't have to take the appointment, but if I do, I'll get to help the citizens of this area turn things around. I think I'd be good at it."

"You will be afraid? You will be in big danger?"

"No. I'm not afraid, and yes, there would be some danger. Every job has its dangers, including farming, but from what I understand, I'll be allowed to appoint deputies to help me. I have a handful of local men I've gotten to know at the lumber camp, also former soldiers, who I would like to have beside me. I think we could make a real difference."

"Where we live?"

"There's another option. I got a letter from Zeb last week. Since we are, for the moment, homeless—they have graciously offered to take us in and share the farm with us."

"What? Why they do this now? After we spend whole winter living with Delia?"

"It could be that my brother has finally grown a spine, or it might be because Barb has had a sudden change of heart, or . . ."

"Or?"

"It has finally occurred to both of them that the farm is still in our mother's name and she could legally have them thrown off the property."

Ingrid gasped. "Mary would *do* that?"

"She has strongly considered it, but ultimately I think she'll just end up charging Zeb and Barb a hefty rent to stay there."

"They would pay?"

"If they think they'll lose the roof over their heads if they don't—they'll pay."

"Zeb and Barb is one place I do *not* want to live!"

"I kind of figured you would feel that way." He chuckled. "So, here's what I'm considering doing—with the pay I'll get from the camp after we bring the logs in, plus whatever Hans pays us for the farm, along with whatever salary I would get as a marshal, I think we could buy a nice house here in town. The children could go to a real school. Mother says she and Hazel are discussing the possibility of pooling their resources and buying a small place here in town since Hazel's house is gone—there's even a chance we could find something close together."

"You will not miss farm?" she asked. "After you work so hard?"

"From what I've been hearing, it doesn't appear that White Rock will ever build back up. The people don't seem to have the heart for it. Most are starting new lives in other towns. I guess I'm like the other people of White Rock. I don't have the heart to go back and try to rebuild. I heard that even Susan's parents, along with her and Lyman, recently moved here to Bay City, where her father has found a church. I think most of us feel the need for a fresh start."

"What about Richard and Virgie's farm?"

"Hans wants to buy that from the children, someday. They

are the only heirs. In the meantime, we could give him permission to work both farms if he wanted."

"Three hundred and twenty acres." Ingrid smiled. "Hans will be very happy . . . and you help Delia and Robert clean up town?"

"I hope so," he said. "Frankly, I'm looking forward to the challenge, but I won't take the job unless you want me to. If this upsets you, I'll tell Delia *and* the president that I won't do it."

Ingrid started laughing. She laughed until tears rolled down her cheeks. She couldn't seem to stop. Every time she tried—one look at him and she would start laughing again.

"What is this?" He seemed utterly mystified by her behavior. "What is so funny?"

"So, you are saying"—Ingrid bit down on her laughter long enough to begin ticking things off on her fingers—"we buy new house, we put children in school, I have many nice neighbors, Susan and family close by, Delia and Lizzy close by, Mary and Hazel close by, plenty nice stores to shop, Hans happy working farm . . . and I not have to carry water to cherry trees no more." She started to laugh again. "Oh, Ingrid so *very* upset!"

He grinned. "I'm guessing then that you approve of the idea?"

She wondered if it was possible to love a man any more than she already did. "I live on moon with you, Joshua Hunter— but Bay City will make me very happy."

He kissed her hard and then glanced over at the substantial wooden door. "Did you lock it?"

"Ja." She laughed. "I lock it plenty good. Children all asleep. Mother and Hazel all asleep. No one bother us until morning unless Polly decides to throw up again."

He took her chin in his hand and looked deep into her

eyes. "You realize that I am going to spend the rest of my life cherishing you, don't you?"

"Ja. I know that good."

He held out his arms to her as a familiar refrain ran through her mind.

*Love bears all things, believes all things, hopes all things, endures all things.*

*Love never fails.*

# AUTHOR'S NOTE

The heart of this novel was inspired by the life of my grand-mother, Elizabeth Allen Bonzo, who took upon herself the task of salvaging a still-grieving dirt farmer's family in the late 1800s. She, too, sat in a neighbor's living room all day and into the night until the neighbor gave up and she was given "her" baby—the widower's infant son. Like Ingrid, my grandmother also forever cherished the fact that her husband once told her that she was a better mother to his children than their birth mother.

Their log home was used as a makeshift courtroom for our rural township in the 1800s. Much of the court trial I write about at the beginning of this book, including the details of the young woman's mysterious illness, were taken verbatim from an 1881 handwritten transcript we discovered among some forgotten court records left in that house.

As in my story, the mystery of the young woman's death was never resolved by the court and was ruled "death by unknown causes."

As I searched for possible causes of death that could

explain her symptoms, I discovered one that surprised me. Patented, herbal, abortive medicines were a big business in the 1800s. The business was so lucrative that in 1870, during a time when earning a dollar a day was considered a fair wage, a Madame Restell spent over sixty thousand dollars on newspaper advertisements alone. The liberal use of these abortifacients caused many deaths.

To the disgust of legitimate logging camp owners, good loggers were sometimes kidnapped and forced to work in dangerous "haywire" camps.

Many believe that the holocaust that swept across the Midwest in October of 1871 was caused by a meteor shower. The fact that so many fires started at virtually the same time, hundreds of miles apart in at least five states, supports this theory. Others believe that it was simply a perfect storm made up of severe drought conditions, hundreds of acres of discarded tree tops, and the habit many farmers had of burning off their fields in the fall.

Most of the scenes I described during the fire, with the exception of Ingrid's rescue and the cross-country journey of Joshua and Hans, were based on eyewitness accounts gleaned from 1871 newspaper clippings. Hundreds of dazed wild animals sought shelter in those towns bordering the lake. Exhausted birds rested on every available surface. Domestic dogs and cats from inland farms ominously abandoned their homes several days before the fire.

The inhabitants of the once flourishing but now phantom town of White Rock tried to save their homes by forming a bucket brigade, only to abandon the effort and run for their lives moments later. The wall of flame was said to have been over one hundred feet high and stretched along the shore for miles. The hurricane-force winds created such havoc in Lake Huron that the people had to fight against being thrown back onto the flaming shore. Some did not succeed and perished. Wet, oaken buckets placed upon people's heads for protection caught fire far out into the water from the heat alone. The scene of Ingrid's wagon being aflame as they hit the water was taken from a true account from a different location.

Most of the farmers in the direct path of the fire tragically chose to stand and fight for their property. Over 1,500 people died. At least forty towns were destroyed. A small fishing boat holding nine adults and several children floated blindly in the thick smoke for three days, during which one child died.

Steamboat captains heroically braved the lack of visibility to rescue hundreds of burn victims and refugees in the days following the fire, dropping food and clothing off to those who stayed behind. A Dr. Johnson from Port Huron worked tirelessly upon the *Moffat*, bandaging and giving comfort to the steady stream of burn victims. Sadly, the long-awaited rains came only twenty-four hours after the conflagration.

The intrepid General George Custer really did have eleven horses shot out from under him. With incredibly bad timing and aim, he managed to accidentally shoot and kill one of them all by himself—while riding it.

**Serena B. Miller** is the author of *The Measure of Katie Calloway* and *Love Finds You in Sugarcreek, Ohio*, as well as numerous articles for periodicals such as *Woman's World*, *Guideposts*, *Reader's Digest*, *Focus on the Family*, *Christian Woman*, and more. She lives on a farm in southern Ohio.

Meet Serena B. Miller at

# www.SerenaBMiller.com

 AuthorSerenaMiller

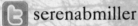 serenabmiller

serenabmiller

Her heart seeks sanctuary in the deep woods.
But will trouble find her even here?

"*The Measure of Katie Calloway* is a fast-paced story with a
generous measure of romance that will have readers cheering as
Katie conquers one trial after another. If you like . . . sharing an
adventure with great characters, this is the book for you."

—ANN H. GABHART, author of *Angel Sister*